LOVE SIGNALS
by
Margie Walker

MARRON PUBLISHERS, INC.

INTRODUCING
MARGIE WALKER

৯ ৯ ৯ ৯ ৯

Margie Walker has held positions in educational and commercial radio, as well as in the print media as a reporter and editor. She considers herself to have been blessed with an understanding family and very supportive friends. She resides in Houston with her loving husband, Sherman, and their two sons.

ROMANCE IN BLACK
MARRON PUBLISHERS, INC.
P. O. Box 756
Yonkers, NY 10703

ISBN 1-879263-01-7

All characters in this book are fictitious. Any resemblance to actual persons, living or dead, is purely coincidental.

Printed in the United States of America

October 1990

Dewra a. Hurdle.

৯ ৯ ৯ ৯

To Joy Kamani

Her faith and constant encouragement has helped to
transform my dreams into reality.

৯ ৯ ৯ ৯

Hi Debra,

How are you? I'm doing a little better. I'm trying to get over you-know-who, but it's tough. He says, he still loves me and he cares, but I'm just taking it slow.

Thanks for listening and I'm working on a new attitude.

Rita

keep in touch!

P R O L O G U E

The history was there for all to see—his life summed up in a single column article in the Atlanta Constitution. And as if that humiliation had not been enough, the trade publications had carried stories about the incident as well. He would never forget, or forgive the person responsible for his ruined career.

"KTOP FM MUSIC DIRECTOR FIRED" read the headlines.

The story linked KTOP's music director and number one jock in Atlanta, J. Don Holly, with BeeBop Record Company promoter, Lance Gilliam, in a payola scandal involving drugs, wild parties and equally wild women. KTOP's General Manager Clark Magness refused to elaborate, saying only that Holly had violated the policy of the ATC Broadcasting Group owned station.

Whether it had been true didn't concern the lone shoe salesman peering out the store windows at Allen Center, a high-rise office building across the street. The result was the same—the end of what had been a long and successful career in radio broadcasting. In essence, the end of his life. And that was always on his mind, second only to thoughts of getting even.

Revenge.

The word brought a smile to his face.

CHAPTER ❧ ONE

*M*arie was the picture of unruffled poise as she stood in the doorway, peering into the swanky conference room, some of its size diminished by the chicly dressed people milling about. But these weren't just ordinary folks. This upwardly mobile group of mostly men and a few women were the prima donnas of the office—the sales staff—who personified the successful image, not only of this room, but of the entire radio station.

But Marie was interested in locating one person in particular. Finally, she spotted her boss on the far side of the room and called, "Patrice? Can I see you in your office?"

There was no mistaking which of the three women present was Patrice Mason, general manager of KHVY FM. Her face was vivacious, and proud. Her light brown sugar complexion spread like rich cream over smooth, oval features. Long eyebrows arched high over dark brown, inquisitive eyes, slender nose, and a wide mouth, suggesting a decisive personality.

The center of attention in the small gathering around her, Patrice was the queen regent of the fastest growing radio station in Houston. She wasn't just another pretty face; radio after all was as much about glamor as any other arena in the entertainment world. But it was a business, for it took dollars and more dollars to keep the glitter bright. No one knew this better than Patrice.

Few were allowed a glimpse of the other side of her personality—the concerned mother and sometimes lonely woman beneath the trailblazer image projected. She radiated a natural energy that showed in her face. Her bold and daring style of doing and getting things done had been one of the main reasons, though certainly not the only one, for her quick rise up the ranks of broadcast management to her current position with the ATC Broadcasting Group.

An astute businesswoman, exceptional leader and dynamic salesperson, she always went after what she wanted, and usually got it. Except perhaps this time.

Patrice picked up on the higher than normal pitch in her assistant's voice, signaling that trouble brewed. She dropped her hands from the pockets of the red double-breasted blazer worn over a slim matching skirt, and looked across the room at Marie. Her quizzical gaze met the strange, wide-eyed look in Marie's eyes. Acknowledging the request with an imperceptible nod, she whispered politely to those around her, "Excuse me."

Her charming countenance remained intact, giving no hints to the guessing game going on behind smiling dimples. She moved with calm, easy strides across the room and stopped only briefly to speak to Mike, the sales manager, who was standing in her path.

She followed Marie quietly through the deserted maze of carpeted hallways to her corner office, inattentive to the walls lined with photos of entertainers who had visited the station. Except for the sales staff and the on-air announcer sequestered in the control room, the station employees had left for the day.

It was already after 6:30 on a Monday evening, and Patrice was exhausted—certainly not up to fielding a crisis. She knew, however, that had it been a minor problem, Marie would have taken care of it.

The cleaning lady met them at the door of the office. After exchanging pleasantries, the stocky woman left, and Patrice firmly closed the door. She leaned against it and folded her arms across her chest. There was a pensive shimmer in the brown eyes as she looked at her assistant, who was toying nervously with the sleeves of a green and white jersey dress.

"What is it?" Her tone addressed both irritation and eagerness to solve the matter so that she could go home. Marie inhaled deeply, then pointed ominously to the folded sheet of paper singled out from a stack of mail on the desk.

Patrice's gaze traveled the length of the younger woman's outstretched arm to the desk and finally rested on the sheet. She stared vacuously at the lone, white stationery a long time before apprehension struck, bringing with it a surge of intense displeasure.

She pounded the door at her back with tightly balled fists, whispering a fierce curse, "Damn!" Just as quickly as her temper erupted, it began to subside. In an effort to compose herself, she closed her eyes, tilted her head against the door and counted silently from one to ten.

Finally, Patrice pushed off from the door, her slender body straightening to her full 5'6" height. She tempered the panic that was threatening, and taking unhurried steps across the room, stood behind her desk. With concern for preserving fingerprints, she picked up the single page by one of its top corners and carefully shook it open. The creased sheet unfolded easily.

With a tight-lipped expression, she critically scanned the composition of misspelled words formed by letters of various sizes and colors cut from a magazine and pasted sloppily onto the sheet. Nevertheless, the message was clear.

"The massaker at sharpville will be childplay compared to what will happen if U dont cancel the 'ANTIAPARTHEID' concert," the note threatened. "Mandela is free. Leve well enuf alone. 'Apartheid In South Africa' aint yo biznes. Lessen U do as we say—we'll blow yo simpetizers away And u wont have no Business to tend to. Sincerely, Supporters of Separation."

"Want me to call Officer Daniels?" Marie asked somberly, her eyes riveted on the paper as it fell from Patrice's trembling hand back onto the desk into its natural creases.

Frightful images began to form in Patrice's mind, making it impossible for her to speak. She nodded her head woodenly, before dropping into her chair. Mindless that she was ruining the make-up accenting her soft brown skin, she passed a tired hand, tipped with long, red nails across her face.

Marie left her staring with anxious eyes at the paper. *You can handle whatever it is, huh?* she chided herself with a sardonic snort.

Patrice felt her confidence floundering, and all she could think to do was kick off her high-heel shoes. She got up and began to wear an invisible trail in the carpet, pacing back and forth in pursuit of answers. But none came. She was frustrated by her inability to solve her first major crisis.

Meandering about the room, she stopped in front of the first floor-to-ceiling window and drew open the blue metal blinds. Staring blankly at the artificially lit skyline painted against the darkened wintery sky, she pressed one hand against the cold glass, longing for a sign, a signal of hope.

The night held strong to its secrets.

Patrice wrapped her arms around herself and closed her eyes, envisioning the end of her nine month reign as general manager. *That is,* she thought, *if I don't make a decision,—the right one. Soon.*

ȥ ȥ ȥ ȥ

Patrice looked at the expensive black and gold watch on her wrist for the umpteenth time. Sighing disgustedly, she dropped her hand to her lap and glanced at the wall clock above the door, part of a ritual that had begun ten minutes earlier. Reversing the crossed-legged position at her ankles, she shifted in her seat, as she examined the gray walled and carpeted reception room. *Didn't anyone ever tell him that it was rude to keep someone waiting?* Awaiting an appearance from Lawrence Woodson, the Vice President of Fiscal Affairs at Banneker University, was not her idea of efficient time management.

Nearly a week had passed before she'd come up with the idea of approaching the university as host for the concert. Once it occurred to her that the campus would be an ideal site, she wondered why she hadn't thought of it in the first place.

Banneker was located in Treeland Heights, a quiet, upper-middle class, suburban community roughly 28 miles northwest of Houston. Having been a resident of the area for a year, she knew it well. Though dominated mostly by white families, a handful of blacks had moved in, residing for the most part unscathed.

The developers had gone to considerable lengths to fashion a town that both complimented and incorporated the natural beauty of the forested acres. Trees lined major thoroughfares, as well as every residential and most commercial properties. The university was situated on the southwestern fringes of a wooded area surrounded by some of the most splendid oaks you'd ever want to see.

"Perfect," she said to herself with a smile. She'd revised the original concept and the concert was now part of a festival. This element would allow the university to earn additional revenue by charging for booth space and drawing an even bigger crowd to the campus. It was a well-known fact that Banneker, like so many Texas institutions of higher learning, needed additional funds for expansion, physically and academically.

She had it all worked out. *Now all I have to do is convince Mr. Woodson.* A scowl replaced the smile when she looked up to check the time. There was no sign of him.

Counseling herself to be a little more tolerant, she uncrossed her legs and sat ramrod straight in her seat. Her eyes began to wander about the professionally decorated area, its elegance worthy and befitting an administrator of fiscal affairs.

The reception area was accented with green vases and ashtrays, and sported black lacquer furnishings such as the chair in which she sat. A large framed black and white charcoal painting of Benjamin Banneker, for whom the university was named, was located on the wall behind her. On the opposite wall was a whimsical set of prints entitled, "Butterfly Women."

She wondered idly if he'd had any influence in the selection, before impulsively discounting the possibility that Woodson would have any appreciation for fine arts, especially for such a delicate and feminine piece.

Patrice was intrigued by what little information she had been able to gather on Lawrence Woodson. Most of it came from a press release that was prepared by the university's public relations office. He was lauded for his proficient business acumen and effective managerial style. There was no mention, however, of his heroism in Vietnam, for which his valor earned him a Congressional Medal of Honor. She'd gotten this tidbit from a column in an old issue of *Black Enterprise* magazine. Unfortunately, there hadn't been a photograph to accompany the article.

He was 39, single, and owned an accounting firm. According to the rumor mill, he was thinking about selling the six-year-old company. Few were surprised when he took leave to head up the fiscal management of the school at the request of Dr. Charles Black, president of Banneker; the two men were friends of long-standing.

He was supposedly a stickler for punctuality, she recalled with skepticism, beginning to suspect that he was purposely leaving her to cool her heels. She chuckled at the irony because her feet were starting to hurt in the three-inch, high-heel shoes.

She smothered a yawn, the only visible sign that she'd gotten very little sleep, having spent most of the night mantally polishing the proposal. *Is he ever going to come out of hibernation?* she thought.

Just to have something to do with her hands, Patrice smoothed the hairs at the nape. As she knew, every strand was in place, for she had gone to the hairdresser only two days ago for a touch-up to straighten the wavy roots of her hair with a gentle relaxer. After a shampoo and blow-dry, her nails, medium length and polished a subdued pink, had been tended by the manicurist.

Deciding to review the proposal one more time, she turned to get her case, then decided against it. She knew it from the first word to the last period, and going over it again would only irritate her. She didn't want anything to interfere with the impression she wanted to make. *No, not wanted to make,* she revised, *had to make.*

Just thinking how important it was to gain his approval was enough to create a festival in her stomach. There was more at stake here than KHVY sponsoring a major concert. Her career as general manager of the station, representing everything she'd worked towards for the past fifteen years and her future, was on the line. If she failed, it would all be shattered into tiny memories.

She slid from her seat in search of a distraction. Her steps took her across the room, drawn by the twin paintings where vibrant colors and intricate details of butterfly wings were exquisitely crafted into a woman's form.

🙶 🙶 🙶 🙶

Lawrence Woodson walked into the room unnoticed. And for that, he was grateful. He hadn't wanted this meeting. Not even the mention of a financial benefit to Banneker had made any difference. Rather, it had been Patrice Mason's persistence that won him over, even as it had repulsed him. Now, he wondered at the quixotic sensations churning inside as he watched her from the doorway that connected the waiting room to his private office.

His eyes catalogued every detail: She was of medium height; he guessed somewhere between 5'5" and 5'7". Nothing else about her, however, suggested the average—her slender frame was poised in front of the glass framed print on the wall, broadcasting regal certainty. Nature had been especially kind, he thought, blessing her tone of blackness with a silky cafe creme complexion. Her thick, black hair, adorned with decorative red and gold combs, was twisted in a ball on top of her head.

The beginnings of a smile tipped the corners of his mouth while his eyes scouted languorously down her back. Her fine shape complimented the dramatic black crepe suit. The shoulder-padded jacket fitted snugly at her tiny waist before flaring over the skirt which tapered to just above the knees.

His rapt attention to her figure caused him to question his propensity for involvement with women who were sedate in temperament and dress, sensing that she was not one of placid emotions. The observation brought to mind another woman he once knew, and the muscles in his face tensed.

"Ms. Mason."

≈ ≈ ≈ ≈

Patrice's hand froze against the glass where she was tracing the wing of a butterfly with her finger. The richness of the manly voice reverberated in her ear and scaled her spine with its mellow overture. *If that voice were on Heavy, our female demographics would go through the roof.* She spun quickly, eager to meet the owner of the dulcet baritone.

Initial contact placed her eye level with a shiny tie pin clasping a blue and white silk tie to a starched white shirt. The expansion of her wide-eyed gaze took in the composite of masculine vigor in the flesh—from his handsome face, and broad shoulders that tapered down to slim, taunt hips. The dark blue suit was finely cut, and a pair of black wing tip shoes complemented his attire.

Her gaze fastened on the set of piercing eyes, staring blankly back at her. Their centers were the most amazing color she'd ever seen on anyone of his dark toast coloring. She blinked, thinking she'd mistaken their brilliant olive glow; the color was more virescent than brown. But when she looked again, a hazel hue dominated his intense, assessing gaze.

Her pulse livened and warning signals flashed in her head, making her question whether she was prepared for a meeting with this man.

Full and earthy summarized the overall effect of his looks. The hairs on his jawline were as thick as those on the top of his head, fashioned in a close-cropped, neat cut. The mouth and chin were firm, effectively casting aside any notions of weakness, but one would always be drawn back to those exotic intense eyes. *Lord, how can anyone prepare for those eyes? They belong in the bedroom—definitely not wasted in an office.*

"I'm sorry to have kept you waiting."

Patrice discovered, to her dismay, that she could not recapture the full indignation she'd felt just moments ago. She cleared her throat before replying, "I was beginning to think"—when their hands touched, her voice dropped to a near whisper—"that you were doing it on purpose."

Within a fraction of a second Lawrence decided she didn't need the make-up, staring at her smooth, clear skin, and the dab of red outlining her wide mouth. Though surprise heightened the sparkle in her almond shaped, brown eyes, he felt certain their fiery challenge spelled trouble for any man foolish enough to dally in their warmth.

He released her hand abruptly, and resisting the impulse to rub his tingling palm against the leg of his trousers, indicated that she should precede into the private office. She retrieved her briefcase and overcoat before following the direction of his outstretched hand.

Everything within the office seemed large, and spoke conclusively of his importance to the university. But it was just a place to work. There were no personal objects, no mementos, no obvious clues to his personality. *He didn't select the furnishings; he probably didn't notice or care about the selection at all,* Patrice suspected.

The long room mirrored the color scheme of the reception area, with windows lining the top half of the entire north wall. A personal computer was nestled over in one corner, while across the room was a gray velvet sofa. A large cherry desk was placed against the east wall, parallel to a glass encased cherry bookcase lined with books.

Lawrence guided her into an armchair that had been placed in front of his desk, cluttered with stacks of manilla folders, before retreating to the large black leather chair on the other side. *That was probably the only thing in the room he'd chosen himself,* she thought, watching him ease into the stiff, throne-like, swivel seat, undaunted by the squeak when he sat.

"Ms. Mason."

"Mr. Woodson."

Each addressed the other simultaneously and exchanged polite smiles. Motioning with his hand, he offered, "Please, you first," then settled back in his chair expectantly.

Patrice experienced an energy higher than the time she'd made her first sales pitch. Her jittery insides were a good sign, she felt, hinting that her wits were renewing themselves.

"In case you aren't aware, Mr. Woodson, KHVY is relatively new in the market as far as radio stations go, but we've captured a substantial size of the market with our innovative programming and community involvement," she began with a great deal of pride.

"Since we've hit the airways roughly nine months ago," she continued, "we have sponsored forums on such issues as education and drop outs, crime prevention and safety, teenage drug abuse and pregnancy, and citizens' rights. In addition, we feature these and other topics on our regular public affairs show, 'Heavy Talk', which airs every Sunday morning. We don't want to stop with our community, Mr. Woodson. We want to be able to positively impact the world community, as well."

With each word she spoke, Patrice became more convinced of the value and plain rightness of the plan.

"As KHVY is part of a chain of stations owned by ATC Broadcasting, we have had the opportunity to be involved with national events, as well as local items of interest and need, as dictated by the ascertainments we've gathered."

Feeling confident in her element, and coupled with the insight of what his decision meant to her personally, she didn't have to force the enthusiasm that animated her features. "This brings us to our latest and the biggest project, by far, ever attempted by KHVY."

Without missing a beat, she passed a blue folder across the desk to him as she explained how ideal Banneker University would be for this event.

Lawrence couldn't help his response to her pitch. *One of these know-it-alls. I should have guessed. Of course, they're the only people who can be trusted to know and do what's right for the world. How fortunate we morons are to have them around to guide us.*

But, she was persuasive, he conceded. Conviction characterized her every inflection and gesture, and as he accepted the shiny blue folder with the black embossed 'KHVY Heavy 106 FM' logo on the cover, he struggled to remain detached from the emotions bubbling inside. He placed the folder on his desk, never once losing sight of the dancing lights of her eyes as she detailed the station's plans for the all-day, anti-apartheid festival and concert.

Yet, the entrepreneurial spirit in him had to admire the air of self-confidence and daring about her. No significant sign of approval, however, cracked his indecipherable countenance. Caution ruled, advising him to wait.

Winding up her presentation, Patrice said as proudly as she'd begun,

"KHVY has established a reputation for its community involvement, and received numerous awards and citations, nationally, as well as locally, as a result of our participation. This project is just a continuation of our efforts to improve and enhance human life and dignity. It's not something we just decided to do."

"And now you're trying to add an international trophy to your award rack, Ms. Mason?" With the challenge came the first apparent sign of emotion, his eyes alight with the love of combat.

Her brow flickered slightly, but she recovered quickly from the unexpected attack, suppressing her surprise in a casual retort. "No, Mr. Woodson. Our bottom line is profits. Community service is a bonus."

"Touche! Why don't you come up with a bonus, to use your word, Ms. Mason, that will serve the community right here at your back door?" A tad of censure colored his tone.

She'd handled argumentative clients before, but she couldn't understand his objection to the station's choice of events. Lawrence Woodson was fast becoming a disappointment. *Please, don't let it be true that he's as shallow as he seems. Doesn't he understand that apartheid is a disease that threatens the fabric of humanity?*

"Excuse me," she said, resting the folder flat on her lap. In spite of her reserve, a faint note of bewilderment slipped into her voice. "There seems to be a problem here. And I'm not sure if it's rooted in some political ideology, or something else."

He looked momentarily abashed, but promptly reverted to the familiar, blank stare. It was not like him to be so openly hostile, regardless of the person or the presentation. He didn't know why he was baiting her, only that he liked the way she sparred. "I'm against apartheid, Ms. Mason, but I fail to see how having a concert . . ."

"And festival," she tacked on.

"And festival," he mimicked, "are going to benefit the people in South Africa. Though I can see your station lining its pockets with money from people who probably couldn't care less about what's happening over there, or even know what's going on."

"That's where you're wrong, Mr. Woodson," she contradicted with triumph in her voice. She bounced up to lean over his desk and opened the folder before him.

He shot her a penetrating look as she rose, then clasped his hands together, careful not to touch hers. Struck by a yearning to taste the lilac-like fragrance that teased his nostrils with its ambrosial scent, he slipped his hands under the desk as though distancing himself from temptation.

Patrice's speech faltered when her eyes met his; she felt herself drowning in his fathomless, light brown gaze. Growing increasingly uneasy under the scrutiny, she lowered her eyes and eased back into her chair.

"The figure in the middle of the page is what we propose to donate to the Bishop Scholarship Fund," she said with as reasonable a voice as she could manage, her eyes riveted on her own copy of the proposal. "And the figure at the bottom is what we propose to donate to the university. That's in addition to what you can earn from the vendors."

"I see," was all he said as he read the figures under the columns marked expenses, earnings and additional revenues on the page. "This amount is fairly generous. Almost too generous."

Lifting her head, she bristled, "What do you mean?"

She made real to him the picture of a proud, defiant Queen Nzingha, fighting colonial rule. Her eyes were slightly round, and bright like shooting stars, her posture stiff and erect. How could such a young woman have been given so much authority? he wondered mildly. His silent answer was not flattering.

"I can't help thinking there's a catch," replied Lawrence, a suspicious line at the corners of his mouth. "You can rent any facility on our campus six to eight times over with what you're offering."

She knew this moment would arrive. "There is no catch, Mr. Woodson." She moistened dry lips. "There is, however, a problem. A minor one, I assure you."

She could almost hear him say, "Ah-ha!", as though he had deduced the villain in a mystery. "The details are on page four in the proposal."

He quickly turned the pages of the proposal, his thick brows furrowed in disbelief. Lawrence sat up in his seat as he scanned each page, his concentration complete.

Patrice watched his profile; it spoke of power and strength, the set of his chin suggesting a stubborn streak. From academician's cloth, he was not cut; the energy he gave off was more like that of a . . . There was no time to complete her assessment, for he raised his head, his eyes riveted on her face.

Patrice swallowed hard as she faced his brooding visage. It lasted for only a second before yet another stoic expression shadowed his handsome face. He drew a deep, ragged breath. Patrice bit her lips in dismay when he closed the folder with finality.

Her heart, however, refused to believe what her mind told her.

The leather moaned as Lawrence shifted in the chair. The tips of his fingers began to rap a staccato beat against each other as he struggled to contain the storm brewing inside him. Then, "wham!", his mighty hands rammed against one another in a single, thunderous clap, causing Patrice to jump in her seat.

"I was wondering what the kicker would be, Ms. Mason."

She flinched at the tomb-like tone of his voice, more frightening than if he had yelled at her. Only seconds ticked off, though it seemed like hours to her before he spoke again.

"And now that I know . . . . " He stopped in mid-sentence to glance out the window, a muscle quivered at his jaw. He was facing her again to explain, "I'm wondering what kind of woman you are. What drives a person like you to gamble with the lives of other people?" She opened her mouth to challenge the pronouncement of guilt, but was swiftly cut off. "Haven't the consequences occurred to you? What if your prank-ster," he leaned across the desk to continue, "is as serious as everyone else, but you," he stressed mockingly, "seem to believe?"

"Mr. Woodson, the concert date is almost three months away. By then, I expect the police . . ."

"How dare you even consider coming to us under these circum-stances?" he asked, the depth of his anger yet to be displayed.

He rose from the seat; his eyes flashed marbles of outrage. He pointed an accusing finger in her face, demanding, "Do you know the power a bomb has, Ms. Mason? Do you have any idea of the kind of devastation to human life and property a bomb can cause in the hands of a lunatic?"

Stalking around the desk to tower over her, Lawrence grounded out, "For your information, Ms. Mason, bombs destroy property. They maim and kill people, Ms. Mason!" He pounded the top of the desk with one angry fist, then promptly spun away from her.

Patrice cringed, feeling as small as she imagined he meant for her to feel. She too had questioned her own motives, experienced moments when she wondered if she were doing the right thing. *Have I let a desperation to prove myself get in the way of common sense and reason? What if I've overestimated the damage a cancellation would have on my career?* The internal list of questions were endless.

You should have seen this coming, her mind taunted. However, nothing in the world could have readied her for this reaction.

She couldn't think of one suitable defense in light of his argument and sat meekly through the detailed accounting on the various types of bombs and their destructive capabilities. He strode about the room, his hands waving to emphasize a particular point, as he continued to reprimand her for selfish greed and stupidity.

But Patrice only half listened as she struggled with her conscience.

Lawrence had no tolerance for ignorance, nor did he care whether he hurt her feelings, and fueled by vivid recollections of the bloody and mangled bodies he'd witnessed in Nam, he reiterated each and every point. No, he didn't give one whit about hurting her feelings. Hundreds of thousands of dead or broken men should be so lucky.

After a while, the ranting words ceased to have an impact, as Patrice was mesmerized by the vigor of his release. *Mercy. Mercy. The man is absolutely magnificent angry.*

Finally, he stopped, and the silence jolted her from the fanciful trance. Indecision, compounded by disorientation, held her immobile, until she looked up and met the icy contempt in the hazel eyes boring down at her.

She treated him to a sudden flash of defensive spirit. "Now wait one minute, Mr. Woodson," rising from her seat. "If you'll stop with the character assassination, I can outline the precautions we're taking and our contingency . . . . "

"I don't believe you, *woman*," he said, shaking his head from side-to-side. "You obviously didn't hear a word I said, so let me make it plain and simple for you. I don't care about your precautions, Ms. Mason. Or your contingency plans."

Lawrence gathered her things and shoved them into her arms, declaring, "You're not going to get a trophy or award or anything else at our expense." Roughly, he then grabbed her by the arm and propelled her towards the door. "Good day, Ms. Mason. I have serious matters to attend to, so if you'll excuse me," he said, looking down at her.

Patrice just stood there, staring up at him in a daze. She felt incapable of bringing forth the fury she believed she should be feeling. She couldn't—didn't want to accept that this was happening to her. He had killed her last hope; the end of an outstanding career built by years of struggle was staring her in the face.

Her eyes mirrored the desolation sweeping through her. She nearly cried out as the painful realization dawned. Then for one precious second, she detected something akin to regret flare in those olive-brown eyes, and her pulses leaped with hope. Soon, she dismissed it as erroneous, wishful thinking for he was again glaring hostilely at her.

Patrice raised her chin, assuming some degree of dignity. She turned around and gracefully walked towards the door and out of the office.

Lawrence returned to his chair. He propped an elbow atop the desk and stared in a fixed gaze out the window. He'd never forget the sad look in those soft pools of sherry. He'd put it there. A stab of guilt pricked his conscience. *I wish it were easier.*

He flung the KHVY folder across the room and swore. "Damn!" Desperately reminding himself that she was not the kind of woman who needed or deserved sympathy. Nevertheless, he was extremely disgusted with himself.

Malcontent was sniping away at his heart.

CHAPTER ❧ TWO

Sometimes, Patrice Antionette, you're gonna stumble.

The knowing words of Patrice's aunt rang in her ears as she maneuvered the car through the downtown streets of the energy capital of the world. Well, she'd been tripped up several times. The most devastating occasion had been when she fancied herself in love the senior year in college, while completing an internship at KFFY, now one of her competitors.

Donald Hollingsworth had walked through the doors and taught her a lesson in love she'd never forget. All of her positive self-perceptions had been replaced with negative ones under his tutelage. If it hadn't been for her Aunt Cleo and best friend Kit, the twins' godmother, she didn't know how she would have survived the ordeal her ex-husband had put her through.

Though her aunt had passed away when the twins were seven, Patrice still remembered Cleo's words of encouragement—"You got to shake off bad and pack it under your feet, real good."

Never had those words meant more to her than now with her career on the line. It was not only her future at stake, but that of Stephen and Stephenie. Every hardship she had undergone had been for them, she mused. And she would gladly do it over again if it were in the cards.

Raising the twins would have been easier had she let her aunt take over right after they were born, for Donald had been unreliable even before then. Instead she had maintained control of their upbringing while completing the last year in the five-year curriculum for a bachelor in Business Management. Scheduling classes around the twins had not been a picnic, but she persisted.

Moving back into her aunt's home was the one concession in which she had no choice. Scholarships were just never intended to cover childcare, and Patrice's barely covered tuition and books. *And thank God I never gave up.*

Patrice popped the steering wheel with the ball of her hand, disgusted with herself for caving in to feelings of helplessness and defeat without a fight. The war ain't over yet, she told herself bravely. *I'll come out of this mess victorious, with or without you, Lawrence Woodson.*

She turned her '88 midnight blue Mercedes into the underground parking lot of the downtown office building where KHVY was located.

Who did he think he was anyway? How dare he tell her how to run her station? What the devil was his problem? And who is this idiot following so closely behind my Benz? was added to her growing list of hostilities when she noted the flash of red trailing behind her. She pulled into the reserved spot marked KHVY GM and shut off the engine.

The car behind her drove on.

She grabbed her briefcase and coat, and got out, slamming the door. She ran to the elevator and luckily didn't have long to wait as a gust of cold wind blew through the opened area. She stabbed the elevator button for the sixteenth floor.

With a free hand, she rubbed the knotted muscles of her shoulders. The notion she harbored for strangling that arrogant, insufferable, maniacal giant didn't help ease the tension created by six little men pounding away in her head.

The doors opened quietly, and stepping off the elevator onto the plush carpet of the hallway, she walked the few steps across the way to the thick glassed doors that brandished the station's call letters.

The young receptionist, Peggy, sitting behind the raised desk talking on the phone, saw her before she could press the doorbell. The buzzer sounded, unlocking the door, and Patrice walked into the station's lobby.

She acknowledged Peggy's wave with a nod, walked through a set of wooden doors, and down the quiet halls to her office. She dropped the briefcase on the black leather couch and hung the coat on the tall chrome coat stand in a corner adjacent to her desk.

Pain favored the back of her neck, and she massaged the area, looking around the teal blue room, undecided about what to do. *I could lose this room to someone.*

On the smoky glass topped desk was a portrait of her children, prominently displayed near the telephone. Numerous plaques and certificates lined the wall behind the desk, testaments to business achievements. There were others on the bookcase in the opposite corner of the room, which also housed her stereo unit, used primarily to monitor the station's broadcasts. All these things represented nearly fifteen years of paid dues—from night sweeper to general manager.

I can do anything.

That had been her automatic response to just about any question asked by an interviewer. And consequently, she had to do just that.

Right out of college with her radio experience limited to the then ten-watt campus station and an internship, her first commercial job had been as the overnight music announcer at a small station in Beaumont, roughly seventy miles from Houston. From two in the morning until six, she played soft "Rhythm & Blues." However, two hours before she went on the air and two hours afterwards, she was the janitor.

It was the best thing I could get, she mused.

Having that kind of access to the station proved essential in learning all aspects of the radio business. Information that wasn't available in school was now within hand's reach—when that hand wasn't clutching the mop and broom she used to clean.

She got back to Houston with just time enough to take the twins to the day-care center, then returned home for a few hours sleep and shower before heading to the "real" job. As a sales clerk at one of the local department stores she was paid more than she was at her job at the radio station, and needed the second job just to survive. That schedule lasted for two years until she'd had a lucky break. Patrice couldn't recall the name of the account executive at the Beaumont station, but was grateful to him for quitting, for it had been her entree into the sales department. The salary wasn't great, but it allowed her to quit the second job and take on more financial responsibility for herself and the twins.

She rode out of Beaumont as the leading salesperson for six months; the length of time she stayed before moving on to Houston. Each job thereafter represented an increase in salary and professional marketability. She had literally broken sales records, and about five years ago, station managers had begun calling her, instead of the other way around. Ironically, the key to Patrice's success had been the development of the then untapped ethnic business market. Few of the radio stations realized how successful some of the smaller Black-owned businesses were. But she had. Many of those accounts were fiercely loyal and moved whenever and wherever Patrice did. This became the word within the industry and was the foundation of her reputation.

Patrice opened the blinds on the window where the view of the northeastern section of downtown was partially obstructed by skyscrapers or limited to the rooftops of older structures. The adjacent window allowed her to see past the freeway that she traveled daily.

She had won what many said the south was not ready for, nor wouldn't be for another ten to fifteen years, if ever. But the handwriting had already been printed on the wall—chiseled there in fact, by the many Black men and women who strove daily to remove the confinements and barriers of prejudice. Since the 1960s, many of Houston's Black residences strove to break the mold of the state's good ole' boy image. The Oiler football team now boasted an African American quarterback; a Nigerian starred on the line-up of the basketball team; the mayor was a woman, as was the chief of police, who inherited the position from a Black man.

Yes, racial tolerance seemed on the horizon in this country, but discrimination was still the mandate of the day. And being a "double minority" meant that Patrice caught hell both ways, for although she was no quitter, she had almost caved in to the beliefs of the skeptics. Almost that is, until she was able to prove them wrong when interviewed by ATC Broadcasting.

At the time, Patrice was the national sales manager at KBBU, a top 40 FM station. The general manager at KBBU proclaimed that Patrice could sell water to fish, and offered her a substantial raise to stay.

She weighed the offer against that from ATC, admittedly somewhat afraid to leave the security she had built. It wasn't until Anthony Russell, ATC's founder and principal owner had flown her up to Chicago (where the company's headquarters was located) for a personal interview that she decided—if given the nod for the general manager slot, she'd take it without looking back.

Even now with the crisis she faced, she knew she'd do it all over again.

Deep contemplation lined her face as she began to pace the area between the coffee table and desk. Calling the home office for advice was out of the question. Such action might be perceived as a sign of instability. No, she didn't want to risk it. The home office had been alerted when the first threat was sent on a computer a week after Christmas, a little more than three weeks ago.

She froze in mid-stride when she heard, then saw the last of a long row of buttons on the phone light up. It was a private number, and the only line that did not ring through the switchboard. It usually meant a call from Mr. Russell.

Patrice hurried to her desk and rubbed moist hands on her skirt before pressing the button. She cleared her throat, and picked up the mouthpiece. "Hello."

Eyeing the phone with puzzlement when there was no response, she replaced the receiver. Though relieved that the call wasn't from Chicago, the hammering in her head did not diminish. With palms raised, she slipped into the chair and applied pressure to the sides of her head.

There was a light rap on the door, then Marie walked in carrying several folders. Marie was in her late 20's, and as usual, she dressed the part of a young urban professional.

Patrice had brought Marie with her from KBBU, where the young woman had been the sales secretary. There was only one thing about Marie which had the power to irk Patrice to no end—and that was bemoaning the absence of a man in her life. Had it not been for Marie's loyalty and attention to detail, which made her invaluable, Patrice wouldn't even have considered offering Marie a position at KHVY. But Marie must have resurrected a waning lovelife because Patrice hadn't heard a peep from her on the matter.

"Perfect timing. Lunch is on the way," Marie announced cheerfully, before observing her boss scouring through desk drawers. "The meeting with Mr. Woodson didn't go well, I take it."

"You got it on the first try," replied Patrice, locating a bottle of aspirins. She opened the safety proof cap with difficulty, then shook two white tablets into the palm of her hand.

"I'll get you some water," offered Marie, about to set the folders on the desk.

"No, thanks," said Patrice, rising, "I'll get it. I need to move around a bit. I'm so mad at that man I could spit," she said with venom in her voice.

She walked from the room and down the hall to the water cooler. She popped the aspirins into her mouth and washed them down with water. While crushing the cup, she couldn't help but think of the satisfaction she would gain from proving Mr. Woodson wrong. *She didn't need his precious college.* But the gesture seemed empty somehow, giving her no pleasure at all. She tossed the crumpled paper into the trash can and headed back to her office.

Marie, Roger, the station's program director and Belinda Cashe, the news director, were already seated on the couch when she returned to her office. Roger, tall and lean, in his early 30's, was sandwiched between the two women.

"You look like the three blind mice," she commented in a mildly amused voice, heading for her desk.

"The ladies are wondering if we should cancel this regular session," Roger said with a hopeful expression.

Patrice's left brow shot up, for she knew the ladies wondered no such thing. And frankly, she was somewhat surprised that Roger would suggest it. "Why?"

"We know about your meeting," he said sheepishly, displaying a chipped tooth. "And you're probably in a bad mood," he cajoled. "And I have a major project going on in production I'd like to return to."

She chuckled lightly, thinking Roger was the only one on the staff bold enough to speak his mind. While she didn't begrudge him his audacity— she also tried to stay in control.

"Thanks for your concern, Roger, but don't worry about my bad mood. Just be thankful it's not directed at you," she replied with a smile to temper the sting of her biting retort.

"Ouch," cringed Roger, joining the laughter that surrounded him. Patrice picked up the folder left on the desk and opened it. There was something about the action that triggered the reminder of being in Lawrence Woodson's office. The smile fell.

"Trice, are you sure you're all right?"

Patrice's head snapped up, and she focused her attention on Belinda, the youngest member of the administrative staff. She had taken a chance hiring B.C., as she was affectionately called by the staff, right out of college. Patrice had recruited her as a reporter, and when the experienced male she had wanted to hire exhibited signs of resentment toward a female boss, B.C. was put to the test. There had been a few tense moments, but the petite, blue-eyed bundle of energy was now working out better than Patrice could have hoped.

"Yeah, I'm fine, thanks," she replied still somewhat distracted, then released a deep audible sigh. "Anything interesting happened while I was away?" she asked offhandedly.

All three stiffened, knowing she alluded to the threats. Roger spoke up, disdain evident in his voice. "If you're referring to the nasty notes we've been getting, no."

Everyone at the station had been privileged to Roger's reaction to the threats. He had moped around, whining that somebody was trying to destroy his reputation in the industry. He had worked as hard as Patrice to secure entertainers for the concert.

Patrice would never admit it to him, but she was just as scared.

"Marie, were you able to get in touch with Officer Daniels?"

"No, I tried several times, but he's been out in the field and hasn't returned any of my calls."

"Try him again after the meeting," Patrice said in a dismissive tone. "Where's Mike?"

Michael Todd Franklin, II, KHVY's immaculately dressed sales manager walked in on cue, a wide grin spread across his face. Mike was in his mid 30's, and with his classically handsome features, golden hair and piercing bluish-green eyes, he could have been a GQ model.

"You must have made a big sale," Belinda guessed.

"Two," he stated proudly, holding up an equal number of fingers. Pulling a chair alongside Patrice's desk, he elaborated, "We got Fruit Juice for another three months, and Heathor for six."

"What's Heathor?" They all wanted to know at the same time.

"A company that produces contraceptives for men," he replied. Laughter erupted from everyone except Mike, who launched into a dissertation on the station's responsibility in helping reduce unwanted teen pregnancies and promoting safe sex.

"All right, all right," Patrice said, trying to restore order, traces of amusement lingering in her voice. "Let's get started."

Having called the meeting to order, she steered away from her unsuccessful encounter with the Banneker University vice-president and channeled the discussion to future promotions and special projects the station would undertake.

❧ ❧ ❧ ❧

Hating lengthy meetings, Patrice called an end to the session after an hour. The sandwiches and drinks delivered for the meeting had been consumed, so all that remained was Roger. He was sprawled across the couch, his eyes closed as he listened to the station's broadcast of a popular female artist singing of the love she threw away for a better one.

Patrice was standing at the floor length, north side window looking pensively out in the direction of the buildings across the way, but unaware of them. The soft rain that started during the meeting had developed into a heavy downpour, blanketing the streets with its intensity.

Its called greed, she thought cynically in response to the lyrics of the song. The melody of the tune and the rain reminded her of a time when she was secure in love: First, her parents until their untimely death in a car accident when she was eight years old, and then Aunt Cleo, who had raised her.

Feeling betrayed when her parents died, she had vowed to never trust anyone again. But Aunt Cleo, her father's widowed sister, wouldn't be denied what she called her "favorite things": love, trust and friendship.

Patrice smiled fondly in remembrance of the eccentric woman who had given her so much. Though there hadn't been a lot of money, Aunt Cleo had a knack for finding things to do and places to go that were fun, inexpensive and more often than not, educational.

Then there was Kit, whom Patrice was closer to than any one of the handful of relatives she had scattered across the country. Kit and the twins were all that was left in the circle of her love. She doubted seriously that it could ever be widened.

The image of Lawrence emerged so vividly in her mind that she could imagine reaching out to run the back of her hand down his strong jaw. Patrice shook her head in denial as she remembered his intellectual maligning and slanderous tongue. And to believe she had sat there so thoroughly mesmerized by his presence that she had been reluctant, even paralyzed to defend herself!

That was simply lust, she snorted inelegantly. *Lust for a pleasing voice and sexy body*, she mused. "Stop it," she whispered to herself.

"What did you say?" asked Roger, startled from his reverie.

"Oh, nothing," she tossed casually over her shoulder.

She didn't see his disbelieving look, but felt questioning eyes boring into her back. The song recaptured her attention: the songstress was belting out a plea for another chance with an old love.

Patrice simply could not afford to associate this song with Lawrence Woodson—for even though it was a sad song, she liked it—and moved to the bookcase to terminate the haunting melody that filled the room.

"Hey, why'd you do that? I wanted to hear the segue," protested Roger.

"Then go to your own office," she quipped, striding to her desk.

"I know you need my company," he retorted.

She laughed as she picked up a handful of messages. "These little slips of pink paper represent all the calls I have to return before the end of the day," she explained patiently, a hint of amusement in her tone. "Now, will you get out of here and let me get to work? Besides, you haven't visited me since you got your laser installed and your new toy in production," she teased.

"And thank you again for modernizing our equipment," he said swinging his legs off the couch to rise. "I can hardly wait for the next book to see how many points we've gained in the ratings. We sound so good it's unbelievable!"

"You're welcome. Now, scram," she said.

"You haven't told me about your meeting with the man at Banneker," he said, resting his palms flat on the desk and leaning over towards her. "I want the full details."

"Roger," she said with an exasperating sigh, rubbing her temples. "If I were you, I'd back off," she threatened in a gentle tone.

"But you're not me," he replied impishly. "And I have as much at stake in this as you do. So give," he added, sticking his hands in the side pockets of his jeans.

She bit down on her lip and briefly hung her head before looking up, literally pass Roger. Her eyes were cloudy with the memory of being forcibly escorted from Woodson's office. Patrice felt then, as she did now, that she had been unfairly judged and convicted. Yet still, she also harbored an awful sensation of having lost something more important than a concert site.

"Earth to Patrice," said Roger, snapping his fingers in her face.

She looked apologetically at Roger, and realized that he was prepared to stay until he received his answer. If there were any way she could get out of having to deal with his tireless interrogation, she would, but she knew better. *He has a right to know where we stand.* Calmly, she began a capsuled accounting of what had happened, but before she finished, outright annoyance textured her voice and gestures. "He lost complete control! It was humiliating."

"My god, is the man blind?" said Roger with indignation that brought laughter and lightheartedness to Patrice.

"Roger, you surprise me sometimes," she said.

"Why?" he said, "Don't tell me you buy into that rumor that I prefer men over women, and don't appreciate a good looking woman?" in a mildly accusing tone, smacking his lips. "If it weren't against my policy, I'd...." he stopped short of completing the thought, a wolfish expression tipping the corners of his mouth up in a grin.

This time her laugh was full. She had wondered about Roger's effeminate ways, but believed his sexual preference was none of her business. As long as he did his job—which he performed excellently as evidenced by the double digit ratings the station had received in the last two books—that was all that mattered to her. The fact that they got along so well was a plus.

"I really don't think looks had anything to do with it," she corrected him primly.

She kept secret her suspicion that Mr. Woodson's animosity had nothing to do with what she had proposed, or even the danger he vehemently insisted was inherent. *No, his objection had been against me personally.* Black females who rose in the corporate structure to decision-making positions have been the targets of malicious speculations and envy. Some men would go to great lengths to bring them down, if not with back-stabbing power plays, then with sly verbiage that raised questions and self-doubt.

"I'm really disappointed that you're sitting here, blowing smoke at me," he said, feigning hurt. "I shouldn't have to tell you how delicious you look in that little black number you're wearing. The man should have been so enraptured that he didn't pay any attention to the proposal."

"You're being chauvinistic," she warned. "Anyway, I think he had something against me personally. He kept me waiting for over twenty minutes for our scheduled appointment."

"And that burned the hell out of you, didn't it?"

"It's the principle of the thing," she started hotly, then caught herself and calmed down. "He agreed to the appointment and should have been there on time."

"He's really rattled your nerves. It's not like you to get so upset," he said with an insightful look in his eyes.

She sighed deeply and agreed. "You're right. I don't know," she said, flinging the messages across the desk. "This whole thing with the bomb threats must be getting to me more than I realized. It's beginning to look like all of our hard work has been for nothing. We may have to cancel."

"There has to be another way," he said, rubbing his jaw thoughtfully.

"Give me a day or two to see what happens," she said in a doubtful tone as she picked up the scattered messages. "Now, let me get to work."

"Ok," he replied, backing from her desk to the door. "If I come up with something before you, I'll come and visit."

"Thanks."

"And Patrice," he added, holding the door slightly ajar. "If your reaction to him is anything to judge by, then I've no doubt the man will call you back, now that he's had time to read through your proposal, without distractions." He smiled knowingly before walking out and closing the door behind him.

🐦 🐦 🐦 🐦

"I told you not to call me at work." Standing behind her desk in her cove-like office, the young woman sorted through papers, holding the phone between her shoulder and ear. "What do you want?"

"Nothing, baby," the man on the other end replied in a voice as smooth as silk. "Is there anything wrong with a man missing his lady and wanting to hear her voice?"

She heard the familiar pout in his voice and regretted her chastisement. This man, her lover, was sensitive and sometimes childish. "No, I'm sorry," she repented softly as she dropped into the chair. "I think it's real sweet of you to call. I was just looking at all these letters I have to type and feeling overwhelmed. Will you forgive me for being so snappy?"

"Sure baby, you're my number one lady."

"I'd better be your only lady," she teased. Theirs was a young relationship—a month and a half to be exact, but the love bug had bitten her quickly. He wasn't the easiest man—he could be mean and had a quick temper—but compared to what she'd had before, he was the best thing that happened to her.

"Want to go out to dinner tonight?" he asked.

"Oh, Jay, I don't know. I'll probably be so tired. There's so much to do. I'll be lucky just to get out of here on time."

"The dragon lady got you running, huh?"

"She's not a dragon lady, and I wish you'd stop calling her that," she said in a mildly irritated tone.

"And I wish you'd stop defending her," he returned bitingly. "Hey look, since you're so busy, I'm gonna let you go."

She'd hurt his feelings; he was sulking, a prelude to anger. Usually when he got angry, his punishment was disappearing for days on end. "Will you call me tonight?"

He hesitated, and she felt as though her heart had lodged itself in her throat, fearing she'd driven him off.

"Yeah, I'll call you tonight," he replied in a grudging voice. Marie breathed a silent sigh of relief.

꙳ ꙳ ꙳ ꙳

Patrice was heedless of the streaks of lightening that flashed brilliantly and the thunder that rocked the cold night sky as she drove out of the parking lot. Gusts of strong winds howled through the open spaces, around the tall steel, brick and glass structures that lined the streets. She steered her car across the smooth pavement made slippery by the light rain—a maze of turns, then a dart onto the freeway that would take her home.

Her work day had ended the way it started—miserably.

Officer Daniels had finally called, but had little to offer in the way of good news: only the same advice he had given her previously.

"Again, the decision to cancel is up to you, Ms. Mason. But I don't think there's anything to these threats. Like I've told you before, professionals don't join causes. They'd wait until the day of the concert, maybe a few hours before the thing starts and demand money. Knowing that if you didn't pay, there would be no way to clear thousands of people from an auditorium without somebody getting hurt. We'll keep working on this and I'll let you know as soon as we uncover something."

She, too, held the belief that a prankster was behind the threats, which was why she hadn't taken the first one seriously. When the second ultimatum arrived, she'd driven her staff crazy, fluctuating between anger and indecision, before deciding the station would go on with its plans.

At least, that had been the case until the manager of the Summit— home of the Houston Rockets' basketball team—called to cancel the rental agreement. He had also received a bomb threat if he allowed the concert to be held there.

It wasn't long afterwards before Patrice discovered that every major concert hall and arena in the city had received a similar warning. Nothing she or Officer Daniels had said could convince any of those managers that the threats were a hoax. That had forced her to seek an alternative.

And even it hadn't worked, she thought, thinking back to the disastrous meeting with Lawrence Woodson. "Damn!" she whispered disgustedly, slapping the wheel with the heel of her hand.

"I won't think about it," she reasoned out loud, trying to talk herself into a calm state of mind. "I came up with one alternative, I can very well come up with another."

After driving several miles through the bumper-to-bumper traffic, the back of her neck tingled as if teased by a feather, and her insides began to quiver as though awaiting disaster to strike. She wet her lips nervously and gripped the steering wheel with both hands.

You're being ridiculous, she told herself with a short laugh, but frequented looks in the rear view mirror.

She turned on the radio, and the familiar saxophone of Grover Washington, Jr., filled the car with one of his popular compositions. She hummed along with the music, a ruse to free herself from the sudden attack of paranoia. She didn't relax, however, until she turned into her circular driveway and was safely in the foyer of her one-and-a-half level home, where a light shone from every room.

"Kids! I'm home," she called out, dropping her keys on the hall table, the vines of a flourishing ivory hanging over one side. Her heels clicked against the white, tiled floor on the way to deposit her overcoat and briefcase in the front closet to the left of the stairs.

Receiving no answer, she stood with one foot on the bottom step of the carpeted staircase, holding onto the handrail and calling again. "Stephen? Stephenie? Are you up there?"

Only a pair of long legs was visible from the top of the stairs where her son called down, "We're doing homework, Mom."

Miffed, she asked, "Don't I get a hello or something?"

"Hi, Mom," he replied dutifully.

"Hi, Mom," she heard her daughter echo.

"All right, if you want to be that way," she said in a conciliatory voice. *Moms have their tactics, too. They'll be down shortly*, chuckling under her breath at her duplicity. She backed down the step, turned, and strolled down the hall to her bedroom.

Despite her nonchalance, she felt a stab of guilt, well aware of the reason for their indifference. After all hadn't she spent the better part of the previous night debating whether she was being too hard on them? This was the part of parenting she liked the least—having to make all the decisions and dole out the discipline.

It is simply no fun being the bad guy all the time, she thought, wrinkling her nose distastefully. *But somebody's got to do it.*

She exhaled a resigning sigh when she reached her room. The master bedroom featured a wisteria pattern superimposed over lavender painted canvased walls. The opulent design was duplicated on the bed's comforter and curtains, which covered the picture window that practically took up the entire wall opposite the door.

She was greeted by a potpourri of pleasant fragrances given off by the dry crushed flowers in the colorful vases set about the room. She stepped out of her heels and wiggled her tired toes in the downy softness of the thick, white carpet on the floor, and sighed a long, soothing, "Awwww."

She had created this room for moments such as the one she was experiencing. It represented a kind of simple extravagance she'd wished for as a child—from the white, gold trimmed nightstands, to the matching bureau, and glass shelved bookcase, where tiny crystal ornaments were displayed. The only pieces of furniture that were out of place in style, but not in sentiment, were the cherry wood armoire and rocking chair which had been a gift from Aunt Cleo when the twins were born.

Moving toward the northern end of the long rectangular room to slide open the double doors of the walk-in closet, she exchanged business attire for an ankle-length, velvet cream caftan with a long stemmed rose design down the front.

She glanced at her watch and wondered what was taking the twins so long to appear. Shrugging off the nagging doubts that maybe her plan wouldn't work this time, she climbed onto her queen-size bed. Reaching over to the nightstand on her left, she pried a magazine from under the lavender princess telephone, then leaned back against the large pillows to read while waiting.

Patrice checked the time again. Minutes had passed, and they had yet to show up. She stared pensively at the door and moved to get up, then changed her mind, deciding to hold off a little longer.

Unable to concentrate on the article she'd started reading, Patrice gave up trying, tossing the magazine aside. There were too many things demanding her mental attention. But determined to free her mind from all unwelcome thoughts, she reclined against the pillows and closed her eyes.

Before long, a sweet musing smile came to her lips as she conjured up pleasant visions of insouciant, spring days. The simple pleasure of a lazy stroll in one of Treeland Height's luscious, forestial parks might do. Or, a weekend fishing trip in the Gulf. Possibly even a short trip to Barbados, where she had a friend whom she hadn't seen in a long time.

"Hmmm," she moaned blissfully, "wonderful."

She hadn't had a vacation in over a year, but plans to take a busman's holiday were forming in her mind. The mere idea of having time for herself—away from the job and her children—was enough to excite her. Even the chiding inner voice taunting that she'd be by herself was discounted as she sighed contentedly, settling on a deep-sea fishing trip.

The picture looming in her mind was one of a golden sunrise overhead, a cool breeze from the ocean spraying her face, and she, strapped in a chair on a yacht, a reel cast into serene, deep blue waters.

"How are we doing, captain?"

Her eyes flew open and she scrambled to a sitting position, her heart hammering in her chest as she looked anxiously about the room. Even as she argued against the remote possibility that Lawrence Woodson was in the room, that mellow baritone of his had seemed so near.

Now I hear him everywhere.

She breathed deeply, shaking her head from side-to-side. Amusement turned up the corners of her mouth. *A vacation is 'looong' overdue,* she thought, unable to shake the image of him standing proudly at the controls of the pleasure cruiser.

She'd had this problem with his image reappearing all day. Not only was it idiotic, but a waste of precious time. She had more important things to devote her attention to—namely the concert. Or even the kids, upstairs sulking. She scooted off the bed to traipse about the room, her hands folded across her bosom.

She picked up the miniature glass scales, mindful of the balance in life they represented. *So difficult to achieve in reality,* she reflected. Replacing it in exchange for her most prized crystal, the bull, she contemplated its exaggerated stubborn characterization.

"Mom?"

She heard her title, one she cherished proudly called softly from the bedroom door. She turned her head to glimpse at Stephen and Stephenie ambling into the room, wearing twin forlorn expressions.

Ignoring their sad, pitiful facades, she asked routinely, "Finish your homework?" She returned the figurine to its place on the shelf, before facing the smaller replicas of herself.

They were almost as tall as she, with Stephen slightly taller and heavier than Stephenie, though minutes younger than his sister. They had inherited Patrice's coloring and facial features—from the cat-eyed shape of her eyes, though theirs were a tawny shade of brown, to her mouth, well-formed and full.

The only outward trait they'd gotten from their father was fine, curly jet black hair; worn in a stylish punk cut on Stephen, while long and frizzy on Stephenie.

"Yeah," her daughter replied, dropping onto the corner of the bed.

She eyed her son, slouched over her dresser, outlining the curves of her round porcelain jewelry box with his finger. She wasn't fooled by his aloof countenance.   "Stephen, how was school?"

"It was all right," he replied, motioning with wiry shoulders and eyes lowered.

"Did anything interesting happen today?"

"No," answered Stephenie, playing with the rainbow colored shoe-strings on her tennis-shoes.

Patrice sat in the rocking chair, her gaze traveling from one twin to the other, pondering the next move. She felt as though she were playing a game of chess, which was definitely not one of her better sports, and losing.

"All right," she said, the sound of a parent's defeat edging her tone. "What's up? Why the long faces?"

"Are you gonna let us go to the basketball game Wednesday night with the band?" Stephen blurted, his tone demanding.

"I'm fairly certain I said that you would be grounded for a week, so the answer is no," she replied patiently.

"Mom!" whined Stephenie. "That's not fair! Colin and Angel are going."

"I don't have any say in how Mr. and Mrs. Westover raise their kids."

"But didn't you talk to Mrs. Westover?" continued Stephenie.

"Yes, I did. And I hope, for your sakes that you don't pull that again." Her tone mirrored the warning as she glared significantly at her offspring. Just remembering the conversation she'd had with Mrs. Westover was enough to set her off. She began to rock in the chair.

She liked her neighbor, but didn't believe in allowing the kind of freedom that Mrs. Westover afforded her kids, who were older than

Stephen and Stephenie. The twins were only fourteen years old, and in her opinion, not old enough to stay out until midnight, riding around with teenagers behind the wheel of the car, no matter how innocent.

"I don't like outside manipulation and I won't respond to it, except maybe to extend your punishment. You should know better. When I say something, I mean it."

"What if Aunt Kit takes us?" queried Stephen, certain that he'd found a loophole in her punishment.

Patrice shook her head in astonishment at his nerviness and chuckled, before retorting in a tone that matched his, "Aunt Kit won't, so don't try to pit us against each other."

"So you're not gonna change your mind, huh?" asked her daughter in a small voice.

"No," replied Patrice firmly, shaking her head after taking a long, audible breath, "I'm not changing my mind."

"Well, that's cool," said Stephen. "Come on, Stephenie."

"Are you leaving already?" asked Patrice, stopping the motion of the chair. "What about a game of 'Rise N' Fly'?" she suggested hopefully, believing they wouldn't pass up an opportunity to show her how little she knew about Black history.

"No, I don't think so," replied Stephenie, sliding off the bed.

"You probably have some station business to work on anyway," added Stephen resentfully.

Patrice pushed herself up from the chair, protesting, "Now, what you're implying is . . . ."

"G' night, Mom." Stephen cut her off as abruptly as he left the room, trailed by his sister.

Patrice threw up her hands in disgust, wanting to throw something, or scream, or fling herself across the bed and cry. She did none of those things, opting to do what she didn't like to do and seldom did at home— work on the station's business.

CHAPTER ❧ THREE

*T*he sound of soft sole shoes pounding against the parquet wood floor on the indoor track was muted as a lone runner jogged with a fluid rhythm in the university's gym. He rounded a curve on the outskirts of the basketball court—his breathing smooth and controlled, his movements coordinated: left arm and right leg, then right arm and left leg lifting in perfect coordination.

It was getting too easy, thought Lawrence, *not enough of a challenge anymore.*

This was not what he'd anticipated when he'd set out for the gym at six this morning, looking for a way to silence the thoughts racing around in his head. He'd been on the track for nearly an hour, chasing simple answers to conflicting emotions.

His modulated pace picked up to a hard and fast all out sprint. Powerful arms and well-toned legs strained, outdistancing physical limitations as he followed the path of the circular racecourse that had no end. Sweat poured from his face and bare chest. The skimpy shorts, covering muscular thighs, were dripping wet—much like his mind—drenched in memories of her.

Four days had gone by since Patric Mason walked into his office; yet he remembered everything about her—the natural exuberance she radiated, those big brown eyes, model-slim body, and even the sweet flowery smell.

He ran harder, bothered by the mere thought of being attracted to a woman like her. *Yes, attracted.* The admission had finally settled home. He'd called his grandmother, needing to hear the voice of someone he knew, and who without question, loved him. The first thing she'd said was, "You must need my advice on a business deal. What is it?"

It was her way of chastising him for not calling more frequently. "No, Nanna," he'd replied affectionately with humor, "business is fine."

"Then it must be a woman."

The guess was standard, part of the ritual they shared in greeting. She'd always sound hopeful.

When he didn't respond in usual jest, she'd continued in her spry, teasing manner. "I'm getting old, you know? The man upstairs isn't going to let me grace this earth forever, waiting for a great-grandchild to hold in these old, tired arms of mine."

Then she'd fallen silent, expectant. When she spoke again, the teasing was gone. "You know son, there comes a time when we have to get rid of the dead weight and get on with our lives. You've got to enjoy your time here."

She'd taken him aback with her pointed perception about the emotional noose he felt around his neck. He'd never shared his feelings—not the self-doubt and guilt anyway—with her or his grandfather during all the time he lived with them.

His speed began to slacken halfway down the track as other images—nightmares of his past—clouded his vision. In his mind's eye, visions of a small boy chasing after a woman flickered and crackled with emotional haze. And every time the youngster was close enough to touch her, she'd scamper out of reach. The years sped back in time, stopping on a day that could have been twenty-four hours, instead of thirty-two years ago.

Even at seven, Lawrence had realized his home wasn't like normal homes. Or, what he imagined was normal.

Lawrence raced instinctively around the track, noticing none of its nuisances. The only sounds he heard was of the angry voices of his childhood:

"*Where are you getting all these things from, Mayrita?*"

"*Leave me alone. Go read your stupid books and stay out of my business.*"

As though trying to outrun the painful memories, Lawrence's feet hit the floor harder, faster.

His parents thought he was outside playing. And he had been, until the

New Orleans' Tobasco-hot sun had chased him inside for a glass of Kool Aid. All he had worn that day was a pair of cut-offs, jeans he had outgrown in length.

"You just take care of your son and mind your own business. I'm tired of having to wait on you to make enough money. You ain't go never have enough money to do anything, go anywhere, buy me nice things."

It wouldn't have mattered anyway, whether his presence was known or unknown. He had heard countless arguments, usually one-sided, as this one was. His mother's loud, piercing tone easily penetrating the paper-thin walls of their small house from the living room, where he imagined she was preening in front of the oval-shaped mirror on the wall.

He stood in the opening between the kitchen and dining room. His feet seemed rooted to the hard floor beneath the cheap, red carpet. He couldn't decide whether to leave or stay.

"Mayrita, I'm doing the best I can. You wanted a house, and we got a house."

"You call this box a house?" she retorted with a snort. Then, *"Just save it, Robert. I don't even want to hear it."*

Lawrence saw the lean, scrappy boy that he had been tiptoe toward the living room. He couldn't remember what had made him decide to linger. He heard a movement from the other room, and stood stock-still, back pressed tight against the wall, holding his breath.

The table was out of place in the dining room. An intricately designed tablecloth of lace, which he knew not to touch, covered the big wood table with eight, big high back chairs. His mother's favorite dishes, a wedding gift from her parents, sat proudly on display in the china cabinet. He had always wondered whether food tasted better when eaten off the delicate porcelain.

On to the connecting opening, he crept, to peek into the living room. He could see them, her more clearly than his father, from his crouched position. She was stunning, and Lawrence envisioned her slim, wild beauty as clearly as he had on that scorching July day. He could almost smell the Cashet powder she used liberally on her satin-soft, almond flesh.

His mother had on a yellow sundress, her delicate shoulders bare and moving in time with the hateful words she spat at his father. She was waving a matching yellow straw hat back and forth, as though it were another medium to help spread the venom inside her. Her long, naturally straight black hair had been combed to lay across one of her shoulders. He used to love touching her thick, silky strands of hair, and sometimes she would indulge him in the luxury.

Dainty gold earrings pierced delicate ears, and this was the cause of the latest disagreement. From the argument, he could tell that his father hadn't purchased them for her. His father couldn't afford them. And by listening to her, that wasn't all his father couldn't get for her.

"I simply asked you where you got them from, Mayrita." Even though his father's voice had rung firm, it held a note of apology, resignation and acceptance.

"It's none of your damn business. You didn't get them for me, that's for certain."

The tone was taunting, a hip thrust forward in teasing defiance. It was enough to crush any man's ego, or drive him to drink. Or even worse. Robert Woodson was a big man, tall and muscular. He could easily have .... Lawrence crushed the remainder of the violent thought. His father had never even raised his voice.

"All right, Mayrita."

Lawrence watched as his father walked across the living room to the old, beat-up roll top desk to get one of the math books. He sat in the rocker near the window facing the side of the house, opened the hand-sewn, blue and white curtains, and then eventually opened his book.

"All right? All right? Is that all you have to say?!"

"What else do you want me to say?"

The older Woodson didn't even bother to look up, but Lawrence knew the pain he was hiding under the polished, experssionless look.

"Well, I'm leaving!"

Mayrita sashayed to the door. She pulled it open with a jerk, then paused in a daring pose.

"Be careful, Mayrita."

With a huff, she had stormed out.

"Daddy?" Lawrence took a hesitant step into the room. *"Where mama going?"*

"I don't know, son," replied his father.

"Is she coming back?"

The older Woodson didn't respond with words, but the look in his eyes said it all.

"Make her come back," Lawrence demanded. *"I don't want her to go. Make her come back, Daddy."*

His father looked up—looked long and hard into his son's wide, fearful gaze. *"I can't make her, son. Can't make nobody love you unless she wants to."*

Lawrence didn't know what made him do it, but he had to catch her, to stop her and bring her back. He ran out the house, leaving the front door ajar as he went.

"Mama! Mama!"

She had to have heard him, but she didn't stop. She didn't even turn around.

His heart was beating so fast, as he raced down the street, the cement hot under his bare feet. Unshed tears stung his eyes, as he called out to her. Again. *"Mama!"*

He wanted his Mama! *Why wouldn't she stop walking away? Why didn't she turn around with her arms opened wide to catch me like those mothers did on TV?* Even some of his friends' mamas did it, hugged their children, planted big, sloppy kisses on the sides of their faces. Told them they were loved. Why didn't his mama do that for him?

He chocked back a tear, calling her name. *"Mama!"*

He didn't dare cry; there were lots of kids playing outside, along the cracked sidewalk and inside small front yards as he raced down the street. His mother was still in sight, hips swaying nonchalantly as she headed for the corner.

He was running out of breath; his little arms pumping hard against the air, feet flying toward the end of the block where the bus stopped. He was a fast runner. He was certain that he could catch up with her.

He saw the big red Cadillac with the top down pull up to the curb. A tall man with slicked-back hair got out from behind the wheel. He had on a white coat, red pants and shiny white shoes. He came around to open the passenger door for Mayrita.

Why was this man touching his mama like she was his? She wasn't his! She belonged to him. To Lawrence. And Daddy.

"Ma-ma!"

Then the boy was no longer a child, but a grown man, and the woman he envisioned bore a striking resemblance to Patrice Mason.

Lawrence wiped the sweat from his face, the salty perspiration stung his eyes. His breathing was labored; easy strides became harder to achieve. His feet slowed until he came to a complete stop. He looked around the big, empty gym, and ironically, felt disquieted by the observation that he was still alone on the track.

"Yes, Nanna. It's time for the running to end."

~~~ ~~~ ~~~ ~~~

Patrice was sitting at her desk signing letters, which Marie picked right up after each signature was scribbled at the bottom of a page. She was grateful the task didn't take a lot of concentration because she was distracted by the anticipation of Lawrence Woodson's arrival.

Roger had been right, she told herself, pausing to stare unseeingly across the room, the tip of the pen in her mouth.

Mr. Woodson had phoned her, full of apologies for his behavior, requesting another meeting. She had truly been surprised by his call: she would have bet money that she never have heard from him again, especially after that damnable confrontation.

"Patrice?" Marie called out softly. "Are you all right?"

"Oh, uh, yeah," was Patrice's stammered reply as she resumed the rote chore. "That ought to keep you busy for a hot minute," she told Marie after signing the last letter and tossing the pen on the desk.

Once Marie left, she walked over to the window to look out. The weather had cleared considerably, though the sky clung to its gray wintery look. She, however, was in sunny spirits, and it shone on her face.

If Woodson hadn't called, she thought reflectively, she would have called the home office, told them she felt compelled to cancel the concert and suffered the consequences. Instead, she had been given a reprieve and accepted it blindly.

Checking her appearance in the glass of the window, Patrice smoothed the wrinkles out of the cream colored, slim-fitting skirt with nervous hands and tugged the double-breasted matching blazer. Clumsy fingers fiddled with the long tie on the emerald silk blouse. Dropping her hands to her stomach, where butterflies were fluttering energetically, she whispered to her reflection, "Stop worrying."

She spun around to check around the room, reassuring herself that everything was in place. The folders were on the coffee table, and a pad and pen rested next to each one. Her desk had been cleared, except for the portrait and a few folders containing sales reports she wanted to review later.

She bit down on her lip and squinted her eyes, trying to figure out what was missing. When she faced the bookshelf, she snapped her fingers, and rushed to turn on the stereo receiver, setting the volume at a low level.

A knock on the door was followed by Marie poking her head into the room. "He's here," she announced with a wide grin on her face.

"Send..." started Patrice, before stopping to clear her throat. "Send him in." *That was better*, she thought; *I sound professional and in control.*

With Marie gone, Patrice laughed lightly, admitting secretly that she was tempted to have him wait twenty minutes. Her conscience, however, frowned on such behavior as childish and immature.

She took a final appraisal of the room, her hands clenched together in front of her. Closing her eyes, she took short calming breaths to harness the galloping excitement. Then she sauntered to poise herself by the end of the coffee table nearest the door, schooling a polite smile on her face.

There was a light rap on the door, and she jumped with a startle. Obvious disappointment and irritation washed over her when Mike rushed into the room.

"I know you're about to have a meeting," he spoke fast, "but I need a quick favor."

"What's the favor?" she asked, placing her hands on her hips.

"Say yes first," he coached.

"Mike," she warned.

"Come with me tonight. Arty Howard's boss is flying in and he wants you to attend a dinner he's hosting at his home."

Arty Howard was one of the station's biggest clients. He was also a first class low-life whom she disliked immensely. But she asked, "Is my presence going to mean more advertising dollars?" knowing if the answer were affirmative, she'd feel compelled to go. After all, business was business.

"Consider it a nice gesture," he said, grinning boyishly.

"Give him my apologies," was her prompt reply as she turned away from Mike to look at the desk calendar. "Tell him I already have plans for tonight."

Mike opened his mouth to protest, and she cut him off firmly, stating, "Next time, give me more notice," with an apologetic smile.

She felt that something more needed to be said, but couldn't for the life of her think of what it could be, for Lawrence Woodson walked through the door. She was utterly speechless. Peculiar, as in conspicuously wanton, sensations rushed through her mind and body like a raft on white water. She tried to act naturally, priming her features behind a look one gives a nodding acquaintance. *You hypocrite,* her mind teased and the veil cracked, producing in its place a flush that enhanced the aesthetics of her features.

The unnerving apprehension Lawrence had experienced while waiting in the lobby faded, and his guarded reserve melted under her glowing regard.

He hadn't known what to expect, had been prepared for the worst, and now, was a little bewildered—more by an increased heartbeat than by her apparent pleasure.

With her hands cupped between his, he could only murmur, "Hello, it's good to see you, again." He faltered as the silence soon engulfed them.

Her hand remained in his firm, yet gentle grasp, far exceeding the bounds of a welcome. But she didn't seem to have the will or desire to free herself from this delectable form of entrapment.

Mike cleared his throat, penetrating the sensual cloud surrounding them. Withdrawing simultaneously, they fixed their gazes on Mike, who returned Patrice's peevish stare with an expression that demanded an introduction. As embarrassment worked its way onto her face, her manners prevailed, and she made short work of the introductions and ushered Mike from the room.

Patrice rested against the door as it closed, giving her pulse a chance to return to normalcy before looking up to catch Lawrence peering mysteriously at her. Annoyed with the thrilling current moving through her, she opened her mouth to say something amusing that would cool the temperature in the room, but her mind drew a blank.

"It's a little different than I thought it would be."

"What?"

"The station. You have a nice size staff. I imagined about ten to twelve people, but you have, what?"

"Thirty-five," she supplied with humor in her voice, relieved that at least one of them had his wits about him. "And I can well imagine what you envisioned—a bunch of weirdos with multi-colored hair, dressed as though they were going to a wild rock concert."

He laughed with her, a shamefaced grin, dazzling against his dark chocolate skin. "No fair, you peeked into my head. I really am impressed."

She felt awed by the sincerity of his compliment and fleetingly wondered why before responding. "Thank you."

Each regarded the other intently in the silence that followed, as though pondering the importance of the moment. Patrice grew uncomfortable under his keen glance and needlessly cleared a dry throat before speaking, a high-pitched laugh coloring her voice.

"Forgive my manners—won't you have a seat?"

"Mr. Woodson."

"Ms. Mason."

They laughed at the dual timing. She then offered: "You first, please."

"I just wanted to apologize again for my behavior last week."

There was more he could have told her, he wasn't in the habit of explaining himself to anyone, and he wasn't about to start. "I hope you don't hold it against Banneker University," he continued in that golden baritone of his.

For some unfathomable reason she had hoped this meeting was taking place because of his desire to see her again. Patrice's smile suddenly lost its former brilliance. She had no one to blame but herself. It was she, not him, who wanted something so badly that she'd placed faith in a vacuum.

Upon seeing the animation flee her expression, he interjected, "It's not the way you're thinking at all," his voice was calm, his gaze steady. "I asked for this meeting because I realized how unfairly I treated you. And I like to think of myself as being fair-minded."

That's mighty big of you, she wanted to say to him, silently mimicking the self-righteous tone in her head. She felt deceived, the tone of his admission sounding as though he had not had a change of mind about the university hosting the concert. She mentally stuck her tongue out at him.

"Can we call an honest truce?"

Lawrence knew this apology stuff would be difficult, especially when she had no real basis to judge his sincerity. It was important that she believed him, for he felt that if she didn't, the loss would somehow be his.

Patrice wasn't sure what to make of the offer. Questions that had gone unasked filled her head: *Will this meeting be a repeat of the other day? What guarantee do I have that he is willing to take me seriously this time? Why is he here?*

"Ms. Mason."

She stiffened, chagrined for having been caught woolgathering. Doubts began to drain from her mind, and she reacted—not to the unanswered questions, but to the hopeful glint lighting his eyes.

"Yes." The voice didn't sound like her own, even the eager, conciliatory reply seemed to have escaped from her brain without the process of logic.

"I had another proposal prepared in case you misplaced the other one and have further questions," she said in as natural a voice as she could summon.

"Not necessary," he replied, pulling folded papers from his coat pocket.

"Have you had a chance to review the proposal?" she asked, smiling as he smoothed the wrinkled papers out on the table.

"Yes, and let me add it's one of the most thorough and concise documents I've seen in a long time," he said. "You can't appreciate those qualities until you've poured through the kinds of proposals I've been not so privileged to read."

She cleared the amusement from her voice. "Well, I'm glad it was good reading. Do you have any questions?"

He hesitated, grappling with how best to say what he believed must be said, wishing he didn't have to test their new armistice so soon.

"Just say it," she coaxed, seeing the mild struggle on his face. "I promise not to throw anything at you."

"You might want to put that promise in layaway until after you've heard what I have to say," he chuckled, smiling back at her with no reminder of his former serious expression.

"All right," she retorted agreeably. "Half a promise now, final payment due upon receipt."

They laughed, both enjoying the spirited repartee between them before getting down to the purpose of the meeting.

It soon became apparent that he had given the matter considerable thought as evidenced by the thorough questions asked. He listened with rapt attention, pursing his lips and nodding understandably to her responses. Only twice did he interrupt for clarifications.

Though Patrice grew more at ease upon seeing that his interest was genuine, she was still no closer to knowing where she stood. The intercom on the phone buzzed, and she exhaled an impatient sigh as she looked across the desk at the irritating object.

"Excuse me a second." She rose to answer the phone. "Marie," she said after picking up the receiver, "this better be good. Yeah? Uh-huh," she said, turning her back to Lawrence, brows slanting in a frown. "All right. Call Daniels, and I'll meet you in the conference room. Oh, have some refreshments sent in for Mr. Woodson."

With a smile pasted on her face, though anxiety and frustration were churning in her stomach, she turned to face him. "Something has come up that I need to take care of. It shouldn't take long. Make yourself comfortable. I'll be right back."

ક ક ક ક

A red bow with ribbons streaming down the sides of a white, square box had been set on one end of the conference room table. Patrice approached it slowly.

A polished nail found its way to her mouth, and she chewed it nervously, pondering the contents of the gift box. When she was a step away from the table, Marie rushed in secretively to stand next to her.

"I had the delivery man wait until after you'd opened it," she said uneasily. Patrice only nodded, then reached to untie the bow. "Don't you think you ought to wait until the police get here?" asked Marie, grabbing Patrice's hand before it reached its destination.

"What if it's nothing? I'd hate to be known for my overactive paranoia," Patrice replied with a feeble attempt at humor. Shaking off Marie's light possession, she moved to untie the ribbon.

The conference door opened and both women, startled, bumped into each other.

"I'm sorry," said Lawrence. "I didn't mean to frighten you. I was just looking around. I hope that's ok."

"It's uh, fine," stammered Patrice, her hand clutching the collar of her blouse. Her heart was pounding so hard she thought it might jump right out of her body.

"Is anything wrong?" His gaze darted back and forth between the two women, who glanced at each other from the corner of their eyes.

"It's nothing."

Patrice's brave words belied the fear that watered her palms and weakened her limbs. She followed his curious regard to the box, then met his sharp, assessing eyes, his brows drawn in contemplation.

She turned her back to him, facing the innocuous-looking box. Shortly, his presence was at her side, but she didn't look up at him. A lump formed in her throat. There was no sense in delaying. She wiped her hands against her skirt, but was unable to hide their trembling as she untied the ribbon and pulled off the top.

A coiled, black object partially hidden under mounds of tissue caused

Marie to shriek and jump from the table. Reacting swiftly, Lawrence grabbed Patrice by the wrist and jerked her away.

He listened keenly for several seconds, and satisfied that he heard no ticking, gently tapped its sides. Experience had taught him that there were no limits to booby traps. Pulling a pen from his coat pocket with his left hand, he held up his right, poised for capture in the air.

"Here's your culprit," he said, holding up a deflated inner-tube from a child's bike.

Patrice heaved a great sigh of relief and stood alongside Lawrence. She searched inside the box, placing tissue paper on the table and found a small white card.

"Be careful how you handle it," advised Marie.

Lawrence took a handkerchief from his pocket and used it to take the card from her hand. He read it, then stared down at her; his countenance metamorphosed to one of cold fury.

She didn't need to read the card to know its contents. Her shoulders slumped dejectedly as she sagged against the table. Patrice straightened to leave the room. Lawrence was on her heels.

ﻭ ﻭ ﻭ ﻭ

"How long has this been going on?"

Patrice looked up to see him standing at the window looking out; she had been holding the door up since they returned to her office.

"The first in such pretty wrappings," she replied in a tired voice. "You already know about the others." Her steps were slow, like that of a tired, old woman when she moved to her desk. She toyed with a pen, then dropped it and folded her hands.

"I guess this means there will be no concert at Banneker," she said, tilting her head to one side to glance at his back.

He turned abruptly to glare at her. "There will be no concert any damn place!"

Patrice started to rise, "Now, you wait one . . ."

The rest of her heated locution died, for she fell back in the chair as she met with the thunderous glare in his olive-brown eyes as he stood like a contentious giant over her desk.

Lawrence sighed with exasperation and took a deep calming breath.

"How can you even think about the damn concert when you've had three bomb threats?" he asked, anger smoldering just below the surface of a controlled expression. "This one warned you to announce the cancellation over the air."

"You know, I was willing to do that before today," she said softly, looking down at her fidgeting hands.

"What made you change your mind?"

"You." At his questioning expression, she explained. "When you requested this meeting, I thought you had entertained the possibility of the concert being at the university. I had hope again. I felt in control of my life," she said passionately, then fell quiet, determined. "Somebody's trying to rob me of that sense of pride, and now, I'm more determined than ever not to give in. Somebody wants me so scared I'll cave in without a fight."

"Damn it woman! You'd better be scared!"

"Why?" she asked in quiet defiance, rising from her seat. "Because I'm a woman?"

"No," he replied, shaking his head. "Because you're a human being who cares about the lives of other people and your own as well."

He caught a glimpse of the portrait of the twins and picked up the picture from her desk, studying it with more than passing interest. He looked at her. "Yours?"

"Yes," she nodded.

"Then be scared because of them," he warned softly.

"That's not fair!" Patrice erupted, slapping the top of her desk as she stood. A wave of apprehension swept through her at the mere thought of harm to the children. But pride drove her on.

"If I were a man you wouldn't throw my children up in my face. That's emotional blackmail. I'm not going to give in to you or anybody else," she hissed, her arms folded as she paced.

She stopped, passing a hand across her face. Her head felt like a battlefield of questions and doubts. Breaking the silence, she stated unevenly, "There are a lot of people, men in particular, who would gladly give their souls to the devil to see me fail in this position." She resumed pacing; the circle of her movement widening "I'm female," she said, and then added in a mocking tone, "and much too young to be entrusted with the amount of authority I have." Her voice turned bitter. "And even after having a solid track record in radio, some people feel I haven't paid my dues."

"Can't you see this has little to do with your gender?" he countered, hiding chagrin. Unfortunately, he was one of those men to whom she referred.

Embarrassment came over Patrice for having blurted her feelings. She turned from his eyes to stare at the ceiling, disappointed she was behaving so unprofessionally.

Career women just didn't share that kind of emotionalism with anybody—except with themselves. Very few men were willing to hear about the problems of women in business, and at worst many claimed women used such problems as excuses for their failure. Emotionalism in females was also an excuse for keeping other women out of the competition for coveted positions.

He watched as she continued to drive home her point. There was a childlike quality about her defiance, a vulnerability beneath the controlled exterior. He'd noticed the contrast the first time they met, but chalked it up to her trade's repertoire of tricks. He didn't feel that way now.

"I think you're a very capable businesswoman."

Lawrence saw etchings of disbelief bathe her face as she stared at him. He knew the exact moment she believed him for her arms fell to her sides.. A smile tipped the corners of her well-formed mouth.

The silence spinning around them like a tightrope was broken by the buzzing of the intercom.

"Yeah, Marie?" she answered. "Ok. Make sure no one goes in the conference room until after he gets here." She replaced the receiver. "Officer Daniels is on his way."

ⁱⁿ ⁱⁿ ⁱⁿ ⁱⁿ

Riding in the mirror walled elevator, Lawrence glanced at his watch. He was running right on schedule. The elevator doors opened at the nineteenth floor with a soft 'whish', and he stepped onto the plush gold carpet of the corridor. The hallway was deserted, which was to be expected at this time of morning.

He inserted the key into the last door on the right, marked "1930" in bold regency letters, and stepped into the entrance of the apartment he maintained in Houston. He flipped the light switch before passing through a short den where light now beamed into the adjacent rooms.

A mirrored ceiling hovered over the white, eight piece setting dining room table to his left, while to his right, black and white striped furniture sat in the middle of the sunken living room.

He crossed the black and white checkered marble floors to the wall length window and pulled open the curtains, exposing the view of misty skies spanning from downtown Houston. More times than not, a visit there was like walking through the United Nations, for the city had become an international gateway to the world, with twenty-three ethnic groups making Houston their home among the population of more than three million.

He shrugged out of his coat and tossed it on one of the twin ottomen footing armless chairs, then crossed the room to the black tiled bar where he poured Scotch in two glasses.

Lawrence hadn't stopped to examine the whys of what he was about to get into, operating on a gut-level feeling that the situation needed his objectivity and expertise. He took a sip from one of the drinks, then consulted the time on his wrist again. He'd left Patrice no more than twenty minutes ago; the decision to do something was reached even before leaving the office. Though he would have liked to wait until that Officer Daniels showed up, he didn't have the time. There was a meeting at the university in a couple of hours, so "this" would have to be done now.

He would rather do this himself, but he'd been exposed, and that factor precluded overt involvement. Furthermore, he had a commitment to the university which would make it almost impossible for him to have the time to do both. *Anyway*, he thought, *with the kind of investigation that has to be done, I need the skills of someone who wouldn't stand out in a crowd. And I know just the person.*

He placed a call to his office from a pay phone in KHVY's building and had Mrs Jansen, his firm's secretary, track down Ross J. Kinney (better known as R. J. among his friends).

Ross was a troubleshooter of sorts. While the accountants for Woodson, Black & Woodson conducted audits for its clients, R. J. was called in to sniff out and resolve any criminal activities.

The doorbell rang.

"It's open," he called out, picking up both drinks.

Ross Kinney, a tall, rangy bodied man, sauntered into the room, his leather jacket poised for tossing onto the couch. He was ruggedly handsome with dark eyes and a secret expression on his pale, baby face.

"What's happening, boss?" he said in a heavy Creole accent, accepting the drink Lawrence held out to him.

Ross was ageless, but Lawrence knew him to be thirty-six. He also had the uncanny ability to mingle in any setting. Lawrence couldn't help thinking that he'd picked the right person for what had to be done.

"I've got a job for you and not much time to explain it," Lawrence said, sitting on the couch.

Ross took a sip of the drink, nodded approvingly, then sat in a chair across from Lawrence. "Okay."

"I want you to make yourself available to a woman."

Ross whistled, a wolfish grin spread across his thin mouth, until he saw the dark scowl settle over Lawrence's features. "Not like that, huh?" The Louisiana accent was noticeably gone.

"No," replied Lawrence, shaking his head affirmatively, "not like that, at all."

"Ok," Ross said seriously, pushing his wavy black hair off his forehead, "what's the deal?"

"Her name is Patrice Mason." Ross rolled the name over in his mind, a thoughtful expression on his face. "She's the general manager of KHVY radio station," said Lawrence, pushing himself up to stroll about the room. "She's been getting bomb threats at the station." R.J. whistled. "I think it's an inside job. The cops are feeding her a line that the threats are pranks."

"Who's handling the case?"

"HPD. An Officer Daniels."

"Daniels is good. A little tired, probably needs a vacation, but he knows his job."

Disbelief marked the look Lawrence cut at Ross. "I saw one of those threats today. Not professional, but effective. And that's what counts in my book."

"Anymore details?"

"Nothing significant."

"Have you told her about me?"

"No," replied Lawrence, adding promptly, "and she's not to know I had anything to do with this."

"Then how do you expect me to make myself available?"

"That's your problem. Just do it, and do it quick. And R.J., make damn sure she never learns or even suspects I sent you, or she'll have my head on a platter. And you can count on the same happening to yours."

"Must be a special lady."

"She is," Lawrence said quietly into his drink.

C H A P T E R ❧ F O U R

*P*atrice was sitting at the oval shaped table attached to the island counter in her spacious, contemporary kitchen. A basket of fresh, yellow mums sat in the center of the table, providing a warming touch to the room which was accented by an assortment of high-tech kitchen gadgety.

Garbed in a shimmering, lapis blue lounging pajamas, she was munching on a spinach salad and sipping wine from a crystal wineglass. She wore the carefree look of someone used to enjoying a pampered life. Only the silent ramblings volleying in her head belied the leisurely picture presented.

It had been another unusually long day. There seemed to be a lot of them lately, she mused. She needed this quiet time to herself, for she had yet another job to perform before calling it a night.

Shortly after Officer Daniels had left, she raced from the station around two o'clock, heading for Treeland Heights Preparatory, the private school the twins attended. The principal, Mr. Carrington ,had called to notify her that they were missing from campus and hadn't been seen since their lunch period.

The cops must have been on a coffee break, she thought, recalling the speed with which she had driven from Houston. By the time she arrived at the school, they had miraculously reappeared. She had been much too angry and still too frightened to utter more than a polite, "Thank you, Mr. Carrington. I'll take care of it."

That had been over six hours ago. She had yet to display the anger that was now at a low boil beneath her seemingly placid composure. And the two criminals had had the good sense not to force the issue, awaiting her next move. Unfortunately, she hadn't figured out what her next move should be.

This was another one of those occasions when a man would certainly have come in handy, she thought, her hands fidgeting indecisively between taking a bite of dinner or a sip from the drink. Dropping the fork into the bowl, she chose the wine. Twirling the stem of the glass between her fingers, she began to entertain thoughts so preposterous that she laughed outright at one outlandish notion.

With an unconscious smile on her lips, she indulged the fancy, *If I had a man around, the problems of being a single working parent wouldn't be so monumental.*

Carried away by the myopic supposition, she began to mold the perfect man in her mind: While a bastion of strength in character and build, he would worship her madly. He'd be honest. Of that, she was uncompromisingly certain. It would be only natural that he loved the twins and shared willingly in the responsibility of raising them. Yes, and supportive of her career, or at least understanding of her need to work. And lastly, he would be a tender, but fierce lover.

Pleased with her creation, a dreamy quality mellowed her face. The faceless man of her whimsy began to take form in the shape and substance of Lawrence Woodson. She gasped, and shivered. The glass of wine was agitated and some of the liquid spilled onto her hand. She rose quickly to get a napkin from the counter and dried trembling fingers.

Panic characterized her features and insides as she quivered with agitation. Cogent denials and protestations dominated her thoughts. *Nothing more than a harmless phantasy*, she excused.

"I must be losing my mind," Patrice said aloud, and shook her head in befuddlement. With the small of her back pressed against the counter and her arms crossed, she stared across the room in a daze.

Memory replayed the first time she'd laid eyes on him. *Bold aggression*. The description came to her from deep within. The very way he stood gave the impression that the unprepared dare not enter his lair, or they'd be chewed up and spat out like a piddling seed. And that tiny, insignificant seed had been her.

But not today, she recalled, a half-smile touching her lips. The seed had grown. At least for a short while anyway, she shrugged with a hollow laugh, before a bittersweet expression shadowed her face.

Lawrence Woodson was a business contact. Period. "You're too old for this," she said, returning to the table. She drained the contents of the glass, then set it down hard on the table. *Didn't Donald teach you anything?* asked a little voice inside.

If there was ever proof that the perfect man existed only in her dreams—it was Don. The man she had fancied herself in love with and married. The ink hadn't dried on the marriage license before he was out chasing women and throwing the escapades in her face. Before long she didn't care about these women and had come to be grateful for the diversion because he also wanted to solve their marital problems with an abusive tongue and fists.

Don had never been a father to the twins. Even before they were born, she realized that the responsibility for their care would rest solely with her, and that had been the best thing that could ever happen to them.

She banished the past from her mind and began picking at the salad with a fork. She felt she had come full circle.

It had been so much easier making decisions for the twins when they were younger. *Or so it seemed*, she thought with indifference. She had learned since their birth that as a single parent her problems would be multiplied. The most telling sign had been the financial situation. She had made nowhere near the money she earned now, so material things were limited while time was abundant. Now, because of the demands of the job, material things were easy to provide, but time was at a premium. She was determined that nothing would infringe on the time she spent with her children. She did not bring the job home.

This was one reason Stephenie and Stephen had not been told about the threats, and she did not feel guilty about keeping this information from them. She wanted them focused on their school work. Her job was her choosing, and the problems associated with it were hers alone to bear.

She leaned back in her chair, peering through the empty glass she held up to the light. *If I had known then what I know now*, she thought, *maybe I would be a better parent*.

"Nah, it wouldn't have been any better."

She set the glass down, and rested her chin on folded arms, mulling over the "what ifs" of parenting. She had once believed that if she gave them a good foundation while they were young, she would escape parental blues as they grew older. Now she didn't know what to believe, or what to do. She was angry and hurt by their behavior and didn't know whether she had a right to be or not.

She got up from the table and went to the refrigerator where she opened the door and picked up a bottle of dry white wine.

"You've stalled long enough," she said softly, replacing the bottle and closing the refrigerator. She rinsed the wine glass, then set it in the sink before tossing the salad remains down the garbage disposal. Taking a deep, cleansing breath, she strode purposefully from the kitchen.

☙ ☙ ☙ ☙

Lawrence was sitting on the couch in Charles' study, a wood paneled room with shelves of books on each wall and two big cherry desks with matching high back leather chairs.

He and Charles had just returned from a meeting at the university, but he couldn't remember one significant piece of information he'd heard. But that wasn't unusual for him of late. Ever since Patrice Mason sashayed into his sedentary life, his concentration on business had been less than the attention span of a two-year-old.

Lawrence looked up to see the man responsible for his presence at Banneker University walking into the room, carrying two mugs of coffee.

"Here you go," said Charles to Lawrence, placing a cup in his outstretched hand.

Dr. Charles Black, a handsome, peanut-butter complexioned man, was in the second year of his presidency at Banneker University. He was slimmer than Lawrence, lean and sinewy looking with sharp features. There was an easy-going, yet commanding manner about him.

His first task on the job had been to have the university audited. He put the job in the hands of the one person he would trust with his life— Lawrence Woodson. He had then set out to secure Lawrence's signature on a one-year contract, believing that one year of work done by Lawrence was worth at least five by any other man.

Charles sat behind the desk nearest the door. He stared at the man with whom he shared not only height, but two years of university and a tour in Vietnam. He knew Lawrence was troubled; he also knew it had nothing to do with the university's financial situation.

"How did the meeting with Miss Mason go?"

"Hm?" Lawrence asked absently. "Oh. Yeah. She got another threat today."

"What?" asked Charles. His thin, straight brows bunched up over piercing deep-set eyes of sable.

Lawrence took a careful sip of the hot coffee. "It hasn't changed her mind about the concert though."

"What are you going to do?"

The loaded question caught Lawrence unprepared. He looked at Charles as if noticing the touches of humor around the mouth and near the eyes for the first time. His pursed lips relaxed, eyes mellowing with an inventive gleam. "What makes you think *I* am," he stressed the singular, first-person pronoun, "going to do anything?"

"Because I know you," was Charles' simple reply, "You haven't been yourself since you told me about her proposal." Lawrence laughed in mild amusement. "So, what's my answer?" Charles probed.

"I've got Ross gathering information on her staff and looking into the list of clients the station services."

"That's going to take a lot of time," Charles commented.

"I know, but we have little choice. Ross has an appointment with her this week sometime, under the guise of having heard rumors about the threats. Hopefully, she'll hire him, thinking it's her idea."

"You'd better hope and pray she doesn't find out." Charles knew first-hand how independent women behaved when they believed they were being manipulated. He'd been married to a little spitfire for two years.

"You're not telling me something I don't already know. She is by far the stubbornest woman I've ever met."

"There's no such word."

The correction came from J. T., short for Jacqueline Teressa Black, Charles' wife, who sauntered into the room.

"What?" asked Lawrence, looking with bewilderment at the very pregnant, but small boned woman with the delicately carved features and mocha brown skin.

"Stubbornest is not a word," she replied, standing behind the chair to wrap her arms around her husband's neck. "Hi," she said softly, kissing him on the cheek. "I didn't know you were back."

"I thought you were asleep," he replied, pulling her onto his lap. "How are my babies?" he asked, rubbing her big stomach tenderly.

"We're fine. How did the meeting go?" she asked, looking between Charles and Lawrence.

"You don't want to know," replied Lawrence, passing a weary hand across his head.

"Then who's this stubborn person you're talking about?" she queried.

"Nobody," said Lawrence, his reply not nearly long nor loud enough to drown out Charles', "A certain radio station general manager."

"Oh, Patrice Mason," said J. T. excitedly. "Still think she's a radio charlatan?"

"I think not," replied Charles with a wide grin.

"Oh. It's like that, huh?" said Jacqueline suggestively.

"No, it's not like that," rebuffed Lawrence, scowling at Charles.

"Well, are we going to be able to help her out?" asked Jacqueline. "It would be nice if we could. I mean, she's been real good to us."

"What do you mean by that?"

"Remember, I told you the other night when you first mentioned her?" said Jacqueline. "She's hired an intern from the communications department every year for the past five years. Even this past summer when she took over Heavy 106. And I'm sure she'll take another one this year."

"I remember you saying you knew her, but I guess I wasn't paying much attention," said Lawrence.

"Ooops!" chided Charles at Lawrence's crestfallen expression.

"Ooops, what?" asked Jacqueline.

"Lawrence turned the lady's proposal down flat," he replied.

Jacqueline pouted at Lawrence.

"Before you say a word," said Lawrence, holding up his hand in defense, "let me remind you that she's received threats to bomb this thing she's hell bent on having. And I saw one of those nasty reminders today."

"Damn!" said Jacqueline.

"My sentiments exactly," echoed Charles.

The conversation turned to university related matters, at which time, J. T. bid the men "good night." But Lawrence was hardly paying attention, his mind on other things. Since leaving the station, he hadn't had the opportunity to call Patrice to find out what that police officer had to say.

Snap!

Charles popped his fingers in front of Lawrence's face, jarring him from his reverie. "Oh, sorry," he smiled sheepishly. "What did you say?"

A line of amusement lifted the corners of Charles' mouth. "Why don't you take some time off and deal with this matter?"

"Deal with what?" asked Lawrence.

"This investigation, for one. And, I suspect there might be some feelings you want to explore."

In all the years he'd known Lawrence, thought Charles, no woman had been able or was even allowed to penetrate his seemingly hard, insensitive exterior—defense mechanisms that were erected a long time ago, compliments of one Mayrita Woodson, Lawrence's mother. She convinced Lawrence that he was unlovable. And with the exception of maybe three people, he gave few a chance to exorcise the dead woman's curse.

Lawrence stiffened, and downing the dregs of his coffee responded, "No. It's not that important."

"Oh, yeah? Then tell me what were we talking about five minutes ago," challenged Charles.

Lawrence opened his mouth to speak, a blank expression crossing his face. He clamped it shut. "All right, so I've been a little preoccupied."

"A little," snorted Charles.

"It's not what you're thinking. This woman doesn't mean anything to me. Except maybe a headache."

"Yeah," smiled Charles reminiscently. "That symptom sounds familiar."

"I just don't want to see anything happen to her, that's all," he defended, sticking his hands in his pockets.

"Yeah, the lady needs someone to watch over her. And there's no one more resourceful than you. She couldn't have done better if she tried," added Charles cryptically, earning a curious glance from Lawrence.

As Charles walked Lawrence out to his car later, he felt good. *I believe things are going to change for Lawrence*, he thought with a smug smile. *This could be just the beginning.* His friend was showing signs of healing from that old infested wound.

ﻌ ﻌ ﻌ ﻌ

The twins had the entire upper level of the house to themselves. It was the attic that had caught their interest in the first place, recalled Patrice, standing outside the door of her son's room.

Her hand froze on the knob, because on the other side of the door she could hear her daughter pleading, "Stephen, you'd better not push it.

We're lucky to be alive, and I'm not sure how much longer our luck is gonna hold."

Pstrice felt the same, wondering if they all could make it through this adolescent stage alive. She was already near the end of her rope, and while she realized that she could not allow their latest escapade to go unpunished, she was certain that grounding them was not the answer.

She heard what sounded like a ball bounce against the wall and knew instinctively that Stephen was the guilty perpetrator. She knocked and did not wait for a reply.

The blue bedroom belonged to a teen who took great care of his possessions, maintaining a neat and tidy room. Posters of rock stars, athletes and movies decorated one wall, while across the room was a built-in bookshelf above a desk where an Apple computer and printer rested.

The hardwood floor in Stephen's room was bare, while Stephenie's room—on the other side of the adjoining bathroom—was carpeted. The twins also shared the wireless telephone sitting atop the Danish wood dresser.

Patrice's gaze shifted from one twin to the other.

Stephen was sitting on his bed with the blue and gray striped bedding, while Stephenie perched on the edge of the desk, her feet resting on the seat of the chair. Neither had changed from their crimson and black school uniforms.

"Hopefully, by now you've had time to think things through and can offer me a reasonable explanation for your behavior," she said in a cool, reproachful tone.

"Ain't nothing to say," Stephen answered in a somewhat belligerent voice, staring up at the ceiling.

"There's plenty to say," she retorted, her voice unhurried and low. "I want to know what's happened to the two, normally well-behavior, polite, intelligent children I used to live with. I thought we at least had a good enough relationship to be able to talk about a problem." Stephen mumbled unintelligibly under his breath. "I beg your pardon?" she asked, setting her hands on her hips, a stoney expression on her face. "Listen young man," she said in a huff, her voice trembling with restrained anger, "if you can't show me some respect, then maybe you've gotten too old to live with your mother."

Stephen began examining his fingers, his head bowed. "I'm sorry," he whispered contritely, before looking up into her face. He started to say more, but caught his sister's wide-eyed warning to keep quiet.

Patrice turned to her daughter. "Do you have anything to say?"

"No ma'am," Stephenie replied meekly. "We're sorry and it won't happen again," she added diplomatically.

"That's not going to cut it this time, little people," said Patrice, stalking across the room to lean against the dresser, turning to look fully into her children's faces. She rested her hands behind her on the dresser. "What do you think I ought to do with you?"

"Ground us like you always do," quipped Stephen.

"Let me remind you that you haven't completed your last sentence," she replied quickly.

She spun around, her back to them and took several tranquil breaths. The neutrality she strived to maintain was rapidly being overcome by the storm inside her, threatening to destroy her composure.

Silence reigned in the tension filled room. She felt as though her children were slipping away. *Am I going about this all wrong?* she wondered, *Am I placing too much emphasis on deciding a punishment, rather than focusing on the cause of the behavior?* She dropped her head and passed a weary hand across a tense face.

She had to be extremely careful or she could lose them forever.

Her head snapped up, for the silent thought had a familiar ring to it. Lawrence Woodson had uttered similar words earlier today, though in a different context. But the fear she experienced was the same. *Is he going to dominate my every thought?* she pondered, feeling besieged by his influence. Patrice drew herself up and turned to face the children. She looked long and hard, first at her son, then her daughter, maternal pride and concern cast a glassy sheen to her eyes.

"I love both of you very much," she blurted, her voice shakier than she wished. She cleared her throat before continuing. "I know you're getting older and you want to test your wings and make your own decisions. That's good. I want that for you."

She paused to swallow the lump that formed in her throat and suddenly felt enveloped in a fog of loneliness. *This is how it feels to let your children go,* her instincts forewarned her. Melancholy touched her face, as she recognized this new phase of the family's development. *This was what parenting was about—preparing your children to leave home. It was a frightening step, but one the three of us had to make together,* Patrice resolved.

"But you have to understand," she said, almost desperately, as she stepped towards them, "in order for that to happen, you have to prove that you're ready to take on the responsibility that goes with that kind of freedom."

"How are we going to prove it when you never trust us?" demanded Stephen, jumping to the floor.

"It's not that I don't trust you, Stephen," she denied passionately. "And let's face it," she stressed, "stunts like the one you pulled today, don't remotely resemble responsible behavior. You were angry with me for grounding you, so you decided to skip classes—knowing how I feel about you getting an education—thinking you were punishing me in some way."

Stephenie hung her head shamefully, while Stephen averted his gaze and stuck his hands in the back pockets of his slacks. Patrice walked over to Stephenie and stroked her hair tenderly.

"All of our friends get to do a lot of things," said Stephenie. "You don't let us do anything!"

"Anything like what?" Patrice asked, folding her arms across her chest, a challenging smile on her face. "If you mean stay out until midnight or leave school without permission, then you're right. I'm not going to condone that."

"That's not what I'm talking about," wailed Stephenie, sliding off the desk to lean against it. "You won't let me have a boyfriend, I can't wear my hair the way I want to. You won't even let me wear make-up!"

"And just about all of my friends have cars," Stephen threw in.

"I see," Patrice murmured softly, as she eased onto the chair. "So you want to be and do like your friends. I suppose if your friends do drugs and have sex, then you'll want to be part of the crowd, huh?" She stared at each of her offspring, her brows raised in inquisitive sarcasm.

"No!" cried the twins simultaneously, frustrated by their failing attempt to make her understand their needs.

"You're twisting our words around," said Stephen grouchily. "You know we're not into stuff like that."

Patrice sighed, wondering how much freedom was enough for them to have at this stage in their young lives. Though she recognized the possibility that she was being overly protective, her mind was set that they would earn their freedom. She was not going to give it to them. Freedom was not just another possession they could walk into the store and buy.

"We just need some space," said Stephenie, dropping her hands around her mother's shoulder and resting her head against Patrice's.

Patrice pondered the idea before stating, "All right. I imagine there are a few things we can negotiate on." Stephen's eyes flashed eagerly. "No car," she told him with finality. "At least, not for another three years. Now," she said, relief evident in her voice, "where do you want to start?"

≈ ≈ ≈ ≈

Lawrence stood outside the front door of Patrice's home, his hands in the pockets of the overcoat that protected him from the cold. It was a modern structure with a circular driveway, set in the middle of a block where each house on the street was designed differently in the upper middle class neighborhood.

It was quiet inside, and he thought about leaving.

Seconds later, the musical chime rang inside the house, and he responded shortly afterwards to, "Who is it?"

Patrice wondered why he was here as she opened the door and politely offered, "Come in."

Maybe it was the fact that he didn't respond immediately to her invitation, or her own unexplainable heightened sense of anticipation that made her feel that time had taken a rest. The porch light illuminated the glow of his bright olive-tinted eyes as they scanned her body thoroughly, from the single braid on top of her head to the pretty pink toes of her bare feet. Silent questions about his presence were forgotten under the delicious shudder that warmed her insides. "Let me take your coat."

It felt as if his tongue was stuck to the roof of his mouth, having been caught off-guard by her overwhelming natural beauty. "I hope you don't mind my dropping by like this," he said, and cursed himself for being trite. The need to see her had been too strong to ignore, and although he wasn't sure what it meant, he'd come.

Neither the rich outlines of his shoulders straining against the hand-knitted fabric, nor the tight-fitting jeans emphasizing the force of his thighs and slimness of his hips escaped her notice.

"No problem," she said, and swallowed the lump that formed in her throat. The sylvan scent of the after-shave on his coat held next to her chest heightened her senses. "Go on in, and I'll join you as soon as I get something to put on my feet."

"Don't bother. You look fine."

Each stared into the other's eyes as if they saw something new and deeply serious.

Patrice felt as though she were about to board a ship for an uncharted journey. She swallowed hard and severed eye contact, turning to hang the coat in the closet. Wordlessly, she led him into the sunken living room done in creamy white and rose, and warmed by the fire roaring in the red brick fireplace. Smells of just-off-the-showroom-furniture intermingled with the slight hickory fragrance from the burning pignut wood. Between the dining area, which was a step up from the living room, was a portable bar located behind a short banister.

"You have a very nice home, Ms. Mason," he told her sincerely, thinking about the house he'd bought but had yet to furnish.

"Thank you, Mr. Woodson. Won't you have a seat?" She pointed to the center sofa of the three-piece velvet sectional facing the fireplace. She sat on the love seat to his left, remembering he wouldn't sit until after she was seated.

"I'm sorry I couldn't stay until the police showed up," he said, looking about the room. His eyes strayed up to the large oil painting of a mother and her children hanging above the fireplace, and noted the absent male figure in the picture.

"You didn't miss anything," she said, following his gaze. "Can I get you something? A drink maybe?"

"Nothing, thanks," he replied, turning to face her. "Have you heard anything from the police yet?"

"They called a little while ago." She shook her head and sighed deeply, explaining, "They found absolutely nothing. No fingerprints. The box was common, as was the card."

"What about the man who delivered it?"

She wrinkled her nose distastefully, not really wanting to discuss the matter, wishing he'd leave it alone. "The box had been left at the main entrance of the building with instructions to deliver it to KHVY," she answered dutifully, "so when one of the guards saw the delivery man, he asked him to drop it off."

"A little irregular, isn't it?" He rested one of his arms over the back of the couch and crossed his legs at the knee.

"Of course, it is," she replied in a tone that held remnants of an anger she had undoubtedly unleashed. "But they seem to think that a radio station doesn't operate like a normal business. I wonder where the owners got those clowns from. They couldn't even give a good description of the man who left the box."

"I'm almost afraid to ask." He exhaled a caustic sigh of disgust.

"A tall, black man of medium build, wearing dark shades, a long coat and one of those beanie hats." She shook her head in amazement, as she folded her legs under her.

"In other words, it could have been anybody," he said. Though he retained affability, there was a distinct hardening of the eyes. "What are you going to do now?"

She sighed before replying in a near whisper, "I don't know. I just don't know."

Both fell victim to clamorous thoughts. With his arms folded across his chest, Lawrence pondered the reason behind her stubborn persistence to hold the concert when the situation demanded that it be canceled.

Patrice watched the baffled contemplation of his expression, and guessed at what he expected of her. She wondered if maybe he were right. *Well girl, the game has moved to another stage, and it's about time you accepted the truth*, she told herself. *If only I had a few more wins under my belt. Then I wouldn't feel so insecure about my standing in the company.* Mr. Russell had been supportive, but even there was a limit as to how far he'd back her. As for her personal self assessment, she knew she wasn't a failure. She'd just have to keep telling herself that for a while, and hopefully it would sink in eventually.

"Ms. Mason," Lawrence started hesitantly. "I understand and sympathize," he emphasized the latter emotion, "with your feelings about how this might affect your career, but I don't believe you're being rational. It simply doesn't make sense to continue with plans for this concert."

He spoke in a tone one would use to chastise a young child who didn't understand the error of her behavior, and it rankled her. It didn't matter that what he said mirrored her own thoughts.

"Look, I know this is none of my business . . . "

"You're absolutely right," she cut him off. "It is none of your business. But I am curious about something. If that threat hadn't come to the office while you were there, would you have permitted the university to participate?"

"That's a board decision," he said evasively.

"All right," she said, staring at him head on, "if that's the way you want to play it, I'll rephrase the question." She sat up straight and planted her feet on the floor. "Would you have presented it to the board?"

"Yes," he replied succinctly. "But not with my approval." He noted the nod she gave in appreciation for his honesty, and though her expression otherwise conveyed no emotion, he knew she was not pleased with his answer. "I'm sorry," he said matter-of-factly, his expression anything but apologetic. "As long as these threats remain a problem, I don't see it any other way."

"You weren't going to allow it anyway, so save your pathetic apology for somebody else," she snapped cattily, springing from the couch to kneel before the fireplace.

"I didn't know you read minds on top of other talents," he said.

Patrice looked at him sharply, then turned to stare into the fireplace, past the amber glow of burning wood. She felt disgusted and unhappy with herself. There was no reason for her bitchy mood and misdirected hostility. She turned to him to admit that, and bumped into the wall of his chest. Patrice cried out in surprise.

He caught her by the shoulders to help steady her, and looked down into an amazed expression. His eyes were warm with understanding and a gentle quality that sent her head whirling vertiginously. She stared up with shocked wonder and felt the air around them thicken with a warmth of emotion that was both comforting and frightening at the same time.

"I'm sorry," she murmured at last and licked her lips nervously. Drawing a ragged breath, she added, "You didn't deserve that."

He smoothed her hair with doting hands before forcing them to fall. "I'll take that drink now." His mellifluous voice sounded unaffected, but his eyes did not convey any lack of affection at all. "Scotch, if you have it."

She was grateful for the opportunity to do something with her nervous hands. They shook as she poured a generous amount of brandy in the drink she prepared for herself.

There was something special about this man—something that made her feel unsure of herself and of everything she ever thought she wanted. She knew with a woman's intuition that he was attracted. It was that same intuition that also warned her that he would not take kindly to a trifling affection; in other words, no flirting allowed. But that was no problem for her, was it?

She watched him saunter round the living room. He was an imposing figure, making the area seem almost like a doll house in comparison. Yet, he moved with the grace of an athlete in an Ernie Barnes painting. He examined the wood carved African warrior; the tiny piece of art disappearing in his hand. He then exchanged it for the mauve elephant flower pot filled with purple mums on the table near the window on one side of the fireplace, inhaled their sweet scent and replaced the fired clay pottery.

"I was in the mood for mums today and bought a plant for just about every room in the house," she said with laughter in her voice, higher than its normal pitch as she approached.

"They're a nice touch," he commented, accepting the drink placed in his hand. "Thank you."

Lawrence noted she was careful to avoid his touch and smiled knowingly as he looked at her from over the rim of his glass. He took a sip from the drink, then raised his brows to express approval of its smooth taste.

"Where are you from, Mr. Woodson?" she asked, comfortably positioning herself with a fluffy throw pillow under one arm.

"We've had far too many disagreements for Mister and Ms, don't you think?" he teased with a smile that made him look boyish and sweet—two descriptions she would have never thought to associate with him.

"I was born in Harlem and raised in Grambling, Louisiana, right around the corner from the university."

"Did you attend Grambling?"

"For two years. Then I dropped out to participate in the scrimmage in Nam."

"You mean to say you volunteered?"

He shook his head in amazement, a strange smile on his face. "Yeah."

Standing in front of the fireplace, he stared absently at the familial portrait, remembering the death and destruction he had seen and his own role in that ugliness. It wasn't an experience he was likely to forget, but he had managed to deal with the stark memories that threatened to eat his sanity away like acid.

"When I got out, I was ready to finish the degree program I had started. There was no reason not to finish since Uncle Sam was paying for it," he added with a shrug.

Guessing, Patrice said, "Back to Grambling."

"No. Not this time," he said, remembering the choice he had almost made. "A friend of mine was in Houston working on his doctorate in education. Texas Southern University, as a matter of fact. So I decided to join him."

"What a coincidence. I transferred to TSU." said Patrice.

"But I suspect I finished before you started," said Lawrence with a chuckle.

"Oh, come on, you're not that old," chided Patrice.

Absently looking down at the ice spinning in the dark liquid of his drink, he replied, "Not really, but I was in a hurry to finish and open up my own business." When he looked up, a hint of pride shone on his face. "I practically had my shingle out before I got the results back from the CPA exam."

"That sure of yourself, huh?" she said, a teasing glint in her eyes.

"Yes," he replied succinctly, a smile of challenge defining his expression. "Enough about me. What about you?" He set the glass on the coaster she'd placed on the marble coffee table and sat on the couch. "How did you get to be such a high powered businesswoman?"

Patrice was curious about what he didn't say, which she suspected was a lot if his expressions were anything to go on. But she, honoring his silence, replied spiritedly, "Hard work, luck, good friends and the grace of God," her features brightening at discussing one of her favorite topics.

"I was introduced to radio my first year in college, and I've been hooked ever since. It consumed a great deal of my time—time my Aunt Cleo felt I should have spent studying to become a teacher. She used to call me a radio junkie," she laughed reminiscently.

"The broadcasting field seems pretty risky," he said with veiled reference to the threat.

Patrice's eyes snapped peevishly and she replied cautiously, "It can be." Her voice lost some of its enthusiasm as she continued, "I took a major in business and minor in communications. Not that I was scared about the risk"—she paused, looking at him significantly—"I loved that part. Anyway, I got a lot of advice that made sense and I went into sales. It's worked well for me."

"Patrice...."

"Lawrence...."

The repetition of the simultaneous name-calling dissolved the tension that threatened to disrupt the easy exchange, and both of them laughed. She opened her mouth to speak when Stephenie called from the doorway.

"Excuse me, Mom." At Patrice's expectant look, she explained, "Telephone."

"Honey, will you take a message for me? I have company."

Lord, I hadn't even heard it ring. Those eyes do mesmerize you.

"It's Roger, and he says it's urgent."

"All right," she replied, standing. "Excuse me, Lawrence." He also stood. "I'll be right back," she directed at him, before turning to Stephenie, "Take care of Mr. Woodson until I get back, please."

Stephenie nodded and mouthed for Patrice's eyes only, "Nice catch." She approached Lawrence with hand extended, "Hi, I'm Stephenie Mason," she said cheerfully.

"Stephenie, I'm Lawrence Woodson," he replied, shaking her hand. "It's a pleasure to meet you at last," he said friendly, noting the physical resemblance to Patrice was greater than the photo had let on. She looked at him curiously. "I saw a picture of you and your brother on your Mom's desk."

"Oh, yeah, right," she said, remembering the picture her mother proudly displayed in her office. "It's a couple of years old, but she says it's her favorite. Can I freshen your drink or get you something else, Mr. Woodson?"

"No thank you, I'm fine."

"Are you one of my Mom's clients?" she asked, sitting on the couch.

"No," he replied with an indulgent smile for her inquisitiveness. "I'm with Banneker University."

"Is the university gonna buy air time on Heavy?"

"No," he answered, laughing lightly. "We've been talking to your mother about the concert the station has been planning. Only I'm not so sure there's going to be a concert," he added, eyes hooded, mouth pursed.

"Why?" While her mother never explained the significance of the station sponsoring a major concert, she had been a radio brat long enough to guess what it meant to the station as well as to her mother's career.

"Hasn't your mother told you what's been going on?" he asked with serious concern.

Her casual reply of "No," with a shrug explained that there was nothing unusual about her lack of knowledge of the station's business.

"She doesn't bring work stuff home," explained Stephenie. "She says when she's there, they get their money's worth. But at home, it's our time. Lately though, there hasn't been much of that," she added petulantly.

He slapped a thigh with one hand, realizing that he had almost put a foot in his mouth.

"Are you OK, Mr. Woodson?"

"Yeah, I'm fine. I didn't know."

"You must think I'm terribly inconsiderate," she continued, voicing her shame with a doleful expression, "complaining like a baby."

He looked at her puzzled, then smiled when he picked up on her line of conversation. "You're entitled," he consoled. "And I'm sure your mother understands," he added sincerely with a glean of approval. Admiration for Patrice Mason rose another notch. "She loves you very much, even if she can't spend as much time with you as you would like."

"Yeah," smiled Stephenie, her voice distant and proud.

He stared at her warmly. Never before had he experienced the kinship, almost paternal feelings he'd felt with this teenager. "I saw two of you in that picture, where's your brother?" he asked, suddenly eager to meet the whole family.

"No, Stephen," Patrice was heard saying before Stephenie could respond. She appeared at the door, followed by her son. She had changed into a bulky sweater and jeans, and was carrying a handbag and a suede boot in each hand. "I'd rather you and Stephenie stay here until I get back," accepting her son's help with her coat.

"But Mom," began Stephen before she placed a finger on his mouth to silence the protest.

"Please. Just do as I ask. I promise I'll be all right," she added gently, then turned to face Lawrence. "I'm really sorry about this. Something has happened at the station and I have to go."

"You're driving to Houston tonight?" shrieked Stephenie, bouncing off the couch.

"Not you too?" Patrice pleaded, tugging on her boots. "You know I wouldn't go unless it was an emergency."

"What if we get another one of those strange calls?"

Instantly alert to the anxiety in Stephenie's voice, Lawrence demanded, "What calls?" He glared back and forth between the twins and Patrice.

"Who are you?" Stephen demanded with a hostile edge to his voice.

"Stephen, this is Mr. Lawrence Woodson."

Stephen eyed Lawrence warily, accepting his outstretched hand. "Hi," he said disinterestedly, then stuck his hands in his back pockets.

Lawrence recognized he had been put in check, but was not offended by Patrice's son dismissal of him. Rather, he found Stephen's attitude touching. "Nice to meet you, Stephen," he said, then immediately refocused. "What calls?" he directed at Patrice.

"Oh, it's nothing. Probably just some kids playing on the phone. Pay no mind to my daughter, she has a tendency to overreact," she explained, adjusting pant legs over the top of her boots.

Lawrence didn't believe her for a moment and made a mental note to have R. J. check into a possible connection between the calls to her home and the threatening letters at the station.

"How long do you think it's gonna take?" her son wanted to know.

"I don't know," she replied, piling the braid on top of her head, then pulling on a wide-rim felt hat. "I'll get back as quickly as I can."

"No!" the twins cautioned.

"Don't rush," said Stephen. "Take your time and drive carefully."

"And call us before you leave the station," added Stephenie.

"I'm going with you."

Three pairs of astonished brown eyes turned on Lawrence. He directed his assertion to Patrice, "Obviously your children are very concerned about your going alone," he said patiently and logically. "They don't need to spend the rest of the night worrying about you."

"Well," she hesitated, not knowing how to respond. His offer—no, his declaration was a total surprise.

Stephenie took the indecision out of Patrice's hands. "Thanks, Mr. Woodson."

"My pleasure," he said, smiling at Stephenie, and then looked at Stephen.

The two males spoke with their eyes, and the distrustful expression that had been on Stephen's face was replaced by one of cautious respect.

"Mom, don't forget to call us when you get there," said Stephen.

"Yes, sir," she saluted, then kissed him on the cheek and repeated the ritual with her daughter. She retrieved Lawrence's coat, and they headed for the front door, the twins at their heels.

"I'll take good care of your mother," he promised the twins. "Try not to worry," he directed at them, before turning to face a slightly dazed Patrice. "We'll take my car."

CHAPTER ✿ FIVE

*T*here was something about the man who got out of the red sports car swinging a gym bag that was incongruent with the shabby surroundings of the apartment complex. Even in the poorly lit parking lot, it wasn't difficult to tell the hard times that had befallen those he passed had not come his way. He was a wide-shouldered man of rangy build who carried himself proudly. The long, gray tweed overcoat he wore was expensive, as was the diamond-studded ring on his hand, and single gold bead piercing his left ear.

The seedy-looking men and women loitering about cast curious glances at the high-yellow, wavy haired stranger who moved with purpose, an air of isolation about him. They wondered, of course, what he was doing here, for they knew him to be a stranger and foreign to their inner clique of people "in the know." But none really cared about his purpose as long as it didn't affect the way "business" and the community operated.

Don was feeling exhilarated; the adrenaline ran high through his veins. He took two steps at a time to the second floor landing where he disappeared into an apartment and turned on the lights.

Though well-groomed and extravagantly bedecked, fast living showed clearly in the light. Only a larger than life self-image and the sure, springy steps remained of the man who once wielded a commanding, charismatic appeal. The planes of his face were angular, but the cheekbones and chin protruded to give him a thin, sallow look. His indulgence and obsession with fast living and revenge had formed pockets under hard, gelatin eyes that were so dark, they appeared black.

His eyes went first to the bed. The yellowed newspaper clipping lay there next to a blue vinyl-backed booklet. It was opened to page twenty-two, where a paragraph had been highlighted with a yellow marker.

Everything was just as he'd left it.

The bag was dropped to the door. He took a pint of gin from a coat pocket and set it on the dresser in the small, three-room apartment—an all-in-one living and bedroom, kitchen and bathroom. He called this place his operation base, for he wouldn't be caught dead in a dump like this otherwise.

He tossed his overcoat across the ugly red velvet couch that might have appealed to him in younger days—before he developed a taste for finer things. The cream-colored paint on the walls was stained and chipped; the thin, gray carpet was ragged and bore signs of age and abuse. It was perfect.

He opened the small bottle of clear liquor and took a big swallow, remembering how easy it had been for him to get into the station. He shouldn't have gone he knew, but was so mad that he couldn't help his rash, revengeful action. Nevertheless, he felt good now that he'd vented his anger.

He lit a cigarette and took another drink from the bottle before dropping on the side of the bed, thinking he'd have to come up with some other way to deal with his ex-wife. She wasn't reacting the way he wanted. He had hoped Marie's fear—which he primed at every opportunity—would rub off on Patrice.

He hadn't counted on Patrice being this unyielding, and faulted himself for that miscalculation, for he had the historical proof of her stubbornness. The harder one tried to steer her in a direction she resisted, the harder she fought.

"Damn, bitch," he spat, dragging on the cigarette.

He fingered the newspaper clipping again; he knew it word for word. Even those which hadn't been printed—the voices renouncing him—remained implanted.

"The rules are clear. You know the punishment for violating the policy."

Though the words had been delivered over six months ago, they rang fresh in the ears of J. Don Holly, one of the aliases of Donald J.

Hollingsworth. Don Juan the Lover, Hal Donaldson, Donald Hall, and Jay Roberts were a few of the other pseudonyms he had used through the years. The practice was an acceptable one in his former trade.

"Get some help, Don. Straighten out your life before it's too late. "

That had been the last of the advice given him. *Clark had almost sounded concerned,* thought Donald with penitence. But the emotion was fleeting, for he remembered how quickly he had been fired—without question and no chance to defend himself.

The word 'drugs' was never verbalized in the conversation. But both knew in addition to the little trinkets, clothes and car rentals, the payoff had also included drugs. He hadn't been a big time user, but he dabbled, and liked to have them on hand for the wild parties.

There was not one "thank you" for the highly rated show or the increase in advertisement revenue, all of which had benefitted the station. *No. Hell no. Instead, a policy book had been shoved in my face,* Donald thought resentfully.

All he had to show for making KTOP the number one station in Atlanta's fiercely competitive market was a goddamn policy booklet! A policy booklet that had been written by one Patrice Mason and accepted by the entire ATC Broadcasting chain covered everything from "programming philosophy" to "appropriate dress and behavior for employees."

Dropping the unfinished cigarette on the floor, Donald smashed it under his heel on the carpet. *To say that I hate the bitch is putting it mildly,* he thought, standing as he ran fingers through his curly hair. Patrice had singularly ruined his career, his life.

Nobody wanted him after KTOP fired the previously hot DJ. He had been blacklisted, and radio, which had been his whole life, was no longer accessible. *Because of her. Because of the former Mrs. Patrice Mason-Hollingsworth,* Don thought bitterly.

Donald could feel the strength of his vendetta—animosity was like an unchecked cancer, eating away reason and reality. He downed the contents of the clear liquor and threw the empty bottle against the wall. It fell into shattered fragments on the floor.

He chuckled ironically, seeing the symbolism between the fragments of glass on the floor and his life. *All because of one unsatisfied woman. She hadn't been satisfied with a new job as general manager. No, she had something to prove. She wasn't content with things the way they were; but Patti never had been one to settle for the status quo,* he recalled. She was always reaching, striving, pushing to be the best, and people seemed eager to follow her lead.

She had to be taught a lesson, and he was looking forward to repaying his ex-wife in kind for destroying his life. If Patti wasn't going to respond to the bomb threats, he would just have to find something else. She had vulnerable spots; all he needed was to tap into one.

He'd used a young college student for the computer job, but she had proven to be worthless. He had the perfect accomplice now—Marie. She was so easy to manipulate—so easy to control. He would have to give that dumb broad a call tonight.

He laughed, remembering just how gullible Marie was, promising undying love. He wondered if she would still claim to love him if she knew that he had been married to her boss. *Marie might forgive me for that,* he thought, *but she wouldn't be as hot she found out I sold women's shoes instead of Cadillacs.* It wasn't his first, nor second or third job choice, but it couldn't have been better if he tried. The shoe store was right across the street from the building where KHVY was located.

He consulted the gold watch on his wrist. It was after nine, but he knew Marie would be up waiting for him. He slipped into his coat, turned off the lights, and slipped out.

 è& è& è& è&

It was nearly one in the morning. Lawrence carefully maneuvered the grey Lincoln on the slippery freeway leading to Patrice's home. Traffic was scarce except for the big eighteen-wheeler trucks that frequently zoomed by on the long stretch from Houston to Treeland Heights.

With Lawrence's coat thrown over her, Patrice was dozing. Unconsciously, she nestled closer to his warmth, resting her head on a solid shoulder.

She feels good. No, better than good, he thought as he looped an arm around her shoulders to draw her nearer. "Shhh," he whispered soothingly when she stirred, and pulled her securely next to him.

A mincing smile grew on his lips as he chanced an adoring glance at her quiet form. Resisting an urge to kiss the top of her head, he returned his attention to the road. The drive was challenging, yet comfortable: not unlike the feelings he was having for Patrice.

Funny, he mused introspectively, *how I've avoided serious relationships for years—always putting on the brakes, a long, long way from commitment.* He wished he could say that he had always exercised diplomacy and tact when ending affairs, but he didn't dare make such a claim.

However, since Patrice's appearance in his life, Lawrence was discovering that he wanted things that he never missed or even suspected he could have. It was as though she held a magical power, luring him on into the unknown. There had been times during the past several days when he realized absolutely that he was no longer in control. It was an inarguable fact he had fought, but seemed powerless to alter. He had been forced to reach deep into his mind, searching for the distinctive link that caused nutured this magnetic attraction to her. For hours on end, he pondered what made her so special to him and why he couldn't just walk away from her. *Whatever it was,* he acknowledged with a contented smile, *I certainly haven't picked the easiest woman in the world. As if I had anything to do with the picking at all.*

Suddenly, lightheartedness gave way to apprehension. He was more concerned about the threats than ever, growing profoundly perturbed as he recalled the nonchalant attitude of the police at the station tonight. They were treating the incident as a simple case of vandalism and assault of the announcer. Attempts at questioning Patrice regarding possible suspects got him nowhere. She clung to a nebulous "they." She was either holding something back, or she really didn't know the identify of the enemy.

He gripped the steering wheel fiercely and hissed a barely audible curse. His eyes narrowed suspiciously, thinking it had to be someone on her staff. The threats and the attack tonight had been too easily accomplished. It had to be someone working for the station, or someone with a contact in the station. But, even as he examined those plausible theories, he knew she'd never entertain either possibility. While he admired her loyalty to the staff, he couldn't help believe that she was carrying it a bit too far.

He took the exit ramp off the freeway, and a short time later, was turning into the driveway. Lawrence stiffened, starring at the sporty, white Jaguar parked behind her car. He was suddenly aware of a sensation that had been totally alien to him, having already assumed the late-night visitor was of the male persuasion. Consumed by a temptation to shake her awake and demand to know who would be visiting at this time of night, he spare no thought to examining what he felt.

The lack of motion caused Patrice to awaken and sit up. "Here already?" she mumbled sleepily.

"Hmm," he replied. "And there's a white Jag parked in your driveway," he added, a question texturing his baritone tones. Patrice sat up quickly and glanced out the window, then sagged in the seat, moaning with disfavor. He instantly demanded, "What's the matter?"

"The twins got Kit to come over," she replied. Though she and Kit had been the best of friends since college, she wasn't up to going through the endless questions Kit was bound to ask.

"Is that bad?" he asked.

"You don't know Kit," she replied with a smile, thinking back to when she met Kit at college.

Patrice had attended a college with predominately white students. That first year, the university had its largest group of freshmen blacks and not enough black student counselors to go around. All of the freshmen and transfers were seated in the auditorium for orientation, waiting for the start of the campus tour. A group of the older students assigned to guide the newcomers got into an argument about their assignments; no one wanted to take the ethnic contingent. In traditional red-hair, green-eyed-temper style, Katherine Margaret McDougall erupted, "I'll take them! They're just students, you idiots!"

Kit's sense of fair play had endeared her to Patrice immediately, and the two formed a bond that had lasted to this day. "She will want to know every detail of what happened," she complained.

She. Kit was a female's name, he deduced quickly. He'd never appreciated the dark as much as he did now, for it concealed the relief washing over his face.

"Maybe she'll surprise you," he commented. In response, she eyed him dubiously. "Come on, let's see if I'm right."

Together, they ran through the misting rain to the front door. As Patrice was about to insert the key in the lock, the door was pulled open.

"Come on in and join the party," invited Kit, a statuesque red head with a booming voice cloaked in mischief. She and Patrice shared a sisterly embrace while Lawrence closed the door and secured the locks.

"Kit, I hope my children are asleep," Patrice lovingly threatened the woman several inches taller than she while removing her coat and hat.

"Aren't you going to introduce me before you start fussing? What happened to your manners?" Kit teased, eyeing Lawrence appreciatively.

"I left them in Houston," was the retort to which Kit huffed and placed her hands on hips in mock anger.

"Katherine McDougall, meet Lawrence Woodson," said Patrice, placing Lawrence's coat and her things in the hall closet.

"Nice to meet you Lawrence Woodson," purred Kit, shaking his hand, before a sly gaze caught the blush spreading across Patrice's face.

"Don't say one word," Patrice growled, unable to control the muscles pulling her face in a wide grin. She pointed a warning finger in Kit's direction.

"The pleasure's all mine, Miss McDougall," said Lawrence. The formal tone was lost to the amusement in his eyes. He took an instant liking to Patrice's friend with the genial mouth and sparkling, feline green eyes, sensing there was little frivolity behind the jocular disposition.

"I think I'm going to like you," Kit beamed, looking at him conspiratorially. She wiggled her brows excessively, earning a rich, hearty laugh from Lawrence.

Patrice watched the playful exchange, noting the years falling from his face while he laughed. *He never laughed like that in my presence*, she thought enviously. Suddenly she was forced to ask herself, *Who had the green eyes— me or Kit?*

She looked up to catch his observant, olive-speckled eyes, and was shocked still by their intensity. Her breathing stopped and a red light flashed in her head, to warn her about the gentle emotions that were transpiring between them. She shook her head, struggling to pull drifting thoughts together, eager to flee his disturbing presence and knowing eyes.

"Come on, you two," Kit interrupted laughingly, leading them down the hall past Patrice's bedroom to the family room.

The glare from the television and a floor-lamp in the far corner provided enough light to see that the sofa bed held the sleeping forms of the twins.

"Here are your babies," Kit whispered to Patrice, who then kissed each on the forehead and pulled the blanket over them.

She led Kit and Lawrence to the living room, but detoured to the bar. "Anybody want to join me?" *I need this drink*, she thought, filling a glass with brandy.

Lawrence requested "The usual," earning an eagle-eyed stare from Kit, who ordered a glass of white wine. Patrice joined them in the living room with their drinks before sitting on the couch across from Lawrence.

"Did you just drop in or did they call you?" Patrice directed to Kit.

Kit noticed the distance Patrice placed between herself and Lawrence and smiled into her glass before replying. "They called me, and at a considerable amount of trouble. I was being paged right after I stepped off the plane."

"What happened in Dallas?"

"Very little. That's why I cut my trip short. And not a moment too soon it seems," she said accusingly.

"Oh no," moaned Patrice. "What did they tell you?"

"I got the full works. From the near beating to the grounding and the new house rules," Kit said with a sneaky expression on her face.

"Kit, you better not go out and buy Stephenie a suitcase of make-up," Patrice warned. Adding, "And no kind of wheels, not even a bicycle for Stephen."

"Spoilsport," Kit retorted with a pout.

"I gather you discipline," Lawrence said to Patrice, then to Kit, "and you spoil."

"You gather right," replied Patrice.

"Hah!" quipped Kit. "You call intermittent grounding punishment?"

"That's all right, they don't wrap me around their little fingers," Patrice said smugly.

"A little pampering never hurt anybody," shrugged Kit. "You could use some yourself," she added slyly, then buried her head in her drink when Patrice's gaze promised revenge. "She has strict rules for them," Kit said to Lawrence in defense. "Somebody has to do something."

"It's for their own good," said Patrice, eyeing Kit from the corner of her eyes. She wrapped both hands around her glass before taking a careful swallow from her drink, frowning distastefully.

"How do you feel about discipline, Lawrence?" Kit asked conversationally.

"I feel a set up," he replied with laughter in his voice. "So, I'll take the fifth, if you don't mind."

"Coward," Kit teased, smiling at him.

"Guilty," he retorted acceptingly.

"What do you do for a living?" she asked casually after silence threatened to settle over the three of them.

He had wondered at the nonverbal communication that had been going on between Kit and Patrice ever since their return. Now, he had a pretty good idea of what was going on. "Is she always this obvious?" he asked Patrice, amusement coloring his tone.

Before Patrice could reply, Kit interjected, "When I want to know something, I ask." Her smile took the sting out of the serious assertion.

Lawrence was slow to reply, watching Kit keenly. He could tell she was enjoying the little game; the half-smile playing at the corners of her mouth was quite telling. He knew, however, that he was not going to appreciate the role of dart board to her pointed questions—he was unused to such brash challenges, especially from females.

He took a measured swallow from the drink, then set the glass on the table. "I'm on leave from an accounting firm I started about six years ago to take over the fiscal management at Banneker University."

"What's the name of the firm—maybe I've heard of it?" she continued doggedly with a smile.

Patrice saw indulgence flee Lawrence's visage to be replaced by a fixed, hazel-eyed stare. The expression was quite familiar to her. He was a proud man, and she guessed he had misinterpreted Kit's intention, probably never having experienced the kind of game she and Kit performed when the other introduced a new man into their small family circle. She briefly debated whether to intercede, tempted to let him suffer for the havoc he was creating with her senses.

It was the "maybe I've heard of it" that struck a raw nerve in Lawrence, unsure of the veiled inquiry. *Is she subtly trying to put me down*, he wondered. *Or is it truly a simple case of her looking out for her friend?*

Lawrence's gaze was fixed on Kit for so long that he was unaware that Patrice had moved until he felt a hand cover his. His eyes flickered with surprise at the protective display, and his whole face relaxed in a smile that conveyed something other than gratitude. He captured her hand and unconsciously began drawing a circle in the center of her opened palm with gentle fingers.

Patrice felt herself grow weightless, as though she were being lifted from the ground in a hot air balloon to dizzying heights. Her eyes traced the curve of his wide mouth, and her insides tingled in expectation of the feel of those firm lips against hers.

Kit felt like a voyeur, for she was certainly enjoying the romantic interplay between Lawrence and Patrice. *It couldn't happen to a more deserving person*, she thought. She could feel the tension building across the room and wondered how much longer they would forget her presence.

"Excuse me," said Kit politely after clearing her throat.

With a jerk of her head, Patrice tugged her hand from Lawrence's possessive grasp, her mouth formed in an embarrassing exclamation that didn't find a voice. She picked up a drink, and settling back on the couch, began to look for an explanation for her strange behavior. Finding none acceptable, she took a sip of the warm liquid. *I really have to get a hold of myself,* Patrice thought.

While Lawrence sipped from his drink with eyes trained on Patrice, he wondered about the thoughts going through her head. *Are they as confused and muddled as those I am having?*

"Woodson, Black & Woodson," he replied absently in response to Kit's question, but neither his gaze nor concentration strayed from Patrice.

Kit was impressed. "Not bad. It has been listed among the top 100 black businesses in the country in *Black Enterprise* magazine for five years running," she added knowledgeably.

Lawrence caught the end of what she'd said and turned to stare at her curiously. Though the magazine had a wide circulation, he suspected even the most avid reader wouldn't carry that kind of information around in her head.

"Kit is in banking and is always on the look out for promising clients," Patrice explained matter-of-factly. "So you shouldn't be surprised by her next question," she added laughing.

"I'm quite satisfied with my bank," he said, robbing Kit of the inquiry.

"Maybe we can discuss it when you get back," replied Kit, undaunted by his pronouncement. Satisfied that Patrice had not fallen for some gigolo, she switched the conversation to the concern that had brought her in the first place. "The kids told me you were called to the station for an emergency." She went on, blithely ignoring the sudden silence in the room. "What happened?"

"Let's talk about something else," Patrice suggested, taking a big swallow of the brandy. She made a bitter face: she guessed she'd never get used to the taste of hard liquor.

"Well, you should know that your children were terribly worried," Kit explained crisply. She drained her glass, then set it on the table. "They were so excited that I hardly understood what they were saying," she added, wrapping slender arms around her legs.

"They do that because they know you're going to come running every time they want something. You've spoiled them rotten, so you get no sympathy from me."

"I'm not complaining. And don't try to avoid the issue," Kit scolded mildly, resting her chin on her knees.

Patrice looked to Lawrence for help. But that unnerving, closed expression was beginning to dominate his features like a dark cloud.

"I don't want to talk about it," she said firmly. "Besides, it's a station problem, and I don't like to bring business home with me."

"You may not like to bring it home," Kit reminded her earnestly, "but face it, kiddo, it has followed you anyway."

Bolting from the couch, Patrice flounced to the window. She opened the curtain to look out into the rainy, cold night, wishing she could lose herself, if only for a moment in the dark.

There was just no escaping from it, from everything. The station's problems had crossed the threshold into her personal life, affecting even the children. Demands were coming at her from all directions—those she placed on herself, the twins, Kit and the station. She stopped short of including Lawrence on the list and drained the last of her drink.

Looking with fascination at the bottom of the empty glass, she smiled. A ridiculing snort escaped her throat, as though warning her that she was fooling no one but herself on that count. Though Lawrence Woodson hadn't exactly demanded her attention, he had certainly captured it.

Kit exchanged a concerned glance with Lawrence. He opened his mouth to speak, but Kit shushed him with a nod of her head, then went over to stand behind Patrice. She draped her arms across Patrice's shoulders comfortingly, and their heads brushed against each other's.

"We don't have to talk about it tonight if you don't want to," Kit said softly.

She knew Patrice had been plagued by uncertainty and worry about the bomb threats. It hadn't been difficult to guess that whatever happened at the station tonight had been a continuation of the same problem.

Patrice squeezed the hand resting across her shoulder and whispered, "Thank you." She turned facing Kit, and the two shared a look that bespoke their friendship and sisterhood.

"I guess I'd better call it a night," announced Kit. "Lawrence, it's a pleasure meeting you. I'm sure I'll see you again."

"I look forward to it," he replied, standing.

"See you in the morning," Kit said to Patrice before leaving the room.

"It's time for me to call it a night, too," Lawrence said to Patrice, taking the glass from her hand and setting it on the table. He held his hand out to her, "Come walk me to the door," he coaxed gently. She nodded acquiescently and placed a hand in his.

"Thanks for coming with me," she said, retrieving his coat from the hall closet.

"It was my pleasure," he said, slipping into his coat. "Next time, I'll provide the entertainment."

She closed her eyes briefly, wishing she could be allowed to forget for even a moment the promise of her unknown nemesis.

"I know you don't want to think about it," he said, "and I wish I didn't have to."

Her shoulders squared, and she stared at him incredulously. "What do you mean by that? It's not your problem."

He opened his mouth to reply, but the threat to R. J. surfaced to the forefront of his mind, and he shut his mouth for fear of letting something slip. Anyway, if Lawrence had his way, and most assuredly he would, he would make her see that her problems were his, and her happiness, his.

"When can I see you again?" he asked instead.

She was shaken by the eagerness of his request and stared open-mouthed, unable to speak.

"I'll call you tomorrow," he said, his eyes holding hers in a steady gaze. He lowered his head and tenderly brushed her mouth with his. "Be sure to lock the door," he advised, opening the door. He stared at her longingly, then with reluctance in his eyes, abruptly walked out, closing the door behind him.

Patrice braced herself against the wall and stared dazedly at the door. Her mouth tingled with the memory of the warm lips on hers. She raised a hand to touch her lips, then let it fall to the side. Her eyelids closed while she considered her involuntary reactions to his gentle, loving looks and touch.

"I can't afford this," she whispered aloud, shuddering inwardly at the warning whisper that told her, *it's too late.*

"You gonna hold the wall up all night?" came Kit's voice from the stairway.

"I, uh, I," stammered Patrice, before pushing herself away from the wall and locking the door. "I thought you went to bed."

"I just wanted to check on you," replied Kit, sitting on the bottom step. "How are you feeling?"

"How do I look?" Patrice replied testily, hands on hips.

Kit's brow flickered a little at Patrice's tone, then she rubbed her chin and looked up at her friend thoughtfully. "I'd say you've been whisked off to a dwelling between heaven and hell."

"Just sleepy," Patrice replied laughingly, hiding her dismay at Kit's accurate diagnosis. She needed time alone to mull through these new sensations and thoughts before she was ready to share the confusion even with a best friend.

"Do you know it yet?" Kit asked to her back.

Patrice stopped and schooled her expression to one of puzzlement before facing Kit. "Know what?" she asked innocuously.

"All right, I'll play," Kit laughed, shaking her head. "What you feel for Mr. Lawrence Woodson?"

"I don't feel anything unusual for him," she said, her fingers crossed behind her back.

"Liar," retorted Kit.

"G' night, Kit," Patrice said rhythmically, spinning away and heading for her room.

"G'night."

ҙ ҙ ҙ ҙ

The tears hadn't stopped flowing from Marie's eyes, still glazed with the fear they'd had during the fight with Jay. Standing before the mirror in the bathroom, she gingerly applied the cold compress to the cut on the side of her mouth with unsteady hands. The wet cloth absorbed the trickle of blood from a bottom lip that was swelling.

The ordeal had been short and was over, but just thinking about it was terrifying—the experience hurting more than her bruise. Marie had no idea that he could be violent—or at least, would be towards her.

He'd arrived at the apartment reeking of liquor, hours late. But she hadn't wanted to ruin their evening and they were spending a pleasant enough time just talking, when there was mention of her job.

She couldn't remember what was said; maybe she defended Patrice against one of Jay's caustic remarks. But whatever it was, he erupted with a torrent of abuse—first, verbal, then physical. And just as quickly as the attack began, he stormed out of the apartment.

The doorbell rang, and Marie's hand froze. When the whining sound was repeated, she cautiously went to the living room and stopped a great distance from the door, afraid to go any closer.

"Who's there?"

"It's me, baby."

That smooth, familiar voice of her lover touched her ears like silk.

Backing away, she shook her head from side-to-side; the words of denial frozen in her throat.

"I'm sorry."

The simple apology was so sincere, so sweet, that new tears rolled down her face. Marie wanted desperately to believe him, for despite what had happened, she still loved him. Yet, fear was still fresh.

"I just had this liquor in me and I just went crazy. I swear to God, it'll never happen again. I'll even quit drinking. Come on, baby, you know how I feel about you. I never meant to lift a hand to you. Come on, Marie. Give me another chance, baby. I swear I'll make it up to you. Please!"

CHAPTER ❧ SIX

"**W**ell, if you can't get it done today, then don't bother calling us tomorrow!" No sooner than Patrice slammed the receiver in its wall cradle, than the instrument rang again.

"Hello," she barked into the mouthpiece. "Oh, Marie, I'm sorry. I just got off the phone with the insurance agent. How is the office clean-up coming this morning?"

She began to circle the table in the breakfast room, her mind operating in thirds: Part of her attention was on Marie's conversation, another, on the list of things that had to be done with regard to the vandalism of the station and assault on her announcer. And finally, there was the meeting she had had with the twins' principal. She felt as if she had already put in a full day of work.

Marie commanded her undivided attention, and she ceased her restive movement.

"No, don't tell him where I am," she said adamantly when informed that Lawrence had called the office. Promising to get in touch later, she hung up. She pushed up the sleeves of her hip-length white beaded sweater and lifted ankle-length turquoise skirt to rest on her knee as she looked over the neat piles of manilla folders, wondering where to begin.

"I told you to take the phone off the hook," said Kit, strolling into the kitchen, carrying a coffee mug.

"I should have listened," replied Patrice with a deep sigh. "You look like you've been in the office," she added, noting Kit's russet colored knit dress, belted at the waist with matching leather pumps.

"I've had my morning fight with Mr. Alderman," she replied, referring to a stodgy associate at the bank, as she filled a mug with hot, steaming coffee.

"What about this time?" asked Patrice.

"The usual. Nonsense." She took Patrice's cup, filled it, then handed it back. "He's been harassing my new secretary. Had the poor young woman in tears when I called." She sat at the table, while Patrice doctored her coffee with cream and artificial sweetener from the decorative glass containers on the island counter. "He's such a pig," said Kit, turning her nose up before taking a sip. "Enough about that. What did the principal say?"

"Nothing that I hadn't already suspected," Patrice replied thoughtfully. "He went into this spiel about newfangled parents whose concept of discipline was to coddle the child with gifts instead of a strap."

"I wonder what his kids are like," chuckled Kit.

"I'm not even sure if he has any. Anyway, they're just flapping their wings, trying to see how far they can go before I haul in the rope."

Though she and the twins had resolved one difference, the principal's child-rearing lecture had made her feel inadequate about fulfilling the dual roles of mother and father. She dropped into the chair across from Kit, setting the mug on the table, and stared pensively into the liquid.

"I'm really concerned about Stephen."

"Why? What has he done?"

Patrice pushed the cup away, then dropped her hands to her lap before answering. "He hasn't done anything that I shouldn't expect, I guess. I don't know. I just feel that I'm not giving him something he needs. And I don't know what that something is—so don't ask. Maybe it's nothing," she shrugged, picking up the mug to take a swallow.

"If you're feeling uneasy about it, it is something," Kit corrected. "Have you asked him?"

"Ask him what?" Patrice retorted. "Am I a sufficient parent? I'm a little scared of what he might say," she answered with a bittersweet laugh.

"Sounds as though you're having a case of the guilts," stated Kit matter-of-factly, sipping from her cup. Patrice shrugged noncommittally and toyed with the spoon, stirring it in the cup.

"I think you're underestimating yourself," continued Kit. "The twins are bright, mannerly, and they're not really bogged down by materials wants. When they're with me, contrary to what you believe, they don't ask me to buy them anything." Patrice eyed Kit from the corner of her eye with a raised brow. "They don't ask," she defended, "they just indulge my need to spend money. And even then, we spend more time playing games and talking than we do shopping."

Kit got up to pour hot coffee over the warm remains in her cup. "When I took them with me to the bank's party, everybody just fell in love with them. Even old Alderman." She imitated a nasal-tone male voice, *"Well, Miss McDougall, I know these fine kids can't be yours, because they're a pleasure to be around."* She and Patrice shared a laugh as Kit slid back into her seat.

"Maybe you're right," Patrice conceded, rising to pour her coffee down the drain. She leaned against the counter facing Kit. "They are good kids, aren't they?" she said, a fond expression brightening her features.

"Did Lawrence Woodson bring this on by any chance?" Kit asked, with a sidelong glance and mischievous grin.

"I don't follow you."

"I think you do," Kit challenged. "I think the entrance of Lawrence Woodson on the scene has made you wonder if you haven't robbed your children of a father."

"That's pure nonsense," Patrice denied. "Absolutely ludicrous," she continued, unwilling to admit that she had been plagued by the very notion that the children, her son in particular, needed a father. "They have a father, for what it's worth." She turned her back to Kit and became engrossed in rinsing the mug. "I'd never marry just so my kids can have a father figure," she said with vehement distaste.

"Part of that is not without some appeal," Kit said softly.

"What?" asked Patrice, turning sharply to stare at Kit. "Tell me you didn't say what I thought I heard you say," she said appalled.

"When was the last time you've even seriously dated? Let's see," she added, not waiting for Patrice's reply. "That Taylor guy from New York. It was what—eight months ago when you broke up with him?"

"I didn't break up with him. He moved back to New York," Patrice said, setting the mug on the drain board.

"After you turned down his proposal," Kit taunted.

"If you'll remember, I'd barely been at the station a month," she said, sauntering to the table. "I wasn't about to saddle myself with a new husband, too. Plus, he seemed more interested in my position than me. Anyway, I don't see where my social life has anything to do with my kids."

"Directly, nothing. But you can't deny that you feel something for Lawrence," said Kit, a knowing gleam in her eyes. "And the feeling is mutual."

"He's a good-looking man, that's all," Patrice said, before her dimples burst from hiding, and she was soon laughing with Kit. "All right, I admit there's something there. What, I haven't worked out, nor am I sure if I want to."

"From what I saw last night, it's already worked out. You just haven't accepted it yet."

"And probably won't. My life is too cluttered as it is. I don't have time for myself, much less for a man as demanding as Lawrence Woodson," she said, voicing the rationale that had played in her head.

"Demanding?" Kit asked, raising fine, arched eyebrows.

"I didn't mean that the way it sounded. I don't really know him at all. I just met him several days ago. And it's hardly time to start thinking of him in terms of permanency."

"Who said anything about permanency?" At Patrice's silence, Kit added, "Aren't you going to ask me what I think about him?"

"No," Patrice replied promptly.

"Good," declared Kit. "That means you like him and don't care what anybody else thinks. He stands a fighting chance. If," she said in parenthesis, "you don't get cold feet."

Patrice fell silent, recalling a time in her life when the refusal to be influenced by someone else's opinion had been a huge mistake. Both Kit and Cleo had tried to caution her about the Don Juan character she worshipped. *If only I had listened.*

"Let sleeping dogs lie," said Kit, guessing the direction of Patrice's thoughts.

"What are you talking about now, Kit?"

"You know," she replied. "You drag up Don's ghost whenever a man shows some interest in you."

Kit would never openly admit how Patrice's relationship with Donald had indirectly influenced her own qualms about marriage. Patrice had enough fear-of-failure to supply both of them. While she didn't believe that she was afraid of the institution of marriage, she planned to make damn sure that the odds would be in favor of a lasting commitment when the time was right.

"I do not...." was as far as Patrice got in her denial. "I guess I do, don't I?"

"Ummm-hmm," murmured Kit. "You can't go around comparing all men to Donald. He wasn't a man anyway. So don't stop eating apples just because some of them have worms."

"It's getting late," said Patrice, pushing a chair under the table. She had too much work to do to spend anymore time thinking about her personal life. "I need to get busy. And you're going to be late for your appointment in Houston if you don't get started."

"I've got plenty of time," said Kit, checking the time on her gold watch. "We haven't talked in a long time, so don't be so eager to get rid of me. I want to know the latest on the concert."

"That will be a short conversation," replied Patrice. "The threats continue. In fact, the latest came when I was trying to talk Lawrence into agreeing to allow the concert be held on Banneker's campus. Last night, somebody vandalized the station and beat up my announcer on his way to relieve my six to ten man."

"Oh, no!" cried Kit, her coffee mug overturned, splashing coffee in an expanding, tan pool. She jumped up to grab a dish cloth. "Certainly you're going to cancel now?!" she said, dabbing at the stain on her dress.

"No," replied Patrice, cleaning the table. "Not yet anyway," she added, tossing the paper towel into the trash.

"Patrice," Kit said anxiously. "These incidents have gotten out of hand. What are you thinking of? I know this concert means a lot to you, but you're not thinking logically about this."

"You sound like Lawrence. I thought you were on my side," Patrice said in a hurt tone.

"This has nothing to do with sides," argued Kit. "My God, Patrice! Find some other way to make a statement against apartheid besides putting innocent peoples' lives in jeopardy. You've never been politically driven before, why now?"

Kit was right of course. She had never before been more than on the fringes of the political activity surrounding her. But there was something about apartheid that struck her more deeply than any other political issue, and she wanted to be a part of helping to dismantle that injustice. So that, coupled with the threats—which she viewed as a warning to "stay in her place"—had made her all the more determined to find a way to hold the concert.

"You're right in a way," she said calmly. "I only regret that I can't make you understand or explain what it is I feel. I hardly understand it myself. But this is important to me, Kit," she added in a soft voice, begging indulgence. She covered her mouth with her hand, then looked into Kit's eyes, dazed with a wish for comprehension.

"It's not about the job, is it?" Kit guessed.

"I thought it was at first," she replied, exhaling deeply. "And in some ways, it still is because whoever is responsible for sending those threats is no more political than I've been in the past. I'm sure of that."

"I don't know what to say," said Kit, clearly nonplused and somewhat frightened for Patrice.

A tiny laugh escaped Patrice's throat, for she'd never seen Kit at a loss for words before.

"I talked Mr. Russell into letting me try one more thing before we announce a cancellation," she said after a while. She leaned over the chair, scraping the back with long nails. "I have an appointment with a private investigator right after lunch." When Kit didn't interrupt, she continued, "I'm going to give it two weeks. That's the absolute latest before we have to finalize everything. If he can't come up with something that suggests the threats are nothing more than pranks, then we call it quits."

"And he agreed to this?" asked Kit in amazement.

"I talked him into it. Hell, I pleaded with him to let me have the final decision on this matter."

"I hope you know what you're in for," said Kit.

"I do, too."

§ § § §

Later that afternoon when Patrice arrived at her office, several message slips awaited her attention—three were from Lawrence Woodson. She didn't believe he was calling to say the university would host the concert. She returned all of the calls, except his.

It hadn't been easy—not returning his calls. There were a number of times when she found the receiver in her hand and her finger poised to dial. But she forced herself to hang up before yielding to temptation, armed with the rationale that there was too much work to get done. When she finally called it a day at the office, she folded up the messages from him and stuffed them in her purse. She took them home and placed them on a spindle on her dresser.

The next several days were tortuous for Patrice.

Lawrence didn't call back, and she underwent a miserable cycle of emotions: First, there was panic. She berated herself for blowing her chance. On its heels followed the feeling of betrayal, blaming his sexual attractiveness for tempting her to abandon reason. Indifference surged as a defense by mid-week. Since he hadn't phoned again, she assumed he had only been interested in a casual fling. That, she told herself, she could do without. Finally, acceptance reigned: it was not meant to be.

However, the memory of his face, his smile, his laugh tantalized her memory and nothing could subdue the niggling doubts that haunted her.

By the end of the week, the brass-plated spike had been cleared from the dresser, and the pink slips torn into jagged shreds. His number, nonetheless, had been committed to memory.

ta ta ta ta

The open curtains rustled to reveal a beautiful, bright afternoon outside, but Patrice's only interest was lounging around the house. And while sitting on the couch in the living room with her feet propped on the table, she absently leafed through a magazine. The twins came quietly into the room and sat on each side of her.

"What can I do for you?" she asked without looking up.

"Why don't we do something?" suggested Stephenie. "You've been sulking, Mom."

"I have not been sulking," she disclaimed, amusement in her voice. She closed the magazine and tossed it on the table. "I gather you're bored and want to do something," she said with a knowing smile. "What do you have in mind?"

"Let's go see a movie," said Stephen eagerly.

"Ah-hah," said Patrice, holding a victorious finger up. "I knew it was something. Ok, let's go."

"Good. I invited Mr. Woodson to come with us," said Stephenie in a small voice, covering her face in anticipation of her mother's ire.

"It wasn't my idea," Stephen tossed in guilelessly before Patrice could gather her thoughts. "Aunt Kit is coming, too."

"And she's bringing her new boyfriend," piped Stephenie excitedly as a diversion. "His name is Martin."

Patrice was paralyzed by the whirlwind of one single thought: I'll see *him again*. She was both excited and irritated in the same instance. Before she could find the words the shrilling sound of the doorbell pierced riotous thoughts.

"I'll get it," her son volunteered, springing up to leave the room.

"Go change clothes quick," urged Stephenie.

"What's wrong with what I have on? I don't have to get dressed up to go to a movie," she said stubbornly. "If," she emphasized, "I go," glaring at her daughter.

Patrice stood to greet the tall, attractive stranger at Kit's side, whom she assumed was Martin . She rolled her eyes at Kit and extended a hand to Martin, smiling gaily into brilliant aquamarine eyes.

"Hi, my name is Patrice Mason. I'm afraid I haven't even heard about you," she said to him, deliberately ignoring Kit, "until a few seconds ago."

"Hello, Patrice. Martin Coppage," he replied, shaking her hand, "and I've heard plenty about you and the twins."

"Have a seat, Martin. Can I get you anything?"

"Patrice!" Kit exclaimed, stomping her foot on the floor.

"Did you hear something, Martin?"

Martin laughed and shook his head, playing along. Kit popped him on the arm. "Is she always this affectionate?" he asked Patrice.

"Who?" she asked innocently.

"Mom!" chimed the twins.

"Mr. Woodson is gonna be here in a little while, and you're not even ready," her daughter reminded her.

"Martin, don't you think jeans and a sweatshirt are dressy enough for a movie?"

"Patrice Antoinette Mason. If you don't get your..." started Kit in a low, threatening tone, which Patrice overlapped in a pleasant voice, "Watch your language, whoever you are."

"I'll show you who I am," retorted Kit indignantly, grabbing Patrice by the wrist and pulling her to the master suite. She slammed the door shut behind them. "Now, what's this all about?"

"Everybody knows everything except me. My best *friend*," she stretched the one syllable word, "brings a black-haired Adonis to my house, and I've never heard one word about him," she replied with hands on her hips.

"Isn't he beautiful?" Kit exclaimed delightfully as she plopped onto the bed. "You wouldn't believe my shock when he turned out to be my appointment the other day. Things have just been moving so fast, even I don't know what's going on," she rattled. "Don't just stand there, get dressed. Lawrence is supposed to meet us here in a few minutes."

"I smell a set-up," said Patrice, folding her arms. "Whose idea was this?"

"It's irrelevant," replied Kit, springing up to slide open the closet doors. "Where's that multi-colored sweater?" she asked, rummaging through the closet. "Oh, here it is."

"I didn't say I was going anywhere," said Patrice, then caught the sweater Kit tossed at her.

"When did you get these?" asked Kit, pulling out a pair of gray trousers. "These will go nicely with that sweater. Hurry up."

Defiance sparkled in Patrice's eyes, a pout fixed on her lips. Kit's eyes flashed a familiar display of impatience, then she released a deep audible sigh.

"Your children were worried about you."

Realizing her defeat was complete, Patrice said, "Well, you might as well fill me in on Martin Coppage." She began changing into the clothes Kit had selected.

Kit's face lit up again. She began to walk around the room as she spoke. "What can I tell you? It's amazing. Even I have to pinch myself to make sure I'm not dreaming. Remember the appointment I had the other day? Well, I was supposed to meet with a Norman Claymore. I wasn't looking forward to it, I can tell you. Imagine what a Norman Claymore looks like," she said, shuddering at the image the name brought to mind.

"What did he look like?"

"I don't know. Never met him," was Kit's reply as she sat in the rocking chair. "He had taken ill and Martin was the substitute. Oh, Patrice, it was so embarrassing," she said laughing. "I babbled like an idiot through most of the meeting and not one ounce of my normal brilliance came out."

"I'm familiar with that state," chuckled Patrice. The doorbell rang, and she froze midway in the act of pulling a pair of long, gray suede boots from the closet.

"That must be Lawrence. I'll fill in the rest later. Hurry up," urged

Kit, jumping from the rocker. "I'll wait for you in the living room," she said on the way out the door.

ఌ ఌ ఌ ఌ

The house seemed exceptionally quiet when Patrice strolled into the living room. She started to call out, then saw Lawrence standing in front of the mantle, staring up at the portrait.

Her body responded in excitement as her eyes drank their fill. Lord-dy, does he ever look *good!* He still was not the most attractive man she'd ever seen, but he had a well-defined face; passionate, sensual features that made him by far the most compelling man she'd ever met. Those lips are so full and inviting. Even in stillness, an air of command exuded from him.

He sensed her presence and slowly turned to face her, the broad shoulders squared, the expression on his face unreadable.

"Hi," she said softly, unconsciously wringing her nervous fingers together. She decided to banish the offensive traitors behind her back when she recognized the nervous display.

"Hi," he said matter-of-factly. "You didn't return my calls. Now, I'm curious," he said, staring at her intently. "Is this really what you want?"

She returned the intense stare, sauntering across the room to stand directly in front of him. "Yes," she replied, in a voice textured with tender apology. "I just wasn't sure," and taking a deep breath continued, "until now."

The admission that spilled from her mouth did not originate from her brain, but replicated her heartfelt emotion.

Lawrence had done little except think of this light-skinned dynamo for the past several days. Her rejection had affected him more deeply than he wanted or cared to admit. And although he'd blamed himself for creating this panic within her, hurt rivaled anger, and he toyed with the idea of walking away from those wonderful open coffee gazes.

Just seeing her again makes me ache with the need to drown in these lovely pools of sensuality. Take me away, Patrice—'ll be a willing victim of those cocoa seas.

"OK, let's go. They're waiting for us outside," he said, a smile of understanding on his face, and tucking her arm under his, guided a supplicant Patrice from the house.

CHAPTER ❧ SEVEN

"*T*his one," said Stephenie, holding up a sequined red dress with a low cut bodice and thin straps.

"No, this one," countered Stephen, pointing to the long sleeve, high neck, blue and white dress lying on the bed.

Patrice, dressed in her robe, critically eyed the evening dresses of her children's choice. She had agreed days ago to attend Banneker's fund-raising banquet with Lawrence, but hadn't given much thought to what she'd wear. She couldn't fall back on the age-old complaint of "I don't have anything to wear." If anything, she told herself, turning to scan the evening dresses that occupied an entire section in the back of her closet, she had too many choices. In her defense, however, everything in her wardrobe represented a necessity. A woman in her position didn't have time to worry about clothes.

Still, it was so uncharacteristic of her to wait until the last minute, even though she suspected why she had. It had been her symbolic way of putting a halter on her feelings. She couldn't afford to let herself be swept off her feet—again.

But this was pushing it, Patrice, she chided herself, a polished nail in her mouth. With less than an hour to dress, she was still undecided.

"Mom, it's cold outside. If you wear that skimpy thing Stephenie's clutching, you're gonna freeze your you know what off," argued Stephen.

"Dinner will not be served outside, stupid," retorted Stephenie.

"Nobody is stupid around here," Patrice chastised her daughter.

"Yeah, Stephenie," mocked Stephen. "I think you ought to wear this one, Mom."

"Mom, don't listen to him!"

"She has to think about her reputation. She can't wear that to a banquet. You want to embarrass Mr. Woodson? Everybody's gonna be gawking," he added, pointing to the revealing red dress.

"You want her to look like a nun?" countered Stephenie, flinging his choice to the far side of the bed. "How would you like your date buttoned up ike a prude?"

Patrice covered her ears, ordering, "OK, OK, enough!" When she had their attention, she drew a deep breath and calmly stated, "Thank you very much for your input, but I'll handle this."

"Which one are you gonna wear?" Stephen inquired, a suspicious glare in his eyes.

"You'll see," she replied, taking the dress from Stephenie, "when I come out. Now, don't you have homework or something?" she added, pushing them out. She hurried to replace the dresses in her closet when the phone on the nightstand rang.

"Hello," she answered. "Oh, hi, Kit. What's up? What am I going to wear tonight? Not you, too! I don't believe you called to ask me that," she said, chuckling. "Why is everybody so concerned about my dress tonight? You'd swear I've never been to a banquet before. I haven't decided yet! I'll look nice, I promise you. No, I'm not going to dress down. Oh, if I wore that, I'd be arrested. Kit!" she said impatiently, "Lawrence is going to be here any minute now, and I'm still in my robe. Yes, I'll call you tomorrow. G'night," she said before ringing off.

She sighed long and hard before heading across the room to the dresser. The phone rang, and she spun around and snatched up the receiver.

"Kit, give me a break," she said. "Hello? Who is this? Hello?" Frowning, Patrice lowered the phone back to its cradle.

With a quick shake of her head, she stalked across the room, mumbling about everybody treating her as if she were a child who had never been anywhere before. She was determined to show her family that she didn't need their help. Look out, *Mr. Woodson, I'll have your tongue hanging down to your lap by the time I'm done with myself tonight.*

Nearly an hour later, Patrice headed for the living room where she could hear the rumble of Lawrence's laughter; the twins were entertaining him. *Good,* she thought. *That's a good sign.* She stood partially hidden behind the wall, peeking into the room to sneak a peek at him.

If it were possible, he looked more imposing than ever, suited in a traditional black dinner jacket, trimmed in black at the lapels and the sides of his trousers.

Raising her arm to check the time and frowning, she remembered opting for the diamond and onyx earrings dangling from her ears. Deciding she'd spied long enough, she took a deep breath and made her grand entrance.

"Oh, Mom!" gushed Stephenie. "When did you get that? It's bad!"

Stephen was too shocked to speak. His mother looked absolutely stunning, but the revealing gown would hardly have been his choice.

Lawrence stared in speechless wonder. He gulped and unconsciously pulled at his tie. His eyes trailed an unhurried path from her lightly made up face and hair, which was styled exotically on top of her head in a ball of ringlets, down to her luscious neck and exposed shoulders. A wickedly black silk crepe gown outlined her slender body, while a white ruffle flowed down the side of the dress, forming a rose at her tiny waist.

She basked under the look in his eyes, and bloomed under the glimmering light green specks of approval. The effervescent sensation bubbling inside her glowed on her cafe au lait face as he narrowed the distance between them in fluid, easy strides. Capturing her hands in his, he murmured, "Patrice," softly—the dulcet baritone caressing her name. "You are absolutely beautiful."

"Thank you. You don't look too bad yourself," she said unable to resist cupping his cheek with her hand.

"Believe me," he joked, pulling at the bow tie, "the country boy from Grambling is still in here."

"You guys are gonna be late," said Stephenie in a voice louder than normal.

Patrice peeped around Lawrence to smile fondly at her offspring. "We get the hint, thank you," she said before turning to Lawrence, "Do we have time for a drink?"

He looked at his watch, then replied, "No, we'd better get going."

"Ok. Stephen, will you get my wrap and bag off the bed, please?"

"Sure, Mom," he replied, galloping from the room.

"Stephenie, I don't want you two waiting up. We should be back, around. . . " she said, looking at Lawrence questioningly.

"Eleven, I imagine," he supplied.

"No later than twelve," she said to her daughter.

"How can we reach you if an emergency comes up?"

"Here, let me give you the number of the security office on campus," he said, pulling a business card and pen from the pocket inside his dinner jacket. He scribbled a number on the back of the card—"Just call this number and the officer will get in touch with us"—and handed it to Stephenie.

Stephen returned with Patrice's small evening bag and a long white fur coat.

"I've never see that before either," said Stephenie, adding indignantly, "When did you buy all these things?"

"Never mind, Miss," Patrice replied, allowing Lawrence to help her into the coat. "You two be good. Stephen, keep her out of trouble."

"Me?!" said Stephenie.

"Come on, give me a kiss so we can go," she said, ignoring her daughter's protest.

"Have fun," said Stephenie, pecking Patrice on the cheek.

"Be careful," warned her son, casting a silent message with his eyes to Lawrence as he kissed his mother.

"Yes, sir," Lawrence said, nodding his head at Stephen.

The twins followed them to the front door, and the phone began to ring. Patrice turned towards the persistent peal and hesitated. "I'm out for the evening. Take a message." Her daughter rushed off to answer the phone, while Stephen pulled open the door. "Be sure and lock up," she advised.

"Will you stop worrying and get outta here?"

Patrice and Lawrence walked out into the dark, chilly night to his car, parked at the front door. He helped her in, then ran around the driver's side.

"Is something wrong?" he asked, starting up the engine.

"No, why did you ask?"

"Because you seemed to have gotten a little jittery."

"No, everything's fine. Just motherly concern rearing its head, that's all," she said with a light laugh.

He cocked his head to the side, looking at her with disbelief, then decided not to let a suspicious nature spoil the evening. "Is there any reason why you're hugging the door over there?" She laughed and moved to sit next to him. "That's better," he said, driving off. "Much better."

ᘒᴥ ᘒᴥ ᘒᴥ ᘒᴥ

Lawrence was to revise his views about fund-raising banquets, having once thought them nothing more than necessary evils. With Patrice at his side, it had been pure fun. And more successful than he or Charles would have imagined. She had inveigled two of the university's more financially able alumni into a competition resulting in over $50,000 in pledges for the university's coffers.

Later the food had been removed and tables pushed against the walls to make room for dancing in the dimly lit room. Conversation was hushed to a low din under the crystal balls circling overhead, casting the dancers in a silhouette.

Patrice couldn't recall the last time she'd enjoyed herself more. *Lawrence has been amorously indulgent, attentive and possessive—everything a woman could hope for,* she thought. She snuggled closer to his solid frame as he guided them in a slow dance across the floor. She couldn't remember the title of the number the band was playing; nor was thought required, for even without words the sentiment of the tune implied "for lovers only."

Their self-absorbed reprieve was interrupted by one of the vice presidents she'd met earlier in the evening, Dr. Kamani, an attractive man of West Indian ancestry. Pausing before the swaying couple, Dr. Kamani tapped Lawrence on the shoulder.

"What do you want, Freddy?" Lawrence asked, clearly perturbed by the intrusion.

"You're not that young that you don't know what a tap on the shoulder means, mon," the vice president replied in a Jamaican accent laced with laughter. "I want to dance with this lovely ladee you've been monopolizing all night."

"No cutting in."

"Lawrence!" Patrice whispered with amused censure.

"There are certain things I don't share," he said seriously, staring down at her. "And you're one of them," he purred, his tone low and purposefully seductive. "Go away, Freddy. Find your own partner," he ordered Dr. Kamani, his gaze riveted on her face.

Reading the message in his eyes, Patrice couldn't help the surge of emotion which responded to the desire in his eyes—no words were required. She responded by increasing the pressure of her arms around his waist and leaning further into his embrace.

🐦 🐦 🐦 🐦

Reluctant for the evening to end, Patrice had issued an invitation to Charles and J.T. to join Lawrence and her for a nightcap at her home. The ambience in the room was one of warm relaxation—friends enjoying after-dinner drinks around a soon to be toasty fire.

Lawrence was replacing the cage over the fireplace. Charles and J.T. were sitting on the sofa, where he was rubbing his wife's swollen feet.

"I love your home, Patrice," J.T. said, looking over her shoulder at Patrice, who was at the bar mixing drinks.

"Thank you. The kids and I were about to give up and let an agent do the looking when we finally lucked out. We must have looked at a hundred homes, trying to find one we all liked."

"Need any help?" Lawrence asked Patrice.

"You can get this tray while I get the hot chocolate," she replied, then headed for the kitchen.

"Think I can convince her to take a leave from the station and come head up our endowment campaign?" Charles said jokingly as he accepted the drink Lawrence put in his hand.

"I wouldn't even let her consider it," said Lawrence.

"You wouldn't let her?" J. T. queried, her brow lifting questioningly. "You have that much power?"

"That's not what I meant at all," replied Lawrence in a tone that marked the end of that conversation.

"What's not what you meant?" asked Patrice, coming into the room carrying a tray with two mugs of hot chocolate with whipped cream on top.

"Nothing," said Lawrence, taking the tray from her to set it on the table. He passed a napkin and mug first to J. T., then Patrice, before joining her on the loveseat.

"We really could use someone with your skills to head up our endowment campaign," said Charles earnestly.

Patrice laughed lightly. "Is that how you got Lawrence?" she asked, looking at Lawrence and smiling.

"He never gives up," Lawrence told her. "He bugged me for two years as if he was a hunter wearing down his prey."

"Nah," discounted Charles, "I just caught you at the right moment. Tell the truth—you were getting tired of traveling and hustling to secure new business."

"Well, let me save you a couple of years, Charles. Now is definitely not the right time for me," Patrice explained, taking a sip of her chocolate, leaving a white smudge of cream on her nose.

"Look at you, just like a baby," teased Lawrence, wiping the cream from her nose with his finger. She wiggled her nose playfully at him.

"Well, I really want you to know we appreciate what you've done for the university."

"I could do more," she said, casting a sly smile at Lawrence from the corner of her eyes, earning a warning nod from him.

"I forgot to ask if the cops have been able to come up with anything on the bomb threats," J. T. said.

"Nothing yet, I'm afraid," she replied, turning slightly to avoid Lawrence's expression. "How's the communication department doing?" she asked, quickly changing the subject.

"Ask the man over there who's sliced our faculty budget in half," retorted J. T. petulantly.

Lawrence chuckled and covered his face with one hand.

Laughing, Charles said, "Well, old buddy, it seems everywhere you turn, there's a bullet whizzing by your head."

"I'm beginning to feel like the duck at target practice," said Lawrence.

The telephone rang intrusively from the kitchen. Lawrence looked at his watch, then at Patrice as she set her mug on the table.

"It's probably Kit," she explained to the tension on his features. "Excuse me."

"What's up?" asked Charles, sensing the introduction of a chill in the warm atmosphere.

"I don't know," replied Lawrence. "Maybe nothing," he said with doubt, placing his drink on the table to follow Patrice to the kitchen.

J. T. looked at Charles curiously, and he shrugged in reply to her silent question. She rested her head on his shoulder, and he wrapped his arm around her. "It's pass your bedtime," he said, planting a kiss on the side of her head.

"I know. And I'm feeling it too. We're not going to want to get up in the morning."

"Ok, when they get back, we'll say our goodnights and get you home."

❧ ❧ ❧ ❧

Patrice was standing in the circle of Lawrence's embrace, fidgeting with his tie. Despite the disturbing phone call, she felt fearless and protected in his strong arms.

"Look, it was nothing. Just a wrong number," she said in an appeasing tone of voice, hoping to erase the worry lines from his forehead.

"I don't think so, and you don't either. My bet is that it was the telephone ringing that upset you before we left. You didn't fool me one bit with that motherly concern."

"Please," she whined. "It's been such a pleasant evening. Let's not ruin it."

Her appealing smile melted his defenses, and he closed his eyes while resting his chin against the top of her head. "All right," he growled softly, knowing he'd been had. Enfolding her close to him, said, "But I want you to know this is not the end."

Standing on tiptoe, she touched her lips to his and gasped surprisingly when he moved his mouth over hers, devouring its softness. His urgent kiss sent her body into a responsive frenzy, and she clutched his sides, holding on to the only solid thing in her grasp.

He had been waiting for this moment, and now that it had finally arrived, he couldn't fathom its end. His hands explored the hollows of her back, pulling her even closer to further intoxicate his senses with her sweet smell and pliant.

She felt his warm breath on her flesh where he placed tiny, delicate kisses from the creamy expanse of her shoulder to succulent lips. "Lawrence. Oh, Lawrence," she whispered into his mouth, her head in a tailspin, her body blazing out of control with want.

Nothing in her experience with men had prepared her for the unconditional and swift surrender he was exacting from her—she gave willingly and fully of her lips. Raising his mouth from hers, he gazed into her desire-glazed eyes before he spoke, his breaths coming in long and deep gulps of air. "If we don't get back soon, our company is going to wonder what's happened to us."

Agreeably, she shook her head and backed out of his hold. She sighed audibly before jesting, "We had better get outside or they'll know for certain what's been going on," earning a quick bear hug from him.

The joy inside her bubbled over, and she laughed infectiously. Her lips were still warm and moist from his kisses when they returned hand-in-hand to the living room.

"Everything all right?" Charles asked, looking at Lawrence speculatively.

"Everything's fine," replied Lawrence, smiling at Patrice.

"We hate to drink and run," said Charles, rising, "but my babies here," he helped J. T. to her feet, "need their rest."

"I'm so glad you could come," said Patrice. "Maybe we can get together again, just the four of us."

"We'd love to," said J.T., sliding her arm into the coat Charles held. "How 'bout dinner at our place next week?"

"Oh, no!" protested Lawrence.

"Lawrence," chastised Patrice, hitting him playfully on the shoulder.

"You don't understand—J. T. can't cook worth a damn."

"Charles, are you going to let him talk about my cooking like that?" J. T. cried indignantly.

"Children, children. Not tonight, please. It's too late," said Charles paternally. To Patrice, who was holding in her laughter, he explained, "They do this all the time."

"Don't worry about it," Patrice said to J. T. "Just give me a call, and the both of us will be there."

She and Lawrence saw them to the door, then he followed them out to their car.

"Be careful," he advised, as Charles revved the engine. "See you in the morning."

"Oh, no rush, early afternoon is soon enough," Charles said casually, a conspiratorial grin on his face.

"Don't blow it," J. T. said menacingly.

Lawrence raised his hands to the heavens and sighed wearily. Charles drove off, and he rushed back inside the house where he found Patrice had already removed the glasses and cups from the coffee table. He was warming his hands in front of the fire when she returned and wrapped her arms around his waist from behind.

"I had a lovely time tonight," she said, lying her head against his back, his coat cold against her cheek.

"So did I," he replied, cupping her hands together in front of him. "Those things usually bore me to death. You made it more than bearable," he said, turning to envelope her in eager arms. "It's late. Time for me to go, too."

"Mmm," she sighed, her head against his chest; she could hear his heartbeat. "I just hate it when a good evening has to end."

"It doesn't have to," he murmured near her ear, nuzzling her neck with warm breath. He was thinking of the future, and the many more days and nights like this they would enjoy together.

She closed her eyes and tightened her arms around him, luxuriating in the feel of his body against hers. She couldn't think past the moment, for nothing could compare to the way she felt right now.

"Patrice."

The seriousness of his tone jolted the languor from her, and she moved slightly to look up into his face. She found lines of concern etched on his forehead.

"I don't like these phone calls you've been getting."

Retreating from his hold and spinning away, she replied, "I don't have any control over them; they're probably just the wrong number. Furthermore, I think you're blowing this out of proportion," she said lightly despite her own misgivings.

His expression spoke volumes about his opinion of the feeble explanation, forcing her to resort to, "You promised we wouldn't talk about it tonight."

"I know I did," he said, stepping forward to pull her back into comforting arms.

Patrice stared up into his face, and her stomach turned over, for he was branding her with the green lights of his warm brown eyes. She was tempted to tell him right then and there she'd cancel the concert.

"I shouldn't have, you know. It's something I can't let go," he finished in a soft, suggestive voice.

She saw the hidden meaning of the words he spoke; they characterized the tender expression on his face. She felt a sharp pang of guilt, for she did not know if she were prepared, now or ever, for that step.

Her distress must have shown, for he said, "I'm not going to ask you to go to bed with me," guessing at the alarmed expression lighting her face. "At least, not tonight," he added, trying to put her at ease.

"I like you, Lawrence. I like being with you. I want you to know that."

She licked her lips nervously. "But I'm not sure I'm ready for anything more right now."

"I see I'm going to have to get you another picture."

"What?"

He nodded to the picture over the mantle-piece. "You're so used to seeing only those three people in that picture that I think you see your life reflected there. I want you, Patrice Mason— in every way. And I'm willing to wait. But let the record show that patience is not what I'm known for." He smiled a mercurial smile that caused a capsule of warmth to break open and spill its heated contents throughout her body. "That said, I think it's time you walked me to the door."

A look of tenderness captioned her expression, and they strolled arm-in-arm to the foyer where he claimed his coat from the closet. His gentle gaze touched her face as they stood at the door, each hesitant to part.

"Will you call me again?" she said, meeting his look with a faint light twinkling in the depths of floating brown eyes.

"You can be assured of it," he replied, then kissed her quickly on the forehead. "G'night." He took a final look at her, and strolled down to the driveway.

Patrice retired to her bedroom after locking up. She picked up her white coat, intending to hang it in her closet. Instead, she sat on the side of the bed with the coat draped around her arm.

It is a poor substitute for the *real thing I held in my arms tonight,* she thought, looking down at the luxurious, white garment. Confusion burned in her eyes. *If only things were as simple as they seem.*

"What's so complicated?" she asked herself aloud. "You either want the man or you don't."

And that is part of the problem, she groaned, burying her face in the coat. She did want him, almost too much.

She flung the coat aside and jumped up, demanding of herself, *"And what's wrong with that?"* She snatched up the coat and stormed to her closet.

Donald Hollingsworth.

Kit's words came back and she froze, the coat falling to the floor in a heap. She closed her eyes, wishing away reminders of Donald, but they weren't easily banished. Retrieving the coat she haphazardly stuffed it on a hanger.

Donald has nothing in common with Lawrence, she argued silently, easing out of her dress. *Lawrence would never hurt me the way Don had.* Such cruelty was not a part of his nature, and he really seemed to care for her.

"*And you're not the same glittery-eyed, impressionable woman-child you were fourteen years ago,*" said the random voice in her mind.

"I'm not," she said to her reflection in the mirror. *This body has mothered two children, this mind has seen to their care, and this heart*—she added, crossing her palms between her bare, brown skinned breasts—*has the capacity to love.*

Yet, with those assertions came the doubts and fear. Could she withstand another failure? What if she were wrong about the feelings that felt so right with Lawrence?

The phone rang, putting an end to her musings.

Patrice gripped the side of the door, wishing the silent intervals between the tinkling sound would signal the last ring. Growing irritated with the constant noise, she walked across the room to answer. Patrice's outstretched hand trembled as she picked up the receiver.

"Hello," she said faintly into the mouthpiece, anticipating the non-reply that usually greeted her.

She gently replaced the receiver back into its bed.

CHAPTER ❧ EIGHT

Sleep was long in coming to Patrice. When the elusive state of rest finally arrived it was of nightmarish quality. Don's mocking face, taunting and cursing her interrupted pleasant interludes and images of she and Lawrence—on the dance floor, holding hands, locked in a tender embrace. Before long, it was morning. Rising sluggishly, Patrice felt as if she hadn't gone to bed at all.

After a steaming shower, she opened the door of her closet and fingered the gown she'd worn to the banquet. Memories of the night before poured over her like a warm summer sun, and she wondered if she dare name this tender feeling.

An urgent desire to see his face, to hear his voice seized her like a tight hug. Impulsively, she picked up the phone to call, dialing the numbers committed to memory. After letting it ring for what seemed like an eternity, she hung up. Before the disappointment had time to set in, Stephenie ran into the room, announcing, "We missed our ride."

Plotting how she would rearrange the day to include time for Lawrence stayed with her through the ritual of dropping the twins off at school and the long drive to Houston. She was sizzling with lunch plans for the two of them and could hardly wait to call him from the office.

Her euphoria was doused as soon as she walked in for Roger was pacing nervously in front of her desk, mumbling insanely to himself.

"What bee got in your bonnet?" she asked, hanging her coat on the rack and almost tumbling the tall pole.

Roger didn't detect the thread of frustration texturing the impatient voice. "Didn't you get my messages last night?" he demanded, irritation marking his tone.

"No, it was late when I got in so I didn't even check for messages," she replied, sitting behind her desk. "Want to tell me what's going on?" she asked with disinterest, leafing through a folder Marie left on the desk.

"Somebody has been driving me up the wall, calling my house and not saying a damn thing!"

Patrice's nerves tensed immediately as letters and numbers on the white page swam dizzily. Roger's news reawakened outrage and fear. Nevertheless, she hid the apprehension under a facade of indifference, for it would do no good to add to Roger's already troubled state. "Maybe an irate former lover?" she speculated.

"No! My lady and I are getting along just fine. At least, we were until the calls started last night," he bit off with disgust. He sat on the edge of her desk. "I think it has something to do with the threats we've been getting at the station," he said.

"Whoa!" she said. "That's like adding one plus one and getting 22. If no one is saying anything, how do you figure the two are related?"

"I don't know," he grumbled, sliding off the desk. "I just do, that's all." While pacing he asked, "What are we going to do about the concert anyway? You've been keeping everything to yourself lately," he added accusingly.

"That's because I can't trust my staff to keep its collective mouth shut," she replied with irritation. "The people from the Free South Africa Movement called, wanting to confirm that we received another threat."

Roger looked at her as if to deny being the culprit, then thought better of saying anything and resumed aimless movement.

Patrice moved to turn on the receiver, piping the station's broadcast into the room. She then pulled a big blue binder from the shelf and returned to her executive chair.

"I'd appreciate it if you'd keep your suspicions to yourself about this," she warned.

"You still haven't answered my question," he said forcefully.

"I have a plan," she said after a while, looking him squarely in the eye. "It's being implemented. You will know my decision in two weeks," she said in a tone that told him he'd received all the information she was going to impart. "Meanwhile, I want you to carry on as though the concert is still on," she said dismissively before rifling through the binder.

"Is there anything else?" she added.

Running nervous fingers through his hair, Roger replied, "No. Except that the KHVY 'Next To Your Heart' nightshirts arrived late yesterday after you'd left."

She looked up and, masking her eagerness to be alone, asked, "How did they turn out? Let me see one."

Roger was more than happy to oblige her request. "Don't go away, I'll be right back," he said with child-like enthusiasm and skipped from the room.

Patrice released her fury by sharply slamming the binder. Just as hastily as she picked up the receiver to call the private investigator, she changed her mind. Taking a chance of calling him from the station. One of her staff might accidentally overhear the conversation. Instead, she would call him later from another phone. She pressed the button on her intercom. Marie answered.

"Yes, boss?"

"Marie, where's Mike this morning?"

"Running late. He called to say that he'd be here in about thirty minutes."

"Ok, as soon as he gets in, send him straight to my office. I want to know who authorized this ridiculous payment schedule on the Smiley Trucking School account." With that said, Patrice pulled a miniature calculator from her drawer, opened the folder and began adding the figures for commercial time on the payment schedule in front of her.

There was one problem after another for the rest of the day, leaving no time for a break, not even for lunch. By five-thirty, Patrice was about to call it a day when she remembered to call Lawrence. She was standing at her door, briefcase in one hand, the other on the knob when Marie entered, nearly bumping into her. "Excuse me, I didn't know you were there."

"Never mind. What's up now?" she asked with exasperation, anticipating more trouble.

"There's a young man here to see you with a package. He says he's from Banneker University, but he won't tell me anything else except, and I quote, 'Mr. Woodson said I was to give this directly to Miss Mason so she'd know it was from him', end quote."

Patrice's tiredness evaporated instantly. Her face lit up, and sparks of jubilance shot through her. "Send him in," she said as excited as a school girl to find out what Lawrence's package contained.

"I thought you'd say that," Marie grinned, then pushed the door open, called out, "Come in, Mr. William Bell, Jr.,"

A tall, powerfully built young man, wearing a Banneker University blue and white cardigan sauntered into the room. He was carrying a small gift box wrapped in a colorful floral paper with a big gold bow capping it.

"Miss Mason," he said to Patrice, extending his hand, "I'm William Bell."

"How do you do, Mr. Bell?" she asked politely as she shook his hand. "You're the young man who was taking pictures at the banquet aren't you?"

"Yes ma'am," he replied, grinning sheepishly. "Mr. Woodson asked me to give this to you," he said, placing the box in her hands.

"Thank you. Can we get you something?" she said, sitting on the couch, her fingers twitching to tear into the box.

"No, thank you, ma'am. I have to get back to campus. Mr. Woodson said I didn't have to stay for a message."

"Oh, but wait," she said, remembering her manners, "let me get you something." She looked frantically around the room. "Oh, Marie where's my purse?"

"Right here, where you left it," replied Marie with a chuckle in her voice as she passed the handbag to Patrice.

"There's no need to do that, Miss Mason. I had to come to Houston anyway, and the station is not far from the firm."

"You work at Mr. Woodson's accounting firm?"

"Yes, ma'am. If I pass the CPA in May, Mr. Woodson promised me a position," he said proudly.

"Mr. Bell," Patrice said in a lecturing tone, "don't think in terms of 'if', only 'when', and I'm sure you'll do just fine."

"Thank you," he said, returning her kind smile. "Well, I better get going if I'm going to make it back before all the dinner is gone," he added, backing out the door.

Marie followed William out, and Patrice zealously resumed her task. She was careful with removing the bow, but the paper was ripped off and tossed carelessly to the floor. Her fingers got stuck on the tape, and she growled with annoyance. Finally, lifting the top off, she pushed away white tissue paper. A delightful gasp escaped her throat as she lifted the six-by-ten size color picture of her and Lawrence encased within a silver frame. A deluge of pleasant memories washed over her as she stared at their images.

Her eyes glistened with tears, and the hand, fondling the glass framed photograph, trembled. She closed her eyes, and hugging the picture close to her breast, remembered the captured moment vividly. The evening had been winding down, tables and chairs were moved to line the walls, allowing room for dancing in the center of the large banquet room. Except for the blue and gold spotlights that infrequently circled the floor where a few couples were dancing, the only lighting had come from the soft candles burning in decorative holders on the tables.

She and Lawrence had stolen away from the hub of conversation to a lone corner to enjoy each other's company. He held her hands across the table, a smile engraved on his face looking deeply into tender brown seas with contentment reigning within his own gaze. No words were required.

God, I have been a fool! Fighting, analyzing, dissecting what she felt for this man when the camera had summarized the emotion in colorful detail. *I am in love with Lawrence Woodson.*

Marie had crept back into the room and placing her hand on Patrice's shoulder asked, "Is everything OK, boss?" Marie looked down at her boss. She was stunned to see the tracks of tears rolling down Patrice's face.

"Oh, yeah," sniffed Patrice, wiping her face with the back of shaky hands. "Everything's fine," she said with a small, self-deprecating laugh.

Patrice sighed deeply and rewrapped the picture back into the tissue before carefully placing it in her case. Then, grabbing her handbag, she calmly announced, "I'm calling it a day." *I want to call Lawrence.*

"But, boss, I wanted to talk to you," said Marie.

"Oh, I'm sorry," replied Patrice. "Can't it wait?"

"I guess, so," Marie demurred. Guessing the reason behind Patrice's eagerness to leave, "Yeah," with an understanding nod of her head.

"Thanks. I promise, first thing in the morning, we'll talk," said Patrice.

The buoyancy that lightened Patrice's steps were deflated when she arrived at the garage to find that all four of the tires on her car had been slashed.

ぬ ぬ ぬ ぬ

There was a twin on either side of Lawrence, looking over his shoulder and peering into a book on the table in the dining room. He was explaining a scientific property, interrupting his discourse periodically to see if they understood.

That's how Patrice found them when she walked into the living room, balancing two large boxes of pizza. She stood motionless, staring across the room at the familial view, amazed at the thrill it gave her to see him like this with her children. She felt tears sting the back of her eyes all over again.

The twins looked up and greeted her, "Hi, Mom," rushing to relieve her of the food after kissing her cheeks.

"Hi, yourself. What are you two rascals up to?" Though the question was posed to the twins, her line of vision locked with Lawrence's gaze.

"Nothing," they replied, dimples pronounced with tongue-in-cheek expressions.

Lawrence rose slowly from his seat, watching her for a sign of objection as he offered a tentative, "Hi."

The elation she felt at seeing him spilled onto her face and softened her features. She took a few steps to meet him and offered a cheek, asking coquettishly, "Don't I get a kiss from you, too?"

Lawrence's pulse quickened at the invitation. He took possession of her hands and squeezed them gently as he briefly brushed his mouth across hers, conscience of their audience. But her soft lips parted under his, and her tongue snaked into his mouth for a kiss that shattered his calm, then left his mouth wanting.

'More', her eyes begged. Matching the action of his emblazoned, lingering gaze, her eyes inventoried what her hands yearned to touch— from the firm jaw, and strong mouth down to a long, muscular torso clad comfortably under a polo sweater, and cuffed, khaki trousers. *I wonder how he looks without anything on?* Patrice wondered.

"We already ate Mom, so we can put these in the freezer," announced Stephen in a piercing voice. Reluctantly, she tore her gaze from Lawrence to look at her daughter.

"We already ate."

"Hamburgers, I imagine," she said, making a distasteful gesture with her nose. "But I guess pizza is not much better."

"No," replied Stephenie, flashing a sleepy-cat grin. "Mr. Woodson made gumbo and rice."

Patrice looked at Lawrence in mischievous disbelief, brows raised high on her forehead and mouth opened wide. "Gumbo?" Head bowed bashfully, Lawrence blushed. It was all she could do to keep from reaching out to pinch him on the cheek. Clearly impressed, she said, "Gumbo as in chicken and sausage, shrimps and crab and okra?"

"Just shrimp, crabs and sausages," he replied modestly. "The other stuff would have taken too long. It wasn't as good as my grandmother's, and you didn't have any bay leaves, but. . . ."

"The gravy was a little on the burnt side," Stephen cut in.

"Roux, not gravy," corrected Lawrence. Defensively, "And there was nothing wrong with it."

"Well, when Mom fixes. . . ." Stephen started in retort.

Patrice put a halt to the Creole-culinary debate, by holding up her hands. "Just tell me this," she said, looking back and forth between Lawrence and Stephen. "Is there anything left?"

Stephenie folded her arms across her chest and cut her eyes at her twin, replying "Maybe you can suck some juice out of the few remaining crab legs Stephen didn't devour."

A look of smug delight came across Lawrence's face.

Stephen captured Patrice and Lawrence in a side-long, sheepish glance. "Well, I didn't say it wasn't good," his face splitting in a wide grin, before joining the symphony of laughter that played around him.

Patrice stepped closer into Lawrence, near enough to smell the remnants of food mingled with his usual ultra-masculine scent. "Are there anymore hidden talents you possess I don't know about?" she inquired, an inventive gleam twinkling in her eyes.

Lawrence beamed, "Infinitely more," he replied in a caressing tone. "And you'll have plenty of time to discover each and every one," dropping a kiss on the tip of her nose. "Plenty of time."

"I guess we can put these in the freezer," announced Stephen.

With a lovely, wide, warming smile trained on Lawrence, Patrice replied, "Yes, I know you're still here." She turned to see the blush and knowing smirks on her children's faces. "How did you con Lawrence over here?"

"Moi?" they chorused innocently.

"Get out of here," she grumbled laughingly, and they frolicked off to the kitchen whispering to each other.

"Your kids are exceptionally bright," said Lawrence, guiding her to the chair next to his, her hand still locked in his possession. "They grasped the conversion problems in a matter of minutes." His tone was full of excitement and happy discovery. "Though I shouldn't be surprised," he added, a lopsided grin plastered on his face as he unconsciously rubbed her hands.

She inspected the pages where the chemistry book was opened, then flipped a few pages. "That's probably because they've already had this assignment," she informed Lawrence with a laugh.

His laughter joined hers as he stated, "Well, I deserve it. I called to talk to you and when I found out you weren't in, I asked if they needed anything."

"To which they replied, food, then help with their homework," she guessed. "I wonder what they would have come up with next if I were any later."

"I'm hesitant to ask," he replied, chuckling, "but I would have been more than happy to oblige," he appended seriously. "By the way, what took you so long? They said you're usually home by seven, it's after eight."

She shook her head, fighting off the dual bouts of anger and frustration she had felt from returning. "You wouldn't believe it."

"Tell me," he implored, recapturing her hands.

The twins returned from the kitchen, each with an apple. Stephen sat on the other side of the table, and took a big, noisy bite from the succulent fruit.

"Later," she promised.

"How 'bout a game of Pictionary?" Stephen suggested, earning a scolding look from his sister and a shrewd one from Patrice. He ignored both females, and stared directly at Lawrence, a beguiling light twinkling in his eyes. Stephenie had hounded Stephen until he caved in and agreed to invite Lawrence over, but he still hadn't formed an impression of the man who gawked at his mother every time he came over. His sister thought it was cute, but he didn't.

Neither Stephenie nor his mother knew what men were like these days, and he didn't want to take any chances on either of them being hurt, especially his mother. Stephenie had laughed at his 'proceed with caution' advice, letting him know that it was not up to him to be the responsible one in the family on this matter.

"Finish your homework?" Patrice inquired casually.

"Yep," replied Stephen, biting another chunk from the apple.

"Are you game?" Patrice asked Lawrence.

"Why not?" he retorted, winking at her slyly.

"Set it up," she instructed.

Rising, Stephen broadcasted to his mother, "Me and you against Stephenie and Mr. Woodson," then looked mischievously at Lawrence. "Stephenie, get the board."

Stephenie propped hands on her hips and opened her mouth to protest. He in turn smiled dulcetly, seemingly quite pleased with himself. Sensing his determination his irate sister threw hands up in the air and marched from the room.

Stephen began clearing the table of tablets and books, declaring, "This is gonna be fun, you'll see," to Patrice and Lawrence.

¿♣ ¿♣ ¿♣ ¿♣

Patrice had wondered how Lawrence felt about the gauntlet her son threw at him, but she didn't have long to find out. He seemed to not only welcome the challenge but relished it, playing a fiercely competitive game.

Lawrence understood and even admired Stephen's protectiveness. He sincerely hoped Patrice appreciated her son's need to test himself, whenever and however the opportunity presented itself. Though he'd never given much thought to fatherhood, the idea of having a son to guide through the rights of passage hit him squarely while watching Stephen competing vigorously to win. He hoped the boy knew how to lose as well, he speculated while he and Stephenie advanced closer to the finish.

The boisterous game was played while consuming the pizzas and soda. After nearly two hours of play, both teams seemed to have gotten stuck on the last square, neither able to correctly guess the word of the picture the other had sketched. Patrice offered a solution that sparked much heated debate from three sides by declaring the game a draw.

"It was a good game," said Stephenie, stifling a yawn behind a hand. She helped Stephen to gather the pieces of the game and store them in the box.

"Yeah, good game," Stephen chimed, a note of surprise in his voice. "Well, g'night," he said, kissing Patrice before turning to leave. "Oh," he said, extending his hand to Lawrence, "thanks for helping us with our homework, Mr. Woodson."

"I was only too happy to help." Lawrence stood to accept Stephen's outstretched hand. "Anytime I can be of assistance, just call."

Patrice sensed a kind of machismo interaction transpiring between her son and Lawrence. In that instant, she finally understood what had been missing from her son's life. It was something she couldn't provide, but was grateful to Lawrence for showing Stephen, even if only temporarily, how a man displays his manhood.

"Goodnight, Mom," Stephenie said, hugging Patrice around the neck.

"G'night, baby," she returned and gently stroked her daughter's face. "I'll be up in a few minutes."

"And don't worry," Stephenie said confidently, "I'll make sure Stephen's not up all night, rambling around."

Stephen grumbled as his sister grabbed him by the arm and pulled him from the room. Patrice and Lawrence listened until the clumsy footsteps and low key grumblings disappeared.

"My kids like you, Mr. Woodson." her relieved tone explained.

"I think your son is still a little unsure of me, but I can appreciate that. I like them too, and don't start with that Mr. Woodson," he bristled good-naturedly while reaching out for her hands. "Now. Tell me what happened."

She pulled her hands back and folded them in her lap. Taking a deep breath, she felt herself being transported back to when she'd first left the office with only one thought on her mind.

A wistful smile slowly warmed her features as she remembered the photo and the candid replica of tender susceptibility it had captured on her face.

"I love it," she said in a low, clear voice filled with wonder.

He read the emotion on her face, but it was off the mark of what he would have preferred to hear.

"I'm glad," he returned, showing nothing of dashed hopes.

"I'm going to fix myself a drink—want one?" she asked suddenly, hopping from her seat.

He followed and arrested her hands on the bottle of liquor. He set the bottle on the portable counter top, then held her by the chin, forcing her to look up at him. Determination rigidly personified his features.

"Somebody slashed my tires," she confessed plainly. "And of course," she added wearily, her voice growing vexed, "none of the security guards saw anything, or noticed anything out of the ordinary." With that said, she broke away from him and strolled into the semidarkness of the living room, partially suffused by the light hanging from the chandelier over the dining room table.

Lawrence swore under his breath and rushed to take the logs she had picked up from the bin on the side of the fireplace. "I'll do this," he said gruffly, pushing restless hands aside. He stacked the store-cut wood in the fireplace and proceeded to prepare a fire before joining her on the couch.

"Any notes today?" he inquired, snaking an arm around her slumped shoulders.

She shook her head in reply while sinking into a cushiony embrace and propping shoeless feet on the coffee table. Each became absorbed in thought over the tire slashing incident—gazes fixed on the growing orange flames.

Only the murderous gleam on Lawrence's face conveyed the violence hovering beneath a placid exterior. *If I catch the coward responsible for disrupting Patrice's life, I will beat him to within an inch of his life. And heaven help the bastard if anything happens to her.*

The logs started to burn with intensity, sparks of blue and gold shooting from the brick encasement. A pecan fragrance began to scent the room.

Patrice desperately racked her brain attempting to make logic where there was none. She repeated the tedious, mind-boggling chore she had undergone on the drive home from work. Over and over, she had asked herself who could possibly hate her as much as the person stalking her every movement. It was a scary feeling, being placed in the vulnerable position in which she was caught.

She shuddered visibly, struck by a spasm of foreboding; Lawrence briefly squeezed her to him and kissed the scented strands of hair tenderly.

"Don't you think it's time to concede?"

He knew the answer before he asked. But histrionics didn't frighten him at all compared to the thought of the danger facing the lovely woman next to him.

She jerked away to meet the expectant, tolerant gaze straight on; firelight heightening the color in her eyes, golden singed and wide with incredulity.

"No!" she said in an adamant but hushed tone. "Not now! I will never cave in to some cowardly little sneak who hides behind little notes he doesn't have the guts to sign his name to."

Patrice moved to get up, but was caught by the steel bands of Lawrence's clamp-like grip. She squirmed and wiggled and her eyes fired bullets of hostility when he effortlessly pinned her to the couch. Like a recalcitrant child, she folded arms across her chest and swung a leg over one knee.

Lawrence was only mildly ashamed of his display of strength, but he wanted her to feel powerlessness in a tangible form, believing she had yet to comprehend the real danger she was facing.

He cut a sidelong glance at her, toying with the idea of telling her about Ross and his involvement. However, in the present black mood, she'd probably toss him out the door. She was a fiercely independent, stubborn woman. His fear had nothing to do with being kicked out; rather, it was the uncertainty of whether she'd let him back in.

Hunched over, he dangled hands between his knees, studying the fluffy carpet. "These little incidents are getting too close to home," he said, twisting slightly to look at her motionless form, her mouth set in a stubborn line. "They've trashed the station, particularly your office. You've been getting weird phone calls. And today, the tires." He enumerated each event on his fingers, his voice growing softer with restrained anger at each recounting. He sat up straight, looking at her with that impatient stare she'd become accustomed to when his disposition bordered on rage.

"How much farther are you going to provoke these people into rasher acts by your refusal to cancel the damn concert?" Patrice averted her gaze from him, and he turned fully, getting closer to her face and forcing her to look at him. "The pattern is set," he added, his voice like an echo from an empty tomb. He left the remainder of the thought to hover menacingly in the air unvoiced.

She felt an uncanny chill run down her spine and rubbed goose bumps on her arms briskly. He'd reached the same conclusion as had Kit— warning that she'd better give additional thought to her obstinacy. She stuck a finger in her mouth in consternation, events and analyses rumbling through her mind like a jumbled ball of uncertainty.

Slapping a hard hand against his thigh, Lawrence pushed himself up to poke at the fire, pondering what he'd have to do to make her understand that she was needlessly endangering her life.

"Damn!" he whispered harshly. She was the most irritatingly obstinate person he'd ever met. But he wanted her in an almost frightening mixture of tenderness and sexual need. He turned to regard her with piercing eyes, poised to speak. He couldn't utter the condemning words on the tip of his tongue—his annoyance couldn't be sustained. Not when her solitary figure looked so small and vulnerable huddled so sadly on the long couch.

Lawrence implored Patrice to look at him with beseeching eyes—soft hazel lights of besotted affection. He knelt on the floor at her feet.

"Patrice. Look at me."

She lifted her head in response to his deep voice, thick and unsteady with an emotion that made her want to both comfort and seek comfort of him. She obeyed his quiet command, placing willing hands in his.

"Look," she said before he could speak, and with a forcefulness in her voice that amazed even herself, "I'm not taking this lightly." She wet her lips before continuing, "I swear I'll reconsider my decision. But not before I'm satisfied that I've hashed it through completely."

Despite the evidence stacked against the prank theory, on some intuitive level she was still not convinced that the threats were anything more than scare tactics designed to frighten her. For what purpose, she couldn't fathom.

"Right now," she said with a deep sigh, "I don't want to discuss it. So please, let's just give it a break," came the plea in a soft voice.

"No way," he responded quickly, standing to tower over her while shocking her with the abruptness. "We're not gonna have that kind of relationship, Patrice," he stated.

Astonishment touched her face, and a warm delirious sensation spiraled from her toes to her head, creating a light headed effect that threatened to overwhelm reason; joy licked closely at its heels. He had taken the decision regarding their future from out of her hands with his declaration—and oddly enough, she wasn't upset. Rather, Patrice was burning with the need to know the full possessiveness implied in his tone and evidenced in the bold stance.

"What kind of relationship aren't we going to have?" she whispered coyly, watching him squirm with delight as he struggled to place the cat back into the bag.

Lawrence looked at her enigmatically when she didn't bolt or balk, then mirth shook his shoulders and flickered briefly in the olive-brown eyes that met hers.

"I'm not going to give in to your whining," he said in a soft, yet firm tone. He sat next to her with their knees touching. "Not on something like this. It's your life, not your career we're talking about," he said, studying her expression. "You may think they're one and the same, but they're not. You can always start over if you have to, but not if you're not around."

Patrice opened her mouth to speak, but the words wouldn't come. She forgot to breathe for her heart pounded an erratic rhythm as he cradled her face between his hands. A delicious shudder heated her body.

"I just found you woman, and I refuse to take any chances on losing you," his voice, dipped in velvet, had dropped to a near whisper.

Lawrence smothered her lips with demanding mastery, siphoning her cry into his mouth. He had been thinking, dreaming of her capitulation for an eternity, it seemed, and ravaged her mouth like a mendicant who had gone days on end without sustenance.

Patrice met his scorching kiss with a hunger that pleased her divinely, binding his hard frame to her. She needed to feel more of the solid strength that was his, needed to know he was as affected as she was. She drank the mellifluence that escaped his throat as her hands began to explore the expansive chest beneath the offensive material.

He reluctantly tore his mouth from hers and put a halt to wandering hands, retreating from the sensuous abyss that was threatening to seal around them. As badly as he wanted her, he doubted that they'd ever finish their talk if he didn't pull away. He cleared his throat before speaking, "You're not going to distract me like this, either."

Patrice let out a delectable laugh, enjoying her ability to excite him. She had once believed, or more accurately, had been led to believe that she did not possess the ability to reciprocate to a loving partner. Lawrence had just punched a hole in this supposition, and she felt doubly invigorated by the newfound self-discovery.

"I want you to carry a gun," he blurted out, though the idea was far from impulsive. "I'll take you out to the range tomorrow and show you how to use it."

His words were like a dash of cold water chilling her warm thoughts. *His timing leaves much to be desired,* she thought, covering her eyes with the balls of her hands. She sighed with exasperation while swinging one leg from over his to cross her own; turning away from him. Rubbing her eyelids with her thumbs, second thoughts about the reasonability of this relationship prevailed. He was more mule-headed than anyone she'd ever met. *With the possible exception of myself,* she admitted with amusement. Her sense of humor took over, and she laughed outright.

"Patrice," he grumbled, spinning her around to demand "what's so damn funny? Do you think having your life threatened is something to laugh about?"

"Oh, Lawrence," she said between fits of laughter. He glared at her as she slowly regained control. "I was just thinking," she said, amusement still in her voice, "you and I will not have some quiet, tepid relationship. We could end up killing each other but at least, we won't bore each other to death."

He made a mocking sound, and a slow smile began to spread across his face until he admitted defeat and joined her in merriment. Lawrence pulled Patrice on his lap and held her tenderly in his embrace.

It is miraculous, he thought, *just how quickly she has become so important to me.* Knowing how he had desperately avoided certain kinds of women made it even more phenomenal; and just having her soft, delicate body pressed against his was enough to set off a series of explosive emotion as well as sexual charges inside him.

Patrice moaned as he buried his head in her neck, the warm air of his breath igniting a yearning inside. She pulled his head upward to touch his lips with her own, placing soft, enticing kisses against his mouth. His response pleased her immensely, and she surrendered to the command of the hot tongue he thrust into her mouth for a kiss that clearly signaled the hunger for her taste.

With one arm draped possessively around her waist, his free hand pulled the feminine tie at her neck. Once the knot fell loose, he unfastened the buttons on her blouse and unsnapped the catch of the lacy bra to reach for one firm breast. His touch was light and painfully exquisite, grazing the nipple of the soft mound with his coarse palm. Blood pulsated through her veins like an awakened river and her skin prickled pleasurably. Sweet, agonizing moans seeped past her throat and into his. She arched against the growing evidence of his arousal and curled caressing fingers around his neck.

She didn't care that her response to his touch was wholly uncharacteristic. Patrice wasn't thinking—no, couldn't think at all.

The twins, the station and the threats faded from reality. She felt protected, cherished and desired. Emotions, like her pulse, were whirling in response to the pleasure nerves he strummed with tantalizing fingers.

Patrice slipped inquisitive hands under his sweater to stroke the fine hairs sprinkled across his magnificent chest, savoring the feel of the fuzzy strands under her hands. His muscles contracted beneath the probing touch.

It was a wondrous sensation—touching her and having her touching him. He had never experienced such an emotional intensity before, never permitted loving emotions and sensations to rule over him.

Awww, but this is more than physical, he thought, a deep, ragged groan slipping past his lips. *I never want to be alone again. Never.*

Gently, Lawrence eased Patrice into a lying position, his patina eyes glazed with desire as he smiled into twin mirrors of yearning. He peeled the blouse from her shoulders to reveal silken brown flesh.

Patrice looked up—her questioning eyes unsure and slightly fearful— she wanted this attractive, sexy man to find her desirable. Her wish came true in his eyes which flickered 'I want you' openly for her to see. She touched his face with feathery fingers, trailing a path from his jaw to lips. Pressing his face against her warm hand, he cradled it to his mouth to plant an open kiss in her palm. He lowered the hand to place it beneath his on one breast; his message clear as he crooned, "So beautiful, so beautiful," and caressed the satiny bosom, before dropping his head to suckle at one dark-tipped, pointed nipple. She gasped and made a litany of his name, "Lawrence. Lawrence." The feel of his hard tongue twirling and licking the fullness of her breast engulfed her in waves of molten, tumultuous passion. His hand slipped through the opening of her slacks, but she froze as reality came crashing down like a giant boulder.

"Oh, Lord," she moaned while her hands fumbled to snap her bra in place. She fiddled unsuccessfully with the buttons and he slapped her hands away to complete the task. "Oh, Lawrence, please forgive me," she begged. "I didn't mean, I mean, I can't . . . the twins," she babbled remorsefully.

He "Shhed" her apology while squeezing her to him. "You have nothing to apologize for," he whispered in her hair. "Shh," he soothed, helping her to sit upright, before kissing her lightly on the forehead. He held Patrice quietly while waiting for his own body to cool.

❧ ❧ ❧ ❧

After leaving Patrice's, Lawrence stopped at the first pay phone he spotted. He parked the car on the side of the all-night convenience store and got out. He inserted a quarter into the slot and waited for the tone. Seven numbers were dialed, then a zero, followed by a three-digit code. He finished the call by punching in the number he was phoning from and hung up.

Within ten minutes, the phone rang, and he snatched up the receiver, answering, "Woodson." With paper and pencil handy, he scribbled a Houston address. "I'll be there within the hour," he said, then replaced the receiver.

Since sleep was out of the question, he might as well relieve R. J.

CHAPTER ❧ NINE

*P*atrice strolled past professionals and students along the trails and curves of Hermann Park; many were simply stealing a moment in the sun. At first glance there was little distinction between Patrice and the other occupants of the park except that she was blissfully happy, and it shone on her face and even in the bouncy walk.

Swinging the makings of a picnic in her hand, she was searching for a nice, secluded area. *Only in Texas,* she thought, *could you enjoy a spring day in the middle of winter.*

She located the perfect spot, a small clearing between two large trees near the foot of the hill edging Miller Outdoor Theatre. She set the basket on the ground and pulled out a colorful patch quilt, which she spread on nature's floor. She kicked off her heels, shrugged out of the jacket of a beige suit-dress and kneeled on the fleecy cover to await Lawrence's arrival.

She didn't have the palate for work today, for planted in her memory was the pleasure of being held against Lawrence's strong, surging body. Her face burned as she remembered her wanton, uninhibited response. Even now, just thinking about him aroused her.

Last night, after Lawrence had left, sleep deluded her. She couldn't remember ever wanting something or someone as much as she'd wanted him. Her self-imposed rule had been really tested for the first time. No man had ever been allowed to stay overnight—her children's presence was her major concern. But her body had hungered so to know possession that she was tempted to abandon the standards she'd set for herself. *Thank God some sane part of my brain realized that I was going too quickly in this relationship.* Unfortunately, Patrice wasn't certain how happy she was about the narrow escape.

This morning when she'd called to invite him to lunch, a yellow light flashed, cautioning her to take it slow. But its impact was fleeting, all but forgotten the moment he came on the line and she heard the baritone timer of his voice. She couldn't get over how easily he had gotten in her blood when she hardly knew anything about him.

There is plenty of time to rectify that, she told herself with a chuckle at the back of her throat. She pulled a blade of grass from the earth and studied the color with squinting eyes.

It is certainly no comparison to the olive hue of Lawrence's eyes, she thought. Patrice wondered from which parent he had inherited the unusual shade as she threw the blade to the ground.

Seconds later, Patrice spotted his car pulling into the parking lot across the street near the Burke Baker Planetarium . She had to fight an overwhelming desire to run and greet him. Patrice cultivated a calm demeanor, but when Lawrence got out of his car and started towards her, she stood and waved eagerly.

He saw her immediately, and even from this distance, his eyes seemed to sparkle with that familiar glow that made her insides tingle. As he neared, she closed the distance with hands outstretched. His touch sent her spirits soaring even higher, and his kiss—an open mouth moving urgently over hers—made blood rush through her veins.

"Hi," he said, his voice a velvet murmur just inches from her lips.

"Hi," she whispered, her mouth spread in superb contentment.

They stood immobile, staring at each other with mellow gazes, as if reassuring themselves the other was real and just as they remembered. He tightened his hold on her hand before allowing her to lead him to their private place in the park. They dropped slowly to the blanket, her hand still in his, each unwilling to breach contact for even a second.

Lawrence had been surprised, though pleasantly so, by her call. His secretary had explicit instructions that if Patrice Mason called, he was to be notified immediately. He'd been in a meeting with the financial committee of the board when his secretary was put to the test. The woman had looked as though she was walking to her death when she'd tiptoed into the board room. "It's Miss Mason, sir," she had whispered tenuously.

His first thought had been that Patrice received another threatening letter. He excused himself abruptly, leaving the board members staring enigmatically after him.

"I'm glad you could make it."

"Wouldn't have missed the opportunity for the world."

Patrice closed her eyes, reveling in the light sensuous touch of his hand stroking her face.

"What would happen if I do this?" Lawrence asked playfully, his hands poised on the ivory shell combs that were holding her hair in place.

He removed them and combed the thick braid out with his fingers, allowing shiny black hair to cascade around her shoulders. He stroked the luscious locks, then sat back to observe what he'd done, a satisfied look set on his face. "I've been wanting to do that for a long time."

"What else have you been wanting to do?" she asked in a breathy whisper.

Lawrence slid a hand up her bare arm, drawing her closer, and kissing her cheeks, one at a time. "The rest," he murmured next to her ear, "I'll have to show you at another time."

If she hadn't been sitting, Patrice just knew she would have fallen. Their closeness was like a drug lulling her. She leaned closer to taste the smile on his mouth with her tongue, stopping to place a kiss at each corner.

Lawrence inhaled deeply, trying to curb the explosive currents racing through him. "Behave," he ordered on an uneven breath.

"Spoilsport," she pouted, then sat back primly and folded restless hands in her lap.

He growled playfully, nuzzling her neck with warm breath and gently wrestling her to the blanket. She laughed, a sonorous sound of blithe that lingered in the air. Reclining over Patrice with one arm under her shoulders, Lawrence stared down into her laughing face with gentle eyes. He should have known he wouldn't have been able extricate this woman from his life—she was entirely too potent and had become vital to him. He didn't know how much longer he could hold out from the emotions she inspired.

Patrice felt as though Lawrence could see right into the core of her heart, and knew of her love. Experiencing a sudden fear, panic surged through her body. What if he didn't want her? She wouldn't know what to do with herself. It wouldn't be easy to pick up the pieces like before—Donald had disillusioned her once; she just couldn't face another go round.

Lawrence interrupted the deep thoughts with, "Hey, come back here."

"Hi, again," she whispered sweetly, reaching her hands up to run over his short hair. Patrice pulled his face down to dart her tongue past willing lips for a kiss that sent shock waves of desire charging through him.

When they pulled apart, she felt his breath tremble in his chest.

"If you don't stop that," he grinned, "I won't be responsible."

"Ok. I'll be a good girl from here on out."

"Fat chance," he retorted, and her gentle laugh joined a deep chuckle.

"Where did you get those eyes from?" she asked with child-like curiosity. "It dawned on me that I know next to nothing about you."

Lawrence stilled; his smile faded into a grimace. Patrice didn't know what to make of the abrupt change. She became frightened, for the mental distance between them was more frightening than any physical separation.

"Lawrence?" He sat up, and she did the same. "We don't have to talk about it if you don't want to," she said hurriedly, her hands nervously fanning the air. "I hope you're hungry," turning to open the basket. "I bought some of everything. I didn't know your taste in deli."

She knew she was babbling, but felt in a quandary of what else to do. Confusion and regret glittered in her eyes, as she silently chided herself for spoiling what was promising to be a wonderful afternoon.

He stilled her hands. "I'm sorry," he mumbled, his mind racing backwards in time. Folding his legs in front of him and wrapping arms around his knees, he stared unseeingly across the park.

"My mother," he said quietly by way of answering. Damn! *I thought I'd rid himself of her ghost.* She hadn't bothered him in a long time, hadn't risen taunt him with his imperfection. Until Patrice.

My imperfection, he thought bitterly. He almost laughed out loud, for it would have been funny if it still wasn't a festering wound. He felt Patrice's comforting, sympathetic hand on his shoulder and knew she had reached the wrong conclusion.

Charles knew bits and pieces of the story. Not even his father's parents who had raised him since his ninth year had been told; though, he suspected they formed a pretty good picture of Robert and Mayrita Woodson's marriage.

His parents had been dead thirty years. Long enough for him to have forgiven and buried the guilt and hurt that scarred him.

"Before I even met you, I thought you were like her," he said, recalling the glowing reports he'd gotten from people who knew Patrice publicly. But he had still been weary because of the realization that a person in the public's eye was not necessarily the same in private.

Something in his tone signaled Patrice that she had not been complimented by the remark, and she stiffened. Lawrence felt her hand lifting from his shoulder and trapped it in place, his hand on top of hers.

"The kind of woman I never wanted to get involved with because you needed, no, wanted things"— he stressed— "no man could provide."

Though the words were voiced aloud, it was as if he were talking to himself. Conjuring the image of a lovely, honey-toned woman with long straight hair and bewitching green eyes, he added, "A woman like that could kill a man."

Patrice didn't know what to say, even if a response was expected of her, which it wasn't. Lawrence had retreated deep into his past, a painful place that was filled with ghosts as evidenced by the dark, brooding expression.

"She was a beautiful woman," he admitted in a grudging tone.

And he, like his father, had loved her to distraction—accepting her faults and eager for the crumbs of her affection. Only, from the very beginning, Lawrence seemed unable to be on the receiving end of any emotion other than disgust or tolerance from her or her parents. Whispers complaining of the darkness of 'the young boy's' skin had haunted his every entrance into a room.

"I used to love going places with her. People were enamored by her looks and friendliness. And like any kid, I was so proud of her. But that wasn't my main reason for wanting to be in her company. I knew how she was at home. And the person the public saw wasn't the woman who did her duty by me. You see, when we were in the public's eye, well, that was the only time she showed me that I was more than a nuisance to her."

Patrice cried out before clamping her hands over her mouth, but Lawrence seemed to have forgotten her presence.

The older he'd become, the more he began to wish for another mother. His father certainly could have used another wife for all the nagging his mother had provided.

"I still can't figure out why they married. They didn't seem to like or want the same things. She wanted to go out all the time, and my dad was content to sit home and read a book or something."

It couldn't have been money; his father didn't have any to speak of and wasn't likely to come into a great sum as a high school math teacher. That, he remembered vividly, had been the source of a great many arguments between his parents near the end of their marriage—his father never had the money to purchase the things she craved.

He snorted disdainfully and grabbed a handful of grass, then squashed the sprigs in one angry hand.

"I can't give you anything that you couldn't give yourself," he said as a warning. Impatiently, Lawrence brushed his hands clean of the blade of grass he'd stripped apart.

Patrice's voice cracked when attempting to speak. She wanted to tell him what he had given her already had nothing to do with material things, but he hushed her by placing one finger against her mouth. He smiled a self-deprecating smile and dropped his hands between firm legs, embarrassed for having voiced the private insecurity.

Financially, he could provide for a woman in a manner that his father had been unable to sustain. *Maybe that's why I have worked so fiendishly to become a success*, he thought retrospectively. The thought of paying a woman to love him—which amounted to the same as giving her everything she desired, in his opinion—made him sick to his stomach. *I'll be loved for who and what I am, not for what I can provide, or I will not love at all. Love has to be earned, enjoyed, nurtured, and savored.*

Lawrence shook his head to remove the cobwebs of the past and turned to Patrice, "My old man tried to purchase the love of the woman who birthed me, and it only brought him pain when he failed. It killed him," he said, rising to circle the park with his gaze, hands buried in his pockets. "She killed him."

At Patrice's gasp, he looked down at her, adding hastily, "Oh, he pulled the trigger, but she drove him to that point. Always wanting more. More, more, more." His voice grew harsh as his ears echoed with the memory of his mother's voice, monotonous with demands for what she considered a better life.

"If you weren't so gung-ho about being a father, we could have a decent life. Children could have waited until later. Now, every time we get a few dollars, we have to spend it on your son!"

His father never uttered a word in reply. He would just sit at his beat up desk in the living room, listening to his wife rant and rave.

"But he loved her so much," Lawrence said after a while, "that he took a night job as a janitor to try and give her some of the things she wanted. It was still never enough."

He sighed deeply and paused a long time before speaking again. "So she found a man who could give her everything her heart desired," he said in a voice so soft that Patrice had to strain to hear. "But she didn't realize," he added, kneeling on the blanket, "until it was too late that nothing in life is free."

His mouth took on an unpleasant twist as he recalled the pitiful creature his mother had become, hooked on drugs and forced to prostitute herself to support a habit

"She died from an overdose," he said plaintively, keeping a tight control over the nightmarish feelings, his expression devoid of emotions. "My dad blamed himself. And so did her parents. So, feeling like the failure everybody said he was, he decided on a way out."

Patrice's insides shriveled a little more with each revelation he had voiced. The vile dislike she had for his mother boomeranged, striking back at her with a repugnance for her own behavior. She had been dogmatic in her pursuit of having the concert, heedless of the danger to others. In her thinking, that made her no better than the woman she silently professed to hate. Tears streamed down her face and the cry she'd been holding stole into the quiet that surrounded them. Lawrence faced her quickly and enfolded her in comforting arms.

"Hush," he said into her hair. "It was a long time ago. And I'm not so sure why I told you, except, I guess it was time that I finally said it out loud and got it out of my system."

"I can see why you would think I was like her," she cried softly into his chest, soaking his shirt with tears.

"That's nonsense!" he said, pulling her back to look into her face. "You're nothing like her. You hear me?" he said, shaking her roughly by the shoulders, "Nothing!" He pulled her almost violently to him and held her. "I admit I was prepared to dislike you, didn't want to like you and tried very hard to keep my distance," he said gruffly.

She squirmed under his brutal honesty and tried to break free, but his hold of her, gentle and possessive, wouldn't allow escape. "And now?" she asked softly, forcing herself to meet his probing gaze.

'Now, I can't seem to help myself,' he admitted silently. "You're not like her," Lawrence replied. "You wouldn't know how to be selfish. Anyway, you're too much of a fighter to demand of others what you wouldn't do yourself." He held her at arms' length to look down into sad, teary eyes, a half smile gentling his lips. "I should know, I've tried everything I could think of to frighten you out of holding that concert."

She tried to laugh with him. Instead, she choked on the tears that continued to roll silently down her face. The hate she harbored for Mayrita turned to pity for the deceased woman. Patrice cupped his face between her hands, thinking she wouldn't make the same mistake as the late Mrs. Woodson.

Lawrence closed his eyes, savoring the moist kisses she placed on his mouth before her tongue slid pass his lips for a slow, drugging kiss that set his insides on fire. He crushed her to him and took command, ravaging her mouth, his tongue alternately coaxing and demanding until she returned his kiss with equal abandon.

When Patrice ran her hands over his chest and felt the cotton shirt instead of his flesh under her touch, she was jolted back into reality. She moaned his name against his lips, and he too, remembered where they were. Their lips parted reluctantly, and tenderly.

"I'm starving," he declared boisterously when he resumed control of his breathing. "What's for lunch?"

"Everything," she replied jubilantly, recapturing her initial excitement for their picnic tryst. They dug into the basket eagerly, pulling out containers of dips, platters of meats, cheeses and crackers. Lawrence held up two bottles of wine, red and white.

"They didn't have scotch," she replied to the questioning brow he raised.

They laughed and talked about any and everything inconsequential as they ate and drank their way through the entire lunch feast. Neither could remember when they'd last had so much fun without feeling guilty for leaving a desk full of work undone.

Lawrence and Patrice were lying on their backs, replete, and looking up into the sunny, cloudless sky, when he asked, "What happened to your marriage?"

"Turn about is fair play, huh?"

"If you don't want to talk about it, that's OK," he said nonchalantly.

"OK," she replied, turning over to lie on her stomach and rest a chin on her hands. With no warning, she felt his hands tickling her unmercifully. "No fair. Foul," she cried, squirming and wiggling while attempting to stifle her giggles. "All right, all right, I give," she cried through the laughter she couldn't contain.

He released her, and she sat up facing him, a pout lining her mouth. He smiled impishly and stared expectantly.

She hadn't spoken of her marriage to Don with anyone except Kit. And even then, she had censored most of what was said. It had been too humiliating, and she hadn't wanted anyone to know of the abuse she'd suffered at the hands of her mean, unfaithful ex-husband.

"It was a mistake," she said casually. "I thought he loved me as much as I thought I loved him. I was wrong."

Lawrence was not fooled by the matter-of-fact tone of the delivery, noticing the tiny hint of anguish in the corner of her eyes. "Is he in contact with the twins?"

She made a sardonic sound in her throat before replying, "He left when they were about three months old. The marriage was over long before they were born."

"What was it about him that attracted you?"

"Can we drop it?" she asked with exasperation. She thought about Donald more in the past several days than she had in the fourteen years they were separated.

"If it's too painful, yes," he replied quietly.

"Painful?" she said, wrinkling her nose and shrugging her shoulders. "No," she finally quipped. "It's not painful, not anymore. Embarrassing, yes."

"Aren't you being rather hard on yourself? You were only, what, nineteen, twenty at the time."

"I was nineteen and thought I could have it all," she said mockingly. "I've long since realized I fell for a mirage. I was so determined to have the love I felt would make my life complete that I didn't pay attention to the fine details."

The evidence had been there; she had been foolish, thrilled because she had gotten the man most women wanted. Disc jockeys as popular as Don always had a group of adoring women hanging around them. He flirted with them, but she had thought it was just part of his deejay persona and allowed it to go unchallenged. That, and a whole lot more, had remained unquestioned for far too long.

"Is he in town?"

"Not likely," she said, playing with the buttons on her jacket. "I used to hear about him from time to time, mostly in the trade journals. It's the nature of the business for music announcers to move around, hopping from one station to another. And in his case, it's doubly true because he can't or refuses to stay at one place for any length of time."

"Haven't you tried to find him?"

"Why?" she asked almost indignantly. "Why are you asking questions about him anyway?"

"He is the father of your children," Lawrence replied in a tone suggesting his curiosity was natural.

"Lawrence," she sighed heavily, "they've never seen him and don't know what he looks like."

Lawrence reached out to capture her hands and held them until she faced him. He examined her with tender, empathetic eyes, as if seeing her unspoken agony.

"He hurt you pretty bad, didn't he?" he said solemnly, wishing he could erase the hurt.

"Yes," she replied succinctly, then took a long, cleansing breath. "But that was a long time ago. I have no feelings for him, good or bad. We just made a mistake."

"Has it soured you on marriage?"

"Are you proposing?" she teased, a mischievous grin playing at the corners of her mouth.

He didn't know where the thought came from, or even when it had popped into his subconscious—it now just seemed like a natural progression.

"Just storing information for future reference," he replied, smiling at her warmly.

Uncertainty lined her forehead, concerned more about her own feelings than his question on the matter. She hadn't thought about having someone to share her life with in terms of marriage. It made her wonder what had she been silently wishing for, if not a long term commitment. Now that the subject had been raised, she didn't know if she were ready to take such a risk. She'd failed once. What guarantees did she have that she wouldn't again?

"Stop thinking so hard." He interrupted her thoughts, tugging at her hands. He pulled her to him and touched her mouth with his before thrusting his tongue between her parted lips for a kiss that was more assuring than passionate.

"You'll know," he whispered cryptically against her mouth.

CHAPTER ✿ TEN

*P*atrice had known Lawrence for a total of thirteen days, and with each passing day, her love deepened and intensified. If seeing him was impossible, she felt bereaved when she didn't get a chance to just speak with him. This turned out to be the case over the next several long and hectic days. Though uneventful as far as the threats were concerned, her job sent her flying in several different directions—including Chicago for a meeting with the corporate bigwigs. What was to be a one-day affair turned into two because the weather put a halt to all forms of travel.

Attired in a white silk gown, Patrice was sitting on the bed in her hotel suite dialing a long distance number. She'd done something this evening that she wouldn't have even dreamed of doing just two weeks ago: she begged out of dinner with the other general managers, all male, protesting that the hard day had zapped her of all of her energy.

Her motivation?

A clamant desire to hear the voice of the virescent eyed man who had managed to rob her of rational thought and behavior.

Lawrence answered on the second ring, and his "Hello," caused a satisfying sense of relief to flow through her.

"Lawrence. It's me," she said, the joyful smile on her face transmitted into her voice.

After a brief silence, they fell into easy conversation. And they talked—about her meeting, the university's fund-raising campaign, the twins, his days in college and her years in radio—long into the night. Though ending their conversation was the last thing on her mind, Patrice's body clock signaled fatigue, and she yawned.

"Is that a cue that you want me to let you go?" he asked with humor in his voice.

"No", she replied, wishing she had the nerve to tell him she never wanted him to let her go. It's still *too soon*, she cautioned herself. The closest she could come to admitting her feelings was, "I wish you were here with me."

She heard him draw a deep breath; hers stilled.

He then cleared his throat, asking, "What would I be doing if I were there with you?" in a tone that barely restrained his need.

The provocative query elicited sinful yearning from her body. She replied with gentle, girlish laughter, "All sorts of things."

"Like what, for instance?" he probed.

"Well," she stalled, passing her hand across the bedspread, closed her eyes to imagine his majestical body filling the empty spot next to her, "first, you could rub my feet."

"Sounds kinky, but I like it. Go on."

"Oh, I kinda figured you'd just work your way up," she said shyly.

"Why, Ms. Mason, is that a blush I hear?"

She denied, "No," but her giggles gave her away. "Don't tease."

"I'm not teasing, woman," he growled. "You can make bet on that. What would I do next?"

"My legs," she replied suggestively.

"Such nice legs, too. Pretty and long," he drawled out before declaring, "They'd wrap around me nicely, don't you think? And you know what would be next?"

"No," she breathed throatily, "what?"

"First, I need to know something."

"What?"

"How are you dressed?"

"Lawrence!" she said in a mild tone of reproach.

"I dare you to tell me you weren't thinking the same thing." When she didn't respond, he demanded as though her answer were of upmost importance, "Tell me."

"Yes," she whispered.

"Yes, what?"

"I have nothing on except a robe."

"I'll settle for that. I like the idea of undressing you myself. When are you coming home?" he demanded brusquely.

She understood his impatience. The sensuous innuendo they exchanged was causing an unbearable ache to thrive in the center of her.

"Hopefully, the weather will clear and I'll catch the first flight out in the morning."

"I'll pick you up."

"No," she countered regretfully, practicality rearing its ugly head. She now wished her plane was flying into Intercontinental Airport, which was nearer to Lawrence as opposed to Hobby in southeast Houston. "I'm coming into Hobby. That's too far for you to drive," she explained, knowing he would have to get up very early to make the long drive.

"Ain't no place on earth that far where you're concerned. What flight are you coming in on?"

She heard him scrambling around for paper before she rattled off the flight number and time of arrival.

"I'll be there."

It wasn't the last thing he said before they rang off, but those three promising words echoed in her head the remainder of the night, resting even in her dreams.

ਤਕ ਤਕ ਤਕ ਤਕ

Luck was on Patrice's side the following morning. The weather changed, and she was able to leave Chicago, but her arrival into Houston was delayed. Lawrence was waiting patiently at the end of the gate.

He spotted her first. When she looked his way, joy bubbled inside her and shone in her eyes. She hurried as fast as her briefcase and shoulder carryall would allow, her heart beating ten times as fast as she could move.

"Hi," she said in low, silvery voice, eyeing him up and down covetously.

"Hi, yourself," he said, pulling her into his arms and kissing her hard on the mouth. When he released her, she stared at him in shock, though immensely pleased by his public display of affection.

"Let's get out of here before they have me arrested for just thinking what I'd like to do to you," he said, relieving her of possessions.

Her giggle developed into full-blown laughter as she linked an arm with his, and they hurried from the terminal.

Lawrence drove crosstown to an elegant western restaurant in the Galleria area whose best features, aside from the southwestern fare served, were the understated lighting and privacy it offered to diners. When they arrived, Patrice excused herself in order to freshen up and make a few calls.

While in the ladies room she made three calls: one to the twins, one to Kit to announce the end or her traveling ordeal, and one to the office. She look at the phone in dread before she made that final call.

"Peggy, this is Patrice, put me through to Marie," she said into the mouthpiece, as she applied a fresh coat of lipstick to dry lips. "Marie, I'm back. What's going on?"

Minutes later, Patrice was weaving, past high-powered execs having late lunches on her way to the table Lawrence had reserved. When he saw her approach, he rose from a corner table which was draped with a white lace tablecloth.

He is *handsome, she thought. Yet* a waning smile shadowed her face, for she wouldn't be able to stay and enjoy the lunch he'd ordered.

"Is something wrong?" he asked, noticing the bittersweet expression.

"I need to get to the station," she replied with a restive sigh.

"What happened?"

She noticed the tensing of his body and read his thoughts. "No, I haven't gotten any of those harassing notes. It's just that some unexpected things have cropped up."

"Anything urgent?"

"Not really, but . . ."

"Then, they'll keep."

His cavalier attitude raised her feministic hackles, and she responded with indignation. "No, Lawrence." Every curve of her body bade resistance. "Look, I know you don't think what I do is important, but *I do*, and so do my kids. I have a business to run, and I shouldn't have to explain to you what that means."

Refusing to be swayed by the tortured dullness of disbelief in his eyes, she insisted, "I want to go." Startled by her own unusually loud voice, she peered around the room with embarrassment to see if any of the other diners were observing their heated exchange.

"You need to eat," he affirmed in a quiet tone. "Whatever the trouble,

I promise you," the smile he trained on her didn't quite reach his eyes, "will be there when you arrive. Now, sit down, our lunch will be here in a moment."

"Are you going to take me to the station or do I have to call a cab?" she demanded testily, her hands on hips.

Very gradually, his mouth took on an unpleasant twist and the olive eyes narrowed and hardened. He passed a composed hand across his face, releasing the deep breath he'd inhaled. Without uttering one word, he calmly circled the table to hold out a chair.

She opened her mouth to protest further, but his adversarial demeanor changed her mind. In a huff, she dropped into the chair and folded arms across her bosom. He returned to his seat and ignored her, taking a leisure sip of red wine in a long-stemmed glass. A Willie Nelson ballad began to play, filling the stiff silence with melancholy.

She was silently cursing the domineering, arrogant, over-bearing, good-looking man sitting across the table from her, paying her no mind at all. Irked by his cool, aloof manner, she tried to duplicate his demeanor. Instead, she grew irritated and unhappy with herself.

"Are we having an argument?" she asked finally, unable to stand the damnable quiet at their table.

"No, we're having an aperitif while we wait for our meal," he replied formally, taking another swallow.

She too drank from the glass in front of her, and as she sipped, guilt welded with confusion. *Why did I choose this moment to make a scene?* she wondered, critically scanning the restaurant. She noted for the first time the subtle romantic atmosphere contained in the western motif.

It was a bout of panic, pure and simple, she told herself while chewing nervously on her lip. The deep feelings she had for the man seating before her was growing so rapidly and in such proportions that she was losing control. *Whether it were true or not,* she mused, *it certainly feels as though I am taking leave of my senses.*

"I'm sorry," Patrice said softly. "I know that doesn't excuse my behavior, particularly since you've gone to so much trouble." Shrugging her shoulders, "I don't know what's wrong with me," her voice was barely audible as she continued "But I, uh, I," she babbled, looking at him for help and receiving it as he reached across the table to still a gesturing hand.

"It's OK."

Tenderly, he planted a titillating kiss in the center of her hand, causing a delicious shudder to course up her wrist.

"Excuse me," said the waiter who'd crept to the table holding a large silver tray laden with food. He waited with the practiced patience of one accustomed to the trysts of the restaurant's clientele. Patrice and Lawrence reluctantly severed their physical as well as emotional contact. He arranged steaming hot dishes of mesquite grilled chicken on the table, then excused himself after inquiring if they needed anything else.

"How did you find this place?" she asked, forking a bite-size chunk of the seasoned chicken.

"I found it out of sheer desperation—I didn't want to eat J. T.'s cooking." At Patrice's puzzled expression, "You know, she may be a dynamo with students in the classroom, but in the kitchen she's a disaster," he said, a trace of laughter in his voice.

"Do you come here often?" she asked before sampling one of the peppers on her plate. Discovering the tiny, harmless looking pepper was incredibly hot, she groped for the glass of water she'd earlier shoved to the side.

Lawrence didn't even try to contain himself and threw his head back, roaring with laughter.

"Why didn't you warn me?" she said accusingly, taking another large swallow of water.

"Sometimes, you just got to let a person find out things for herself," he said with a knowing look.

ॐ ॐ ॐ ॐ

With his coat and tie removed, and shirt sleeves rolled up muscular arms, Lawrence sat slouched in one of the high-backed chairs in his office. Loosely clasped in a left hand was a black and white, glossy photo of Ellen Conway, the sales secretary of KHVY.

Rubbing his shoulder with one free hand, he rolled his head around at the neck, causing the stiff muscles to pop. He had been going through the individual reports, complete with photos that R. J. had sent by courier. That was shortly after he'd dealt with a problem at the university, which prevented him from fulfilling his intentions regarding Patrice.

Lawrence dropped a hand to his knee, thinking about the plans he had made to hold her hostage for the rest of the day. He was going to take her to his apartment—to get some much needed rest, of course, and later, they would be joined by the twins for dinner. He had already arranged for Kit to pick up the twins from school and drop them off at his place.

He sighed wistfully over the best laid plans gone to pot, and reverted his attention back to the photo in his hand. This was the ninth profile. It was becoming more and more difficult to concentrate with each piece of information studied. He found himself guessing at Patrice's relationship with each employee, looking for the smallest thing that could possibly set someone against her.

Let this be a warning, he told himself, reminded of the sage advice given doctors about operating on close members of their families. He felt certain that he was overlooking something—emotions were blinding him to clues he might have detected if Patrice had not meant anything to him.

It was far too late to question or bemoan his feelings. Acceptance had already been fully rooted.

He closed his eyes, then opened them slowly to stare unseeingly across the room, pass the open blinds at the darkness outside. *Patrice.* The photo slipped through relaxing fingers, and he was snapped back to reality. Reaching down, Lawrence snatched it up and resumed the tedious task of studying what had been so far insignificant information. Nevertheless, he appreciated R.J.'s style—detailed, but succinct. The third sentence caught his eye, and he poured over the brief with a more than mild interest: Mrs. Conway had been separated from her husband for over a year, he read, then shrugged, thinking there was nothing criminal about that. However, what was interesting was her financial status. She was trying to raise four boys, all under ten years of age, on the thousand dollar a month salary she earned from the station. According to R. J., the woman had creditors lined up at her two-bedroom apartment door. There was more, but Lawrence had read enough. He tossed the report to the coffee table. It landed next to a brown envelope, bulging with similar reports.

He rubbed his chin thoughtfully, mulling over the possibilities—motive, opportunity, means. Opportunity was easy; she had unquestionable access to the station. Whether she had the means was debatable. *Unless,* he thought suddenly, his hand frozen on the back of his neck, *someone else was in on the deal. But this doesn't make sense,* he argued.

He brought a disgusted hand down on the arm of the chair and sprang from the seat to pace the room.

There had been no demand for money, only the cancellation of the concert. Ellen Conway needed money; she couldn't afford to be an altruist. And passing a tired hand across the top of his head, Lawrence concluded that her name could be scratched from the list of suspects.

He consulted the timepiece on his wrist and whistled. It was after seven. He hadn't talked to Patrice in three hours and thirty-one minutes, he calculated, as one corner of an engaging mouth pulled into a lopsided smile. She had called to let him know they were invited to dinner at the Black's; the four of them were expected in twenty minutes.

He strode back to the coffee table and shoved the photo in the package with the other reports. Heading for his desk, he sealed the envelope before concealing it between the files in one of the bottom drawers. But as he was rolling down his sleeves, the phone rang. "Hello? Yes, I know I'm running late, J.T.," he chuckled indulgently. "Yes, J.T., I'm leaving right now. We'll be on time."

A smile eased across his face as he replaced the receiver. There was but one thing on his mind now; how he'd spent the past couple of hours.

Grabbing his coat from the back of the chair, Lawrence hurried from his office, humming the melody of an old fashioned love song.

ža ža ža ža

Lawrence strolled from the living room into the foyer of Patrice's home. She was sitting with arms folded under her head at her desk. He bent over to kiss the back of her neck, and his arms spread like wings to envelope her. He heard the smile in her sigh before she stood and turned into the welcoming circle of the embrace.

"I'm not going to stay, you're dead on your feet," he said, rocking them from side-to-side, his chin resting on the top of her head.

"No monsters lurking about?" she asked, her words muffled against the cashmere pullover.

They had just returned from the Black's home, and Lawrence insisted on checking the house before leaving. Too tired to argue, Patrice had agreed. The twins had marched straight off to bed the moment they walked into the house.

"No, everything's fine, though I want to see about getting another lock for that kitchen door."

"Yes, sir."

"Don't be smart," he said, holding her face by the chin to drop a kiss on her lips.

She smothered a yawn with a right hand and returned to nestle against him, replying, "I'm too exhausted."

"I know." His hand slid gently up and down her arms before hugging her tightly. "Why don't you stay home tomorrow and get some rest?"

It felt so good, the way his fingers stroked the small of her back over the raspberry chiffon top she wore. She could have almost fallen asleep on her feet—almost. Her body was quite conscience of the hard strength pressed against her, his manly scent filling hungry senses. She sighed mellowly, enjoying his presence.

"I wish I could."

"Why can't you? I'll pick you up for a late breakfast, and after that, we'll do whatever you want." His honeyed voice lowered to a beguiling register, causing a sweet sensation to build within her. "Hmm," she murmured dreamily. "It's tempting, but I have a million things to do," she added lazily.

"Such as?" The alluring tone was replaced with a challenge.

Returning a sharp eyed stare, she put a little distance between them, palms flat against his chest. "You'll be happy to know I've decided to cancel the concert," she said in a mildly accusing tone.

He wasn't surprised by the announcement because R. J. had informed him of her decision, but it hurt that she was so annoyed with him.

Patrice could have kicked herself for turning him into the guilty party. "I'm sorry, I didn't mean that the way it sounded," she added contritely. She was really dissatisfied with herself; this was one time she had made a decision that went against conscience.

"No, I'm not happy about it," he said.

"No?" she said, backing out of his grasp. "I thought that's what you wanted. We've certainly had enough arguments about it."

His gaze followed her as she spun pass him to drop on the bottom step of the stairs, the shadows of the incandescent light falling harshly over the frustrated features.

"Yes," he retorted, exasperation in his tone.

Lawrence knelt in front of her, his hands slid possessively down her arms and tightening around a wrist. "I encouraged you to cancel for the reason I gave you. I don't want to see anybody getting hurt. And that includes you, too." His eyes held her dearly before speaking again. "Plus,

I know you well enough to know that if anything happened, you would never forgive yourself."

Though issued ages ago, the disparaging remarks he made about her character had stayed in her mind. He couldn't have known what his acknowledgement to the contrary meant to her—a delicious balm filled her senses. It took a while before she could find her voice and simply stared at him.

"Thank you for that," she said softly, stroking the side of his face.

He nearly groaned aloud; her engaging touch and almond eyes brimmed with quiet passion. He closed his eyes, and holding a hand to the side of his face, imagined the rest of her softness cuddled next to him. Before Patrice knew what happened, he was at her side, crushing her to him.

"Oh, God, Patrice, if I had my way, you could have anything— everything." he confessed. He wrapped her hair around one hand and gently pulled to look into her face. "Don't you know that, woman?" he added in a lower, huskier tone.

"No, I didn't," she replied in a weak and tremulous whisper.

"Now you do."

This time he did groan and claimed a quick, hard squeeze from her. He wanted her so badly that he hurt, but he didn't dare do more than hold her, or he wouldn't be able to stop.

"Give me my goodnight kiss so I can get out of here and let you get some sleep," he said gruffly, loosening the tight hold.

Patrice tightened her arms around his waist, head resting against his heart. Its erratic beat matched her own. "I don't want you to go," she groaned, wanting only to savor the closeness they shared a little longer— forever.

"Then marry me and solve this social dilemma."

"Don't tease," she whispered, eyes wide and alert as they scanned his face.

"I'm not teasing," he replied smoothly, staring directly into her astounded countenance, brows drawn in serious intent.

"Not because of the twins." she said adamantly. "I won't use them as an excuse."

"Then for what excuse will you marry me?"

Their gazes locked, each searching, reading the signals aflame in the other's eyes.

The many nights and days spent in cumbersome thought over whether she had the courage to follow through with this relationship raced through Patrice's mind. If the inexhaustible feelings she had for him weren't those of a woman in love, then she was at a profound lost to describe her emotions; but that was no longer an issue as she gazed at him. There were no shadows across her heart now, only sunshine. The very air around them crackled with anticipation. Lawrence felt as though he were standing at the door of some wonderful discovery—merely waiting for it to open. The waiting was almost unbearable.

"No excuse, my darling. Only one reason."

Patrice stressed each word distinctly, confidently, her eyes shining brightly in the shadowy spot where they sat.

"Which is?"

"That I love you."

Though he saw the answer written on her face, felt it in her touch, he was shocked at how desperately he needed to hear the words repeated. And remained stock still, waiting.

"Do you?"

She understood the origin of the soft query and caressed his expressionless visage with a tender hand.

"I love you."

She said the words plainly, without hesitation, canonizing the declaration in her own heart and mind. Visceral sensations—the likes of which Lawrence had never known—exploded inside him, dispersing fireballs of euphoria. Words lacked their usual eloquence, and governed by fully charged emotions, Lawrence crushed her to him and devoured her mouth.

Trembling limbs clung to him as Patrice gave herself freely to the wild passion of his kiss, his tongue sending wave after wave of desire coursing through her. Then the pressure of his mouth softened, and they shared a series of slow, shivery kisses that were no less potent.

When her breathing began to settle down to a more even rhythm, she asked, "Now where does that put us?"

He let out a whooping laugh, like a child who had been granted a treasured wish—his heart was satisfied.

"Always the business woman. Get the details outlined up front," he teased, an indulgent grin characterizing his features.

She smiled. "I'm sorry. It's just that ... Everything ... This seems so sudden. I'm ... unbalanced. I don't, I mean I ...."

A smile crinkled the skin around his eyes, glazed familiarly in their glowing hue as he finally cut off the apologetic babbling by placing a painfully sweet kiss on her lips.

"No apologies needed," he whispered against the pulsing hollow at the base of her throat. "It's what I would have wanted to know." Dropping a kiss on her forehead, he straightened. Now's the time, he urged himself.

She watched curiously while he outstretched long legs to stick a hand into his pocket, then placed a closed fist on her jean-clad thigh. Her eyes sought his for explanation, but he gave no hint as to the mysterious object.

"I got this," he said finally, "after the first time you called me from Chicago. I was very tempted to fly up there, as you well know."

A warm, reminiscent smile spread across her face. She remembered it well. Patrice had had to talk Lawrence out of accompanying her, and jokingly suggested he keep an eye on the twins. He'd taken the task to heart, treating them to breakfast every morning before dropping them off at school, picking them up afterwards, and overseeing homework and dinner. Both Stephenie and Stephen had informed her that Lawrence was a lot more fun than she, meaning, of course, that he let them have their way.

"I didn't want you to think I didn't trust you out of my sight," he continued. The word "trust" brought an embarrassing smile to his lips and earned a chuckle from her.

"I know it's corny and all of that, but I was jealous." He licked full, well-shaped lips nervously before reluctantly adding, "And scared . . ." She placed both hands over his fidgeting ones. ". . . that some other man would snatch you away, and I don't think I could bear losing you. In fact, I know I can't. I want any man who looks at you to know you've been taken off the market," he said with pure male possessiveness. One at a time, his fingers spread open, and a cluster of sparkling diamonds surrounding a splendid sapphire stone was revealed.

Patrice's hand flew to her mouth. "Lawrence?" Her whisper was incredulous, her breathing instantly unsteady.

"Here, let me," he said with an outward calm. His hands shook ever so slightly as he slid the white gold engagement ring onto the third finger of her left hand. "Patrice Antionette Mason, will you marry me—be my lover, my wife, the mother of the children we'll add to the two we already have? Be mine forever?"

CHAPTER ❧ ELEVEN

*P*atrice was much too excited to sleep. *And that isn't the worst of it,* she thought, lying in the dark of her bedroom. Lawrence had been gone for less than an hour, and she was suffering the dull ache of desire—wishing he had not gone, but nothing she had said could convince him to stay the night.

"You're forgetting the children," he had told her, holding both hands between his, while laughing at her useless struggle to break free.

She'd mounted an argument of her own, countering in her a most persuasive voice, "But honey, the children are asleep. They're going to be out until the alarm goes off at 6:30 in the morning."

"Well, that's good, but I'm too old to be sneaking out of my woman's home before her children rise."

"Lawrence!"

She had begged, whined and protested, but he wouldn't budge.

"I'll pick you up for breakfast and we'll talk then."

And with that, he'd kissed her on the mouth, released her hands and walked out. After long, frustrating moments she had finally pushed herself off the stairs where he had left her in near tears, and quietly screamed.

As the ache brought on by the sweet longing began to subside, she began to put the fairy tale events of the evening into perspective. A marriage proposal was the last thing she had expected, though she should have counted on some demand for absolute commitment from him. Not only was he a man who made up his mind quickly and decisively, but one of deep emotions. And he certainly wouldn't waste them, especially those of the heart, on a casual affair.

And what of her acceptance to this quick decision of his?

Well, she thought with her face splitting into a wide grin, *I am in love.*

As she fingered the big stone, she refused to allow herself to think about what they had done. Experience had shown her that thinking wasn't her long suit when it came to Lawrence.

The need for the strong loving possession of this tender man was still so much with her that she groaned and pulled her body into a tight ball. She'd never get any sleep of what was left from the night.

❧ ❧ ❧ ❧

Standing at the phone booth, digging into his pocket for a quarter, Lawrence looked across the parking lot of the all-night convenience store. Several passersby were gathering to observe the debris of a car accident in the middle of the intersection, and although he was only involved as a witness, in a way the collision had been his fault. So, like two of the drivers involved, he was waiting for the police to arrive to take his statement.

While he waited, he felt an overwhelming need to hear Patrice's and to make make sure she was all right. After all, she was partly involved, too, he suspected, though he hadn't figured out the connection.

"Hi babe, asleep?"

"No, and it's all your fault. Had you stayed, I'd be resting peacefully by now," she chided teasingly.

Chuckling, he retorted, "I doubt that very much."

"Well," she conceded with a giggle, "you're probably right about that. But I still wouldn't be lying here, in this big bed, in the dark, all by myself."

"That will change soon, babe. Real soon."

"Speaking of which, when are we going to tell the kids?"

He hesitated before answering. "Not yet."

Picturing the disquiet his news was bound to create, Lawrence massaged throbbing temples, wondering what wild thoughts were running through her mind. Heaven knows she had a good reason to jump to the wrong conclusion, and he couldn't blame her in light of his exit from her home. He wished there was a more tactful way to do this.

"Are you at home?" Patrice's attempt at sounding casual failed.

"No." He swallowed hard before speaking again. "Look, honey, I want to keep our engagement just between us for a while. I don't even want you to tell Kit."

Silence crackled over the phone lines, and he swore viciously to himself. He'd like nothing better right now than to get his hands around the neck of the driver who left the scene of the accident.

Frankly, he was a little scared. He began to feel that his and Patrice's young relationship was being put to a quick test. He believed she loved him, but love had a strange way of eroding over the slightest provocation. He heard her stirring on the other end, and his heart stilled.

"Something has happened, hasn't it? Did you get hurt? Are you OK? You're at the hospital, aren't you?" She rattled off the barrage of questions in a panic-laced voice.

Lawrence's breathing eased with the feeling that comes from knowing someone, particularly the woman you love, is concerned about you above all else. "No, no, I'm fine."

"Will you please stop making me ask all these damn questions and tell me what the hell is going on?!"

"Testy, aren't we?" he laughed.

"Lawrence!"

"It's nothing, babe. I swear. There was a wreck, but I'm just a witness."

"What happened?"

"A car ran a light."

When he didn't say more, she said warily, "There's more, isn't there?"

Damn! She read him so well. "Yes."

"But you're not going to tell me?" she guessed perceptively.

"No. At least, not just yet."

He hadn't wanted to alarm her unduly, but had ended up doing just that with his half truths. Nevertheless, he wasn't going to tell her that someone had been parked outside her home in a red car. Or, that this mystery person had driven off in a squeal of burning rubber when he had walked down the driveway. He remembered being so intent on getting home to cool his ardor under the cold spray of a shower that he almost hadn't noticed the car. What had drawn his attention to the vehicle was the movement of a huddled figure sitting there in the dark. The person looked up and saw him approaching and immediately revved up the car and sped off. Without a second thought, he had jumped into his car to give chase.

The red car had weaved recklessly through the residential neighborhood before finally managing to get to the main street. When the driver ran the red light, he also sideswiped another car and sped away. However, the domino effect of this first accident caused the car that had been hit to ram into the back of a second automobile.

It is a miracle no one has been seriously hurt, Lawrence thought as he looked at the twisted metal and broken glass littering the street.

"Are we still on for tomorrow?" Patrice asked at the other end of the phone.

"Yes. And I definitely don't want you going into the office."

"But . . ." she started.

"No, buts. I mean it, Patrice. You're not going and that's final."

≈ ≈ ≈ ≈

The car came to a screeching halt on the graveled-incline off the freeway. Cars above whizzed by in excess of the speed limit, other drivers were either unconcerned or too fearful to stop and inquire whether the driver of the red car was experiencing car trouble.

Killing the engine under a nearby lamp post, Don jumped out from behind the wheel and rushed to the front of the car. The moment he saw the extent of the damage—a small dent near the cracked headlight—he let lose a viscous, guttural scream. The cold, midnight sky cringed under the torrent of expletives that erupted from him.

"I will make you pay for everything you bitch. . . ."

He kicked the tire, then pivoted circularly in one spot, enraged over the damage to his prized possession—the sporty red Camero with mag wheels, bucket seats and leather-lined interior.

A combination of disbelief and rage marred his expression. Burning with anger, he unbuttoned the long, black leather coat, then placed a frustrated hand on his hip; the other gripped his hair.

He wasn't to blame. *It was Patrice's fault—plain and simple.*

Pulling a crushed pack of cigarettes from his shirt pocket, he shook one out and tried to light it against the windy turbulence created by the fast-moving traffic. After several tries, he succeeded, and took a long drag off the cigarette. Sitting on the hood to the car, he remembered that all he had intended to do was to get a look at the place.

He had been so thrilled with obtaining the address that all he could think to do was drive over. A smile came to his features recalling Marie's timid behavior. *The bitch is just like a timid kitten around me.* He laughed, musing at his own mix of metaphors: *Cats and dogs—cat and mouse games. Just like I'm the cat and Patrice the little mouse in my maze.*

Still, no one could imagine his surprise at his stroke of luck when he commented about Patrice probably living in a mansion, while she, Marie, could barely afford rent on a two-bedroom apartment. Predictably, Marie had come rushing to Patrice's defense before she even realized it. It was an old habit, hard for him to break her of—even after he had demonstrated that he would not tolerate his woman questioning his opinion on any matter. But this time he had played it cool. This time he didn't erupt, rather, he simply seized on a golden opportunity:

"Well, where does she live?" he asked with a hint of disgust lining his tone. And it had worked, for although wary, Marie had given him the address. He had actually hung around her place for another hour before fabricating an excuse to leave.

"Look baby, I need to call it a night. I've got a sales report that's due in to the manger tomorrow." Hell, he mused, *I could have told Marie anything and she would have believed it.* Don held the smoke laced with nicotine in the cavern of his mouth, and then blew it out in rings that evaporated. After driving through the neighborhood, he couldn't resist parking out front. That was when the tantalizing idea took hold. *Why not check out the house a little closer? It was dark enough.* The side door of the garage in back of the house had been child's play to unlock. The one leading from inside the garage to the kitchen was even more difficult, but not enough to deter him. A rush of blood had made his heart beat like a kettledrum; its flow was rapid through his veins. It's *a better high than drugs*, he had though as a playful smile floated across his face.

He wandered around aimlessly. *Ah, Patrice and her children.* He had found the picture over the fireplace particularly amusing. *No man in her house, no man in her life.* It had made him feel. . .well, powerful. He had forced her into such an existence; he had beaten the desire for other men out of her for good.

Don tossed the cigarette onto the ground. He began stalking around the car, growing increasingly agitated by what he had learned after letting waiting outside the house. He stopped at the rear of the car, hands stuffed in the coat pockets.

After driving around the neighborhood, he had psyched himself into thinking he could get used to living in an area like this, a house like Patrice's. He was anxious for her to return home, then he had planned to walk up to the front door and ring the bell. He wondered what she would have said; what she would have done; the expression on her face. I would have loved to have seen the expression on her face.

I did not get to do any of that, he mused bitterly.

The picture had turned out to be just a showpiece, a lie. There was a man in Patrice's life after all. . .And that man had nearly caught him tonight.

Don strained his memory, trying to recall the name Marie had mentioned in passing. He remembered that he had heard it while still in college. *No*, he corrected, *it was at a Black History program.*

"What was it?"

It had to do with peanuts or something like that. Woodson. Carter G. Woodson. That was it. No, not Carter. No. . . .The first name was something else.

Snapping his finger, Don smiled with satisfaction, "Lawrence Woodson!" Pulling open the car door, he happened to look over his left shoulder and saw it. As big as daylight, and waiting like beacon of truth—high above the freeway on the other side was a big, green sign. The writing in bold white letters read Banneker University—next exit.

Yeah, that was the place Marie mentioned. Yeah. . . that was it.

ða ða ða ða

With a cup of coffee in front of her, Patrice was sitting at the table in her kitchen, staring pensively across the room pondering her new engagement. Or more specifically, the fact that it had to be kept a secret and the gorgeous ring hidden away in a bottom drawer. Unconsciously, she began to rub the finger that had briefly been adorned with the diamond and sapphire ring—its naked state was like a blemish on what should have been a joyous occasion.

A sigh of resignation passed her lips. Something had happened to cause Lawrence to request this silence, and she accepted it, because she instinctively knew that this mysterious something had to do with the threats.

Patrice ran her fingers through her hair, thinking about the insanity of the situation and her only recourse. With her decision finally made Patrice planned to phone in the announcement to Roger and have him put it on the air.

However, remembering why she wasn't going to the office brought a smile to her lips and a dreamy mist to her eyes. *I get to spend the whole day with Lawrence.*

As her mind wondered over the events of the previous night, Patrice failed to acknowledge the "Good morning, Mom," from the twins who came into the room.

"Mom?" called Stephenie, waving a hand in front of Patrice's face.

Patrice looked up disoriented, then blushed. "Good-morning," she said with a warm glow. "What do you want for breakfast?"

The twins glanced at each other with bewildered brows.

"Is everything OK?" asked Stephen.

"Yeah, everything's fine," she replied.

"Then why aren't you dressed?" he continued suspiciously, eyeing the ivory satin robe with tiny pearl buttons . The elegant garment had been a gift from Stephenie and he for Christmas. As far as he knew, she had only worn it once. Stephen looked to Stephenie for an answer, but she was busy pouring cereal in a bowl. As he prepared a similar breakfast of cereal and milk, he continued to stare at his mother peculiarly.

She doesn't look sick, he decided. *She looks fine—although something is definitely different about her this morning.* The struggle to pinpoint the change he noticed was evidenced in his squinted eyes and wrinkled brow. She seemed soft, maybe? Lovely? The description made him feel uncomfortable. He had never thought of her in those terms. His mother was a good-looking woman. Intelligent. Tough. She had to be.

Anyway, he liked it when her glossy black hair was down around her shoulders and not pinned up in that ball she preferred. Her face was lightly made up as usual, but there was a faraway look in her eyes—not sad, but not cheerful either.

"I'm fine. Really," she said firmly with a smile, wrapping her hands around a coffee mug. Hesitantly she added, "I'm not going to the office this morning," timid brown eyes avoided the two pairs of curious stares hawking her every movement.

"Oh? And why not?" Stephenie wanted to know, her mouth full of Rice Crispies.

As if on cue, the doorbell rang. The twins looked at her, then at each other and back at their mother. She had already sprang from her seat and was dashing from the kitchen, the folds of her robe flowing in her wake.

Lawrence was surprised when the door was opened with a jerk, and Patrice rushed into his arms. Instinctively, he held her close to him and surprise quickly gave way to the other emotions associated only with her. He felt her soft lips fasten on his, her tongue greedy as it darted inside his mouth for a kiss that heightened his blood pressure.

In his arms, Patrice felt light headed and carefree. Nothing else mattered but the two of them, and she kissed him enthusiastically, releasing some of the pent up hunger she had had to store. His mouth was firm against hers and strong arms wrapped endearingly around her. She didn't care whether she was making a spectacle of herself. A quick study, she learned to accept the unexpected from herself when it came to Lawrence and being truly in love. It was just the way things were—the way things would be for a long, long time to come.

"We'd better get inside before the whole neighborhood shows up for the show." he murmured with a voice that was thick and husky as he gently guided her back into the house.

As he turned to lock the door, her eyes feasted on the outline of his muscular build, her imagination filling in the fine details hidden from sight beneath the maroon hooded sweat-suit.

Facing her with outstretched arms, he said with a provocative command, "Now, come here, woman."

Obeying gladly, she sashayed into the inviting circle of hungry arms. She stared winsomely at the expression alight on the gently carved face before they blurred when he lowered his head to claim her mouth.

"Hmm," he moaned and buried his head in the soft neck. "This is what I want for breakfast every morning," he murmured against her warm flesh, inhaling her morning fresh scent.

"You're so easy to please," she said saucily and stood on her toes to brazenly rub rhythmic hips against his, eliciting the desired tormented groan.

"We'll see if you still feel that way after, say, fifty years."

Her hands cupped his face. "I know I will. Fifty years and more. Make no mistake about that, Mr. Woodson."

"Yes, ma'am," he mumbled before reclaiming her mouth for a slow, drugging kiss that sent a shot of heat inside her. His tongue teased her lips apart and slipped between the opening hungrily.

Lawrence nourished appetite on her taste, a combination of coffee and tooth-paste. He pulled the pliant body tighter against him, and she moved closer to the part of his anatomy pulsing with life against her satin covered thigh.

"Mercy woman, what you do to me."

"Mmm, oh yes," she whispered, her body temperature rising.

"If you keep that up, your kids will stumble in here and catch me ravishing their mother."

"I trust you," she replied, her lips trailing along his. "And anyway, would that be so bad?"

"What are you up to?" Lawrence murmured, with suspicion characterizing his gaze.

"My darling, I love you and I simply want them to see that. I want them to see how two people in love behave. I want my son to see how a man is supposed to love a woman, and my daughter to see how fulfilling a woman in love can be, as long as she doesn't confuse love with something else."

Lawrence had no difficulty synthesizing the intent behind Patrice's words. Having poor, or rather no, examples of what love can be contributed heavily to many of the problems affecting his relationships with women in his life—his own childhood had provided a disastrous vision of the effect of loving and of being loved. If not for Patrice, he would have remained a helpless, emotional cripple who was paralyzed by a diseased vision of what a woman wanted from a man.

"You're something else. You know that?"

"As long as I'm your something else," she replied with laughter in her voice, as she resumed the delicious position against his lips.

The twins stumbled into the foyer, catching Patrice and Lawrence entangled in a kiss that was rapidly propelling them out of control. Stephen cleared his throat, and the lovers jumped apart.

Patrice swallowed hard, stains of embarrassment colored her cheeks— so much for her bravado a minute ago. She waited until she'd regained some semblance of regular breathing before facing the twins.

"Uh, it's Lawrence," she explained ineptly, looking very much like a child who'd gotten caught with a hand in the cookie jar.

Ever the tactful one, Stephenie said, "Good-morning, Mr. Woodson," politely but with laughter trembling on her lips.

"Good morning, Stephenie," Lawrence returned, then to her twin with a respectful nod of his head, "Stephen."

Ambivalence swarmed inside Stephen's head. What he had witnessed provided the answer to the subtle changes he noticed in his mother's appearance and behavior. *Mom is really, truly in love with this man.* Though Stephenie had been trying to get him to see and accept what was happening between their mother and Mr. Woodson, he had refused to believe it. Until now.

"Good morning," Stephen said, pausing slightly before adding, "Lawrence."

A strained silence loomed briefly over the foursome until Stephenie asked matter-of-factly, "Who's taking us to school?"

≈ ≈ ≈ ≈

"Want to come with me?" asked Lawrence as he parked the car on the lot adjacent to the university's administration building. "I'll only be a minute."

"Sure, why not?" replied Patrice. She had accompanied him to drop the twins off at school after changing into a rose jumpsuit that made her look like a college coed. "Unless you'd rather I wait in the car."

"No, I wouldn't rather you wait in the car," he growled playfully, pulling her into his arms to gingerly nip the side of her neck. They laughed with the satisfaction of good feelings and expectations as he politely held out a hand to help her from the car.

This day will be be a beautiful one, mused Patrice, for already the sun was promising to shine high in the mildly cool, blue skies. The parking lot was nearly full, signaling the start of another busy day on campus. Students were scurrying to get to class on time, while faculty and staff hurried to their respective places.

With her hand in his and their heads close together in conversation, they crossed the lot on route to the building. Affectionately called the "Ivory Tower," the four-story, two-toned marble and glass structure was surrounded by a well-kept yard and healthy trees on three sides.

"Good morning, Mr. Woodson."

The greeting was issued by a tall, gracious-looking woman in her mid-to-late thirties who met them on the steps of the building. She was professionally dressed, complete with briefcase.

"Good morning, Dr. Butler," Lawrence returned, seemingly oblivious to the woman's lingering stare. He tugged gently at Patrice's hand to match his long-legged strides as they continued on their way.

"You're ruining my reputation, Miss Mason," he whispered in her ear as he opened one of the glass doors into the building.

"Oh? And how's that, Mr. Woodson?" she retorted, blushing up at him.

"Everybody's going to think I'm dating a freshman half my age. Before the day is out, I'll be a condemned, dirty old man."

She laughingly replied, "Let them talk."

"They will definitely do that," he said, more or less to himself, surprised that he really didn't care.

They passed several other people in the hall who spoke to Lawrence, more out of curiosity then anything else he suspected. He acknowledged the greetings with a slight nod, but never once let go of Patrice's hand.

Patrice caught more than one of the females they passed casting sly glances in Lawrence's direction, while they looked at her with a mixture of congratulation and envy. She smiled proudly and tightened her hold on his hand.

Lawrence opened the door to his office and ushered her in, his hand on the small of her back. Seconds after he closed the door, his matronly attired secretary, Mrs. Jenkins, came blustering out of his private office.

"Oh, Mr. Woodson, Mr. Woodson! It's awful! Just awful!"

"What is it, Mrs. Jenkins?" he asked patiently, going to the woman's side.

"In there—in your office. Somebody's broken in and made a mess of things."

Lawrence rushed into his office. A cloud of disgust came over his face as he looked around the room which had been trashed beyond belief. The couch and chairs had been sliced, books torn apart and thrown about, windows broken and the computer smashed. As if that hadn't been enough vandalism, the photos and profiles on KHVY employees had been strewn about, along with other papers he'd left on his desk.

He swore bitterly and passed a frustrated hand across his face, wondering why someone had gone through all this trouble, this risk to merely trash the place. Sighing resignedly, he began to carefully pick up the incriminating papers first, although suffering no illusion that he'd get them all before Patrice walked through the door. It was probably just as well, he told himself, because he had already postponed talking to her about the investigation longer than he should.

"Oh, no! Look at this mess!"

Lawrence looked up from where he was kneeling and shrugged nonchalantly. "Don't worry about it." Patrice bent to pick up some papers and photos at her feet. "Don't touch..." he started, but it was too late, "anything."

"I'm sor..." her voice trailed off as the familiarity of the face in the photo she had picked up captured her attention.

With head bowed, Lawrence released the papers he held, a shower of white fluttering slowly to the floor. His body tensed while waiting for her volcanic eruption.

Patrice was speechless—clear thought was impossible. She stared wide-eyed and open-mouthed at Lawrence, then back at the photo of Roger clutched in a closed fist. She looked around the room and noticed the back of another five-by-seven size, slick sheet of paper and stooped to pick it up. It was a picture of Marie. She scooped up another of Belinda, then Mike. *My entire staff must be littering the floor of Lawrence's office,* she thought.

As time silently passed, the air grew tight as if a small rubber band were being stretched to contain a large object.

"Lawrence?" She whispered quietly and hesitantly while she straightening. Her emotions were a crazy mixture of opposing desires: hope for a simple explanation, and fear that there was none. She inhaled deeply before continuing, "What's going on? What are pictures of my staff doing in your office?"

Lawrence closed his eyes tiredly, *God, what am I going to do?* Patrice's calm demeanor did not bode well—he had been expecting screams and histrionics, and could deal with that. But this solemn, cautious performance scared him.

"Baby, it's not what you're thinking," he said as calmly as possible while he rose to look down at her.

She'd forgotten about his uncanny ability to go so deep inside of himself that it seemed he was the only person around. Somehow, his behavior seemed damning to her, but she refused to jump to hasty conclusions. At least, she tried not to. But even with this determination, she had to hold a tight rein over her emotions: she couldn't think of one plausible reason for this—this spying.

"Oh, no? That's funny," she replied. "You know what I'm thinking when I don't." Her voice, an octave higher than normal grew unsteady. "Why don't you tell me what I'm suppose to think?" she said in a tone hardening with sarcasm.

Her posture alerted him to the fact that whatever his defense of good intentions were, they would not be accepted in a like manner. Panic struck a chord within his fragile composure and an overwhelming loneliness washed over his mind. He hadn't felt this way since his parents died—abandoned, and knowing there was nothing, nothing he could do to change things.

"We'll talk about it over breakfast," he said commandingly, reverting to a tactic with which he was most familiar and comfortable. "Just let me get security . . ."

"No."

There was no compromise in her tone, yet she felt composure seal like a fragile shell around her. She had been betrayed by the one man she thought she could trust, the only man she'd loved in mature, realistic commitment.

She glared at him with burning, reproaching eyes, then down at the photos, slipping freely from trembling fingers. It took more strength than she knew herself capable of to keep the stinging tears at bay. She drew herself up quietly and quickly backed out of the room.

There was something about the fallen photos that signaled a finality to Lawrence, causing an icy fear to twist around his heart. Seconds ticked by before he summoned ladened feet to function.

Rushing past Mrs. Jenkins, who was on the phone, he caught up with Patrice at the outer door. He tried to shove it shut, but she kept her foot planted between the slight opening.

"Let me go or I'll pitch a fit like this campus has never seen," she murmured between gritted teeth.

"Baby, I swear . . ."

"Don't baby me," she snapped, snatching the door open to crash into his knee and storming out.

Lawrence bumped into several people in the hallway to reach Patrice. When he caught up with her, he grabbed her securely by the wrist. She tried to break free, staring at him with an implacable expression. He reluctantly dropped her hand.

"Please come back to my office," he said, easily keeping up with her hurried steps. "Give me a chance to explain."

"I don't need the explanation now," she said in a chilly tone, not looking at him. "My eyes told me all I need to know."

Jerking her to a halt, Lawrence grated harshly, "You know nothing."

"All right, go ahead, explain," she placated, folding her arms across her bosom.

Curious to see the usually proper, unruffled Mr. Woodson in a public argument with a woman, onlookers slowed their movements to eavesdrop. Lawrence grabbed Patrice by the hand and pulled her roughly through the nearest open doorway.

"Well, morning," said Charles, who was bent over his secretary's empty desk. "What brings you to our campus, Patrice?"

"Charles, will you take me home?"

"Oh-oh," said Charles.

"You're not going anywhere until you hear me out," affirmed Lawrence. "Charles, let me use your office." In the second he released her hand and took his eyes off her, Patrice darted from the room.

"Problems with your woman, buddy?" teased Charles with a snicker.

Lawrence bit off a curse, then stormed out of the room to return to his office while Charles' laughter rung in his ears.

ra ra ra ra

"What's so important that I had to take an early lunch?" asked Marie, sliding into the booth at McDonald's.

The fast-food restaurant, which usually did a brisk business, wasn't crowded at this time of the morning. Breakfast was no longer being served, and it was still a little early for lunch. Marie and Jay had the entire smoking section to themselves.

Jay replied, "Things were going slow at the dealership, so I decided to take an early lunch, and wanted to spend the time with you. Is that important enough for you?" She merely smile a lopsided, tender smile which brightened her wry eyes. "Frankly," he tacked on, "I'm surprised you agreed."

"Things are kind of slow this morning," explained Marie. "Patrice won't be in today."

"Oh?" he asked.

"Yeah. Must be a first. I've never known her to miss a day of work."

"Did she say why?"

"No. She wanted to talk to Roger, but he hadn't gotten to the office yet."

Jay's heart accelerated to a lively beat in his chest. He cautioned himself to remain calm. *Cool out.* "What do you want?" he asked casually. *Be patient Jay boy, be patient with the pigeon.*

"Huh?"

"Food," he replied with a chuckle. "What do you want to eat?" he clarified while rising to his feet.

"I'm not really hungry," said Marie. "How about a juice and a danish?"

He got in line behind a woman with two bratty kids, but their endless chatter didn't bother him, for his thoughts were on Patrice. He wondered whether she had decided to cancel the concert. He would be disappointed if she did, for it provided a good guise for him to make her life miserable. While she may have suspected a prank, no one else was willing to risk calling his bluff. But if she's canceling, he was definitely going to have to figure out something else that would hurt her. He placed his order, then returned to the table with juice, danish and a coffee.

"Do you think she's finally seen the light and decided to cancel?" he picked up on the line of the conversation casually while stirring cream into the coffee.

"She didn't say one way or the other, but I would imagine so," replied Marie, sticking the straw through the top of the juice container. "I could tell she wasn't in a talkative mood. But I think," she added with a conspiratorial grin, "she's going to spend some time with Lawrence Woodson."

Feeling an electric sparkle weave its way down his spine, Jay remember the thrill of the previous night. Marie didn't know how fortunate she was last night, for if I didn't trash that office, I would have used her as my sweet, little punching bag.

"Who's Woodson?" Jay asked, pretending ignorance.

"The man in her life. I thought I told you about him," she replied, sipping the juice. "He's a vice-president at Banneker University."

"I don't think so," said Jay. "I would have remembered news like that. The impervious Ms. Mason takes time out for a man in her life," he snorted. "I guess she's human after all."

"Patrice is really a nice person," said Marie as she bit into her danish. "I don't understand your hostility toward her."

"I'm not, not really," he said, taking one of her hands and lifting it to his mouth. "It's just when I think about her, I think about you doing all the work, while she sits back and gets all the credit," he whispered as he kissed her hand.

"That's sweet of you to think so, but it's not true. Yes, I work hard, but only because she works hard. I've never had a more dedicated, fair-minded boss than Patrice. She doesn't do anything she's not willing to do herself."

"Yeah, right," he said with a calculated expression and tone. "Didn't you tell me she had a kid?"

"Twins. Stephen and Stephenie."

"I bet you they're spoiled brats," he said, trying to disguise his envy under a disinterested look. His mind drifted back to the rooms upstairs in Patrice's home, both lavished with expensive toys and furnishings. "She gives them everything they ask for so she won't feel as if she's neglecting them."

"That couldn't be farthest from the truth. If you knew her better, you wouldn't say that. She has the most well-behaved children. At least, most of the time."

"What do you mean "most of the time?" Jay queried.

"A couple of weeks ago they skipped a class at school, and she stormed out of the office ready to kill. And the next day, I overheard Roger offering her a pair of tickets for them to go to a Luther Vandross concert, and she said they were still on punishment."

"So, you're telling me that she's a good mother, on top of all her other accomplishments." He smashed the cigarette in the tin ashtray, then tapped a fresh one on the table.

"Yep," replied Marie, biting into another corner of the pastry. "In fact, the only thing she loves better than her job are her children.

Jay cocked his head to the side as though more interested in lighting another cigarette than Marie's disclosures. In one quick breath, he blew out the fire at the end of the match, then dropped the wooden stick in the ashtray. Feigning utter contentment with the cigarette, he listened intently to Marie's babble, storing information as a computer would store input.

"They mean the world to her. She doesn't like to take work home with her. Says it interrupts with her quality time with the twins. When she leaves the office, it may be late, but she's usually finished whatever she had set out to do for that day." Marie paused to reflect, "I wish my mother had been that devoted to me," but she no longer had her lover's attention.

Jay puffed lightly on the cigarette, a distant gaze in his eyes. *Stupid! I'm so stupid sometimes. Those damn kids! It was there all along. The weakness I've been looking for. The kids: Patrice's Achilles' heel. My darling children.* A smile turned the corner of his mouth upward.

CHAPTER ❧ TWELVE

"*I* don't know what to think, or what to believe anymore," said Patrice with agonized frustration. Her heart told her one thing—Lawrence would never do anything to hurt her; yet her mind couldn't discount what she'd seen.

She was pacing about the balcony just off the living room of Kit's high-rise apartment. Kit sat quietly in one of the chairs of the white patio furniture sipping coffee from a clear crystal cup while listening—she'd been doing so for the past hour.

Patrice had caught a bus near the university to walk two blocks from the bus stop home. She didn't want to speak to Lawrence. Figuring that he'd try to contact her, Patrice phoned Kit at work. They had mutually agreed to meet at Kit's place.

"It seems my instincts regarding men are still in a teenage mode or something. My best bet from here on out is to chuck the possibility of ever having a man in my life. I was better off without one in the first place. I guess I needed this lesson to prove that, once and for all." Patrice fell silent, looking down at the traffic twenty floors below, then up at the clear and sunny morning sky.

Still, not a word was said by Kit. She understood Patrice's need to talk, convinced that idle rhetoric was the extent of her friend's indulgence.

The wretched expression on Patrice's face had inspired contradictory reactions: the need to cry and the need to shout with glee. She chose the latter, for despite the pain with which Patrice now suffered, gone was the woman who had been a victim of a man's so-called "love". Yes, some good had come of this. Patrice was finally free from the shackles of diffidence and humiliation to which Donald Hollingsworth had subjected her. *Lawrence is a good man and worthy of Patrice,* she reflected. *However, right now I would like to strangle him for stupidity.*

Passing a careful hand over the single thick braid of long red hair, Kit waited patiently for the catharsis to continue. The initial rage had been vented; the self-castigation was almost over. Kit glanced at her watch, *I'll give it another minute for the waterworks.*

"Damn, Kit, I trusted him," Patrice lamented, turning to face her friend. "And God help me, I love him so much," she whimpered as the tears she had been determined to suppress flowed. She dropped in a pathetic heap into a chair.

"It's going to be all right," Kit commiserated, rising to go to Patrice. She kneeled next to the chair and took Patrice's hands in hers.

"Damn!" swore Patrice chokingly. "I said I wasn't going to do this. Cry over some man. Now look at me," her hands fanning the air helplessly.

"Get it out of your system," advised Kit with an understanding smile. And Patrice did.

Shortly afterwards, Kit sent Patrice inside to wash her face. When she returned, quiet and withdrawn, a fresh cup of coffee awaited her on the table. She reached to pick up the cup of liquid caffeine with hands that shook so badly that she feared dropping the dainty crystal, envisioning shattered glass all over the balcony's brick-tiled floor.

Patrice snatched her hands back and clasped them together over her mouth to quell the dirge of another bout of tears. She inhaled deeply and began to wander from one end of the small area to the other, trying to coach herself out of misery.

After all, I still have my job, my kids, my health. That's all that matters now, she told herself.

Cutting through her silent soliloquy was a cynical inner voice, demanding, *Who are you trying to fool?* and she ceased ambling. Dropping both hands to her sides she lifted her head to stare at the sun as though answers were to be found in its golden brightness.

Kit began to worry. It seemed she had underestimated the extent of the damage Lawrence's faux pas caused. *Whatever*, Kit decided firmly, *I am not going to let Patrice wear a martyr's cloak for much longer.*

"You know Lawrence has a place not too far from here," announced Kit by way of breaking the silence.

Patrice tried not to look surprise, but her expression fell flat, and Kit laughed. Easing into a lounge chair, Patrice drawled, "Seems he's full of surprises."

"He said you hadn't seen the place." A sly grin flitted across Kit's features in memory of how she came to learn this tidbit. She would have to tell Patrice about it one day.

"He also said you wouldn't like it. And from what he described, he's right," Kit added, twitching her nose in distaste. When Patrice didn't rise to the baiting, she continued, "You know, he's a classical chauvinist."

Patrice snorted bitterly. "Heaven help the next woman who gets involved with him." A flash of grief ripped through her at the mere thought of him with another woman.

"Yes, she'll need heaven's help, the poor dear," Kit taunted.

"I know what you're trying to do Kit, and it won't work."

"All I'm trying to do is get you to snap out of it. I thought after you'd vent your rage, you'd be ready to see reason. But you're sitting there like a stone, convincing yourself that he's the worst thing that has ever happened to you!"

Electing to ignore Kit's outburst, Patrice said, "Since we're into surprises, I can tell you now that it no longer matters. Lawrence proposed last night, ring and all," she said attempting a sardonic chuckle that came out like a whimper.

Patrice cupped her mouth, trying to hold on to a semblance of composure. She swallowed the lump that had formed in her throat before speaking again. "He wanted to keep it a secret for a while."

Kit stared at Patrice with an impatient look, shaking her head from side-to-side. "I wouldn't be so quick to impart with my lover's secret if I were you," she said, reproach in her tone. "By the way, congratulations."

"Congratulations are not in order," Patrice returned. "At least, not anymore, thank you."

"Oh, damn it, Patrice! I think you're making a big deal out of this. Lawrence didn't do anything other than try to help."

"By going behind my back, spying on my staff?" she yelled. "He had pictures of everybody. I fail to see how that kind of exercise translates into helping me."

"Think, Patrice. What else would he use them for, if not to help? Don't tell me you believe he was behind the threats?" When Patrice didn't respond, Kit asked, "Is that what you believe?"

"Of course not," said Patrice. "That's not what I'm saying."

"Then what are you suggesting he did that was so terrible?" Kit demanded to know. "I think it was rather sweet of him."

"I don't know," moaned Patrice rising from her seat. "If he'd just explained when I asked him about the photos."

"Did you give him a chance?"

Patrice started to issue a prompt and firm "yes," but held her tongue, weighing an answer. She began to wonder if she hadn't convicted him with her actions, if not her words. Guilt lodged itself in her breast, and she replied, "I did and I didn't," in a barely audible voice.

"Which is it? Did you or didn't you?"

"I tried to," she answered, running agitated fingers through her hair, her defensive back to Kit. "He just looked at me with that vapid look of his, then tried to order me about," she added snappily, then wrapped her arms around herself.

"Order you about," Kit quoted knowingly. Her brows lifted fractionally, a half smile teased the well-shaped corners of her mouth. Yes, Lawrence would revert to something *like that,* she thought. *He is a lot like Martin in that respect—each have this penchant control.*

"We'll discuss it at breakfast." Patrice repeated Lawrence's words in tone and cadence.

Yes, that was him, Kit said to herself, her smile threatening to erupt, but it was hidden behind the rim of the cup as she sipped lingeringly. "I see," she said.

"If he wasn't guilty, he certainly acted the part," said Patrice petulantly.

"Sounds like you reacted irrationally to me."

Patrice turned to look at Kit with her mouth open in denial.

"I mean, after all," Kit said, shrugging silk covered shoulders, "he did offer to explain, but you had already condemned him. Imagine how he felt," she posed, setting the cup on the table to swing her legs together on the floor in front of her.

"First"—she said, brandishing a finger—"he was stunned to discover that someone had broken into his office. Then," she continued, furnishing another finger, "to have you stumble in and see those photos." Kit retrieved the coffee and mumbled, "That was incredibly dumb of him," she mumbled into the cup. "He must have known if you found out about them that you'd be upset."

Patrice opened her mouth to speak; Kit cut her off, offering speculatively, "And maybe, just maybe he wanted you to find out."

"Your logic escapes me," retorted Patrice, turning her back to grip the railing.

"Well, he didn't have to invite you in. He could have asked you to stay in the car, and you would have been none the wiser."

Facing Kit, Patrice responded gloatingly, "But you're forgetting one thing: he didn't know the office had been trashed."

"Doesn't matter," returned Kit nonchalantly. "There's no way you can convince me that he would take the slightest risk of having you discover those pictures unless he intended to tell you himself."

"When?" challenged Patrice in disbelief, though she desperately wanted to cling to that possibility.

"That's irrelevant," replied Kit promptly. "You'd better be sure you're not making a mistake by throwing the fish back into the water. For such a normally, perceptive business-woman, I don't see how you could make such a hasty decision without all the facts."

Before Patrice could respond, Kit amended, "Well, I do understand how you feel, but I've also been around Lawrence with your kids. I don't believe he could have faked the kind of genuine devotion I saw him display. And you know it too. Your ego is bruised and you're just too angry and hurt right now to admit it."

Even while she agreed with Kit's assessment, Patrice couldn't help the thought that came out, "Listening to my heart has gotten me in trouble before."

"That was before, this is now. And you know what?" Kit asked in a lighter mood.

"What?"

"You still haven't asked me what I thought of Lawrence, nor have you asked me what I would do if I were you."

Patrice smiled a smile that brightened her entire face, and Kit breathed a tremendous sigh of relief. The two women exchanged an expression of secret understanding: It had been an unspoken ritual that neither sought the other's outlook. If the shoe of crisis were on the other foot, they knew that each had to come to an independent conclusion. Advice usually arrived from very subjective outlooks—their pact was one of solid objectivity in the face of grave decisions.

"Now, I am curious," said Kit. "What are you going to do?"

Patrice thought about her answer before replying. "I know I'm not going to throw my fish back." After a brief silence, she added with the growing confidence she felt, "But neither am I going to let him off the hook so easily."

Kit looked over her shoulder into the apartment as she stated, "Good for you."

"What is it?" asked Patrice, following Kit's gaze inside.

"I thought I heard something."

"You think somebody's at the door?"

"You think they'd have the good sense to ring the doorbell," said Kit, while rising to head inside.

Patrice leaned over the railing, wishing she were back home in the comfort of her bedroom. Some of her best thinking was done there—and it was certainly time that she used her brain. She could kick herself for intimating that Lawrence had anything to do with the threats. It was something she knew instinctively without the need for proof. She had just been so stunned by those photos that it had destroyed all rational thought processes.

Whoever was behind the threats had prior knowledge of the concert. Lawrence, on the other hand, hadn't the faintest idea about the station's intention when approached. He could have cared less, of this she was sure.

Not that he wasn't concerned about the political issue that had the entire world in hot debate, but he'd fought his war. He was satisfied and committed to ensure the future of Banneker University and making it an institution worthy of its name.

There was something else about him that should have warned her off snap judgements: Lawrence possessed an old-fashion quality known as integrity. He was respectful of her and her kids, and he hadn't forced the issue of consummating their relationship despite her obvious willingness.

Realizing that she had a lot to atone for, fear like a piercing stiletto plunged into her bosom. *What if he doesn't forgive me as quickly as I've implied his guilt? What if he can't forgive me at all?*

I have to reach him before more time has passed, thought Patrice as she spun quickly to leave. When she reached the living room, she spotted Kit ushering in an uncharacteristically meek Lawrence, "What took you so long?" Kit demanded.

"Lawrence," Patrice whispered.

Lawrence had already spotted her over Kit's right shoulder. Whatever he was going to say halted on his lips before he mumbled a reply—undecipherable to Patrice's hearing.

Patrice's heart lurched excitedly, her eyes feasting on his magnificent presence. In spite of his set face, clamped mouth and fixed eyes it mattered little to her that he was obviously irritated and angry. The only thing that mattered was that he was here.

"Patrice," he said with a tense nod.

"What are you doing here?"

"You're here, aren't you?"

"I mean, I, I was just on my way to find you." She was horrified to hear herself stammering like a simpleton.

"If you hadn't run away that wouldn't be necessary, would it?"

He's not going *to make it easy for me*, she thought, noting the righteous indignation that had come over his countenance. Though he had every right to be angry with her, she was not going to let him intimidate her. After all, he had a lot of explaining to do himself!

Planting her hands on hips, Patrice said with more bravado that she felt, "You lied to me. And heaven knows what else you've been up to behind my back. I'm not so sure I should have anything to do with you anymore."

"You had the opportunity to make that choice a long time ago. Now, it's too late for anymores, Ms. Mason."

Not wanting to remain in the path of the electrical currents shooting back and forth across the room, Kit interjected lightly, "Excuse me. I need to get back to work." She picked up her purse and suit jacket from the couch, "Be sure to lock up when you leave. Or stay here if you like," she invited while heading for the front door. "Martin is picking me up for dinner and I don't expect to be back tonight."

"Kit, wait a minute," begged Patrice.

But it was too late, for Kit was already making good her escape. "I'll talk to you later," she waved, then pulled the door shut behind her.

"I made a mistake leaving you last night," said Lawrence, slowly approaching Patrice. "I won't make that mistake again."

"Lawrence, ah, listen. I've had time to think," she said anxiously while backing away and nearly knocking over a lamp table. In the instant she turned to correct it, he was upon her.

"Where's the bedroom?"

With hands braced against his sweater-clad chest, Patrice tried unsuccessfully to shove him away. "Lawrence, wait, we need to talk," raced the words from nervous lips.

"Later for talking," he growled, entrapping her in an intractable hold, and making it impossible for her to retreat before the assault of his kiss. He smothered her mouth with driving urgency, forcing her lips to part for the invasion of his masterful tongue.

She managed to wrench her head aside. "No, Lawrence! We need to get things straightened out, first."

"Does it really matter?" he asked, gazing into her face with the memory of what he'd almost lost. He'd been like a wounded animal when she raced off the campus, and everyone around him had suffered from his grief-stricken mania.

"My mind was made up to let you go. And then, I started to remember how I felt before you came along." His voice trailed off, abbreviating his thoughts, and he took a deep audible breath. "Then I started thinking about all the good things I've felt since you've come into my life. I'm not willing to give all that up because of two errors in judgement, are you?" At the slight shake of her head, he added, "So, it really doesn't matter what we do first, does it?"

No, it really doesn't, she thought with a newfound sensation of wonder. With everything that was the essence of her, she wanted him—wanted to know the sensual expression of being loved. *I want to know what it's like to be loved by this caring, gentle, vulnerable man. I want to kiss away the wants and seal the ache of any previous pain.* "No," she whispered aloud, "No."

Patrice sensed his relief. Not another word passed between them as Lawrence scooped her up in his arms. "Which way?"

ya ya ya ya

Save for the large bed on a platform in the center of the room, scant attention was paid to the mahogany furniture. Lawrence and Patrice stood facing each other, held captive by a timid tension that had begun to surround them the second he set her down on the floor.

Watching his face rapidly grow dark and serious, she frowned, her mind alive with questions. His hands were clenched at his sides and beads of perspiration were popping out across his forehead. She wondered anxiously whether he was having second thoughts.

"I won't be able to let you go, Patrice." He spoke at last, his baritone-pitched voice rasping a warning. "You're the only woman I've ever really wanted. Needed," he amended. "And I know I'll never be able to let you go."

Now she fully understood his hesitation: his vulnerability endeared him to her even more. *Emotions run deep in my man's soul,* she mused. However, so did the painful reminders of the brutal rejection he suffered at the hands of an insensitive and uncaring mother. Patrice couldn't blame him for wanting to ensure that he would be wholly received, for once the final threshold had been crossed, he would be committed to the end.

Lawrence knew he'd come after her with a determination that bordered on insanity, but he had his pride, too, and he'd never beg or force a commitment from her. The next step was hers. He willed her to take it towards him.

I know what I have to do, thought Patrice.

While watching the tender desire shining from Lawrence's eyes, Patrice pulled the straps of her jumpsuit slowly off both shoulders and wiggled out of the one-piece garment. The remainder of her clothes followed until she stood before him with nothing on but a sure expression—her brown eyes illuminating bold confidence. She saw him inhale deeply and close his eyes while his hands flicked open, then close again.

"There's no turning back for me, love," she whispered.

Patrice took a step towards him to take his hands and enfold them, palms open, over her smooth round breasts, her nipples firming instantly under his touch.

"I'm here for you. And I plan to be for a long time. I have a lot to give and I'll always give you the best that I've got. So, if you have any doubts about my love for you, be rid of them right now."

Her love pledge was like an emollient, healing the sore of doubt that had marred him for so long that he'd given up on ever experiencing an unselfish love.

"Patrice." His voice simmered with barely checked emotion.

The need to feel her naked brown splendor covering him like a silky cocoon rose like an intemperate, sweet ache. His hand, warm and damp, trembled against the side of her face. She held it in place, then pressed her lips into the salty palm before following the dark line of life there with a wet tongue.

Lawrence's insides seethed with ardent need, and a tormented moan gushed pass his lips under the onslaught of the teasing tongue. "Patrice," he whispered gravelly, lifting her off the floor to crush her to him.

He took her mouth with a savage intensity, forcing her lips open with a thrusting tongue, urgent and exploratory in her mouth. She clung fiercely to him, returning his kiss with equal abandonment.

As he lowered her to stand on the floor, the pressure of his mouth lessened, giving a dreamy intimacy to their kiss now. He tilted her chin and caressed her with his look; her lids were heavy with longing, her lips swollen from his ravishing kiss.

Her insides melted under the hot glow burning in his eyes, enlivened in a yellowish tint she'd never seen there before. They poured over her in an obsessive gaze that would have frightened her had she not shared the same keen need to know his possession.

"I don't have the right words to tell you how I feel inside," he murmured awkwardly. "How you make me feel. I wish..." his voice trailed off. "I wish I knew some of those flowery words that come so easily to those fantasy heroes."

She tried to still his apology, but he captured her hand. "No, I have to say this, my beautiful, precious woman." He paused, and for the first time since he'd stepped into the apartment, he smiled the smile that made her go weak in the knees. "I love you."

Tears formed in her eyes and began to stream quietly down her face. She raised on her toes to wrap her arms around his neck and smiled through the tears, caressing him with a radiant, watery gaze. "I don't need pretty words—simple ones will do. Simple words will do just fine."

And then she kissed him, lingering, savoring every feel of the strong hardness of his lips, warm and pliant under hers.

"I love you. I love you. I love you," he murmured munificently, his lips searing a path down her neck, her shoulders. "You are beautiful," he whispered reverently, his hand shaking slightly as it trailed down the middle of her chest to her abdomen, its feathery touch scorching her skin.

"Better than my dreams," he moaned, his lips continuing to explore her smooth flesh as he slid to his knees. Unrestrained whimpers echoed from her lips, and she clutched at his shoulders, a liquid heaviness settling in the center of her femininity. "Everything is so much better than my dreams."

His tongue flickered along the insides of her slim legs, and his lips brushed across the curly hairs at the junction between her thighs. Her whimpers grew into guttural moans, crying his name repeatedly as he tasted the secrets of her womanhood.

Lawrence wanted to love her as no other man ever had before. Or ever *will again*, he decided. He pushed his restraint to its limit until he could no longer bear the wonderful self-inflicted torture. *I have to have her. Now.*

Patrice moaned as he lay her down in the center of the bed where she watched while he stripped the sweats from his body and dropped them carelessly to the floor. Her breath was suspended in her heaving chest, her eyes consumed with need.

She had reached the brink of her endurance. She wanted to learn the feel of his velveteen flesh, the rich brown color of the earth; she was awed by the power and beauty of his wide chest and muscular well-toned thighs. "Lawrence." His name became a plea on her lips, a slender hand extended and welcoming.

She gasped, and genuine rapture lingered in the air as he lowered his body to settle between her parted thighs. He reclaimed her lips in a surprisingly tender, yet urgent kiss. Patrice embraced him with the force of the delirious hunger that was inside her.

She pulled her lips from his to place tingling kisses about his face and neck before teasing an ear with her hot, ragged breathing. Her body squirmed beneath him, her hands frantic as they moved downward, skimming both sides of his taut body. She traced the fullness of his mouth with a moist tongue and with a gentle hand began to stroke the hard maleness throbbing between her legs.

Lawrence groaned, long and hard, raining kisses about her face. She pleasured him in a pure and explosive manner, surpassing anything he'd every wished to experience. He covered her hand with his, encouraging her to guide him into her. She cried out as she took him into her warmth and clutched his shoulders, thrusting her hips upward to accept him fully.

"Mine," he groaned in impassioned possessiveness before a tongue slipped past her lips into the wet welcome of her hot mouth.

Marveling at the fit of their bodies in exquisite harmony with one another, she matched each powerful thrust he made into her. Gasps of sweet agony filled the air. Patrice wanted the sensations, like a tidal wave of pure pleasure, to last forever and wished she could prevent the inevitable.

Her body began to vibrate with liquid fire, and she cried out his name only seconds before he groaned rapturously, joining her in divine release. His slippery body collapsed atop hers; his shattered breathing mingled with the soft pants coming from her throat. He wrapped his arms around her and touched her with his eyes, before tracing the path of each glorious tear that rolled down her face with his tongue.

There was so much she wanted to tell him, but the words were misty thoughts in her head. She placed a finger on his mouth as she searched his gaze, her eyes incredulous beacons of wonder, signaling her love.

"Are you all right?" he asked, rolling on his back and cuddling her in his arms.

She smiled at him shyly, her face a blossom of ultimate happiness. "I'm fine," she said softly, before throwing her head back in a peel of laughter, declaring, "No, I'm better than fine." She quieted, adding in a tone of awe, "I, I never . . . I didn't believe . . . ."

He interrupted her stammering by placing a lone finger against her lips. "Shh. I know babe. I know," he said with a slight tremor in his voice, bathing her with loving eyes.

Lawrence felt he had captured a piece of heaven and never wanted to let it go. He kissed Patrice lightly on the mouth, then settled her comfortably in his arms and covered them both.

CHAPTER ❧ THIRTEEN

*P*atrice was storing the goods from one of the several bags of groceries the twins were carting into the kitchen. This was the last of her Saturday chores, and she was ready to claim time for herself before calling Lawrence. She leaned her back against the counter and hugged the bag of coffee to her bosom as her thoughts drifted, reliving the paradisal moments spent with him.

After enduring rabid teasing that he'd created a sex fiend—though her monstrous desire for him hadn't been all one-sided—they'd finally left Kit's around noon, driven by a hunger of another kind. Lawrence drove to an off-the-beaten-path seafood restaurant in Kemah (midway between Houston and Galveston) where he then explained about the photos and the incident of the previous night over stuffed crab and baked salmon.

"You might as well know it all now," he'd begun, preparing her for a revelation that was bound to set off her temper. "The private detective you hired, well, he handles the investigations for my firm."

"Your accounting company, you mean?" she had said, knowing she wasn't going to like the rest of what he had to say. Upon learning he had been responsible for Ross Kinney's sudden appearance, she was in no mood to follow his advice to "calm down."

"Then you can damn well pay for his services," she had thrown at him, stabbing at one of the cherry tomatos in her salad.

"You were right about one thing," he said.

"What's that?"

"Our relationship has never been and never will be dull, and we may well end up killing each other. You are by far the stubbornest woman I have ever met. And don't tell me there's no such word!"

She hadn't been able to contain her outburst of laughter, and even now, she chuckled over the incident. He'd gone on to speculate about the possible relationship between the red car that had been parked outside her home and the trashing of his office.

"Unless you have another jealous lover stashed some place," he had concluded jokingly, "then I'm at a loss about what's going on."

They'd had a good laugh about it, and that had ended the discussion about the threats, though she felt he had yet to disclose everything. But satisfied with their enthralled hand-holding atmosphere, she really hadn't cared.

After lunch they headed back to Treeland Heights and stopped off at his recently purchased town-house. He wanted to change clothes before picking up the twins from school. It was there that he made the casual remark, "I'm glad I haven't started furnishing this place," while giving her the grand tour of the barely furnished rooms. "I think we'll need something much bigger. And fairly soon."

To her suggestion that there was no need to buy another home, he replied in a tone that brooked no argument, "I provide for my family."

"His family." She could hear his voice, unflinching and proud, referring to her and the twins as his family. It made her proud too, and a little nervous to think they'd come to this point so quickly.

She was snapped from her woolgathering by a teasing Stephen, calling out, "Earth to Mom," his hands cupped like a megaphone. She laughed and socked him playfully before resuming her duty.

"We'll finish this, Mom," offered Stephenie, who began stacking can goods in the pantry.

"Oh, thanks," she replied, grateful to be rid of the tedious chore. Pulling the ribbon from her hair to let it fall around her shoulders, she began to think about upcoming plans.

First on the agenda was a long, relaxing bath, for the late-night hours were beginning to exact a toll. She yawned before announcing, "If I drown in the tub, don't move me until Monday," while stretching her designer-sweatsuit clad body.

"What if Lawrence calls before then?" Stephenie said tongue-in-cheek.

"Tell him...." She was about to quip, *Tell him to come over and join me,* but thought better of it and instead added, "I'll see him when he gets here."

The phone on the wall rang and her son said, "That's probably him now, so you can tell him yourself."

"Smarty pants," said Patrice before answering the phone. "Hel-lo," she said into the mouthpiece in a sultry, rhythmic tone for her lover.

But it was not Lawrence, nor anyone else she wanted to talk to. She gripped the phone with both hands as a chill shot up her spine, and her pulses accelerated to a quick, staccato beat. She covered her mouth with her hand to prevent the cry building in her from escaping. Her hand shook as she tried to calmly set the receiver in its cradle.

"That was quick," observed Stephen. "Must not have been Lawrence. Who was it, Mom?"

"Uh," she stammered, her mind racing in several different directions. Telling the twins is out of the *question,* she instantly decided.

"It was a wrong number," she replied with an indifferent shrug, and unconsciously began to help the twins put away the provisions.

Stephen and Stephenie exchanged puzzled glances before training concerned examinations on their mother. "Mom?"

Startled, she jumped, and the can of tomato sauce she was holding fell and rolled across the kitchen floor.

"Mom?!"

Stephenie cried her name anxiously, elongating the one syllable word into two. She grabbed Patrice's hand. "What's wrong?" she begged to know, sensing her mother's distress.

"Nothing. I just remembered something I was supposed to do," she lied hurriedly. She looked at her watch and exclaimed, "It's twelve-thirty. If you don't hurry, you won't be ready when Kit comes to pick you up."

That's good, thought Patrice. At least her wits had returned enough to remember that Kit was coming. *The twins would be safe with their godmother until I can figure out what to do.*

Stephen stared at her with skepticism before turning his back to place some packages of meats in the freezer compartment of the refrigerator. "I've changed my mind. We're not going."

Stephenie gave her brother a grand look of disbelief and opened her mouth to challenge him, but changed her mind. "I better call and tell her not to come then."

"No! No! No! You won't do any such thing," declared Patrice vehemently. She glared at her offspring with exasperation. Stilling nervous hands, she said in a steady voice, "I don't want you to cancel your plans. I happen to know that Kit has planned a big surprise for you, and I don't want you to spoil it for her. Do you hear me?"

A muscle twitched in Stephen's jaw. He inhaled deeply, staring at her defiantly from the corner of his eyes. "I said," he countered in a quiet, stubborn voice, "we're not going."

"And I said you are," retorted Patrice heatedly, shaking her finger at him.

Mother and son eyed each other combatively before Stephenie stepped between them, asking innocently, "Is Lawrence coming over?"

"What does that have to do with anything?" Patrice snapped, losing the little control she had on her temper.

"Well, if he's coming, you can get him to stay with you until we get back tomorrow," Stephenie replied as if it were the most natural solution to a difficult problem.

"Of all the arrogant, non . . ." Patrice shouted before she was interrupted by the ringing of the phone. She froze momentarily, then stomped across the room to answer.

"Hello," she barked impatiently after snatching the receiver off the hook. "Oh, hi." she said as she amended her tone considerably and leaned against the wall. "It's nothing. I'm sure," she said imploringly. "Really, Lawrence. No. Lawrence, wait!"

She sighed dismally and hung up the phone, then glowered at the twins, hands on her hips. "Now, see what you've done. He thinks he has to come over here and save us from something," she ranted, throwing her hands up in the air in bitter defeat.

"Good," declared Stephenie. "He can help you finish putting these groceries up while we pack." She grabbed Stephen's hand and pulled him from the kitchen, leaving Patrice stuttering unintelligibly.

ༀ　ༀ　ༀ　ༀ

Lawrence had arrived over thirty minutes ago, just as she was completing the task the children had abandoned.

His suspicion that something was troubling her was confirmed despite the gaiety she had pretended when he looked into those big brown eyes glazed with agitation. She had also been as skittish as a frightened cat, even cutting her index finger while slicing an apple.

They were now sitting silently at the dining room table, munching from a snack tray she insisted on preparing. He watched intently as she examined a slice of the pale yellowish Swiss, squinting her eyes to peep through the large holes before rolling it in a tubular shape. She held it to her mouth, but instead of taking a bite, dropped it onto the plate and wiped her hands on the napkin.

Quietly, the twins came into the room. The bright colors they wore, red, purple and yellow, contrasted sharply with the somber atmosphere. They spoke to Lawrence and plopped down on the chairs opposite the adults.

"Is it settled?" Stephen asked after a while, reaching for a cracker.

Patrice choked on the drink she was sipping, and Stephenie kicked her twin under the table.

"Ow, what did I say?" he asked, rubbing his ankle.

Restored from the slaps on her back by Lawrence, Patrice looked at her son menacingly. "If you say one more word, I swear I'll make the rest of your life so miserable . . ." The threat slipped past her lips before she realized what she was saying.

"Mom!" scolded Stephenie.

Patrice covered her face with her hands, then folded them on the table and apologized quietly to her son, "I'm sorry." But she was angry with him for assuming she had discussed her problem with Lawrence. It seemed that after fourteen years of taking care of her family, they suddenly decided she was no longer capable for the job.

Lawrence looked from Patrice to her son and back again. His mouth took on an unpleasant twist as he spoke. "All right, I've waited long enough for an explanation. I think somebody had better tell me what's going on," His patience had worn thin.

The twins' brows rose fractionally, otherwise they didn't move, shocked by the ominous sound of the hard, yet soft-voiced demand. They then risked curious glances at their mother's outwardly serene composure as she nibbled on a cracker.

"Patrice." Lawrence's deep voice resonated in a tone promising, *this is your last warning.*

She stalled, taking a sip of soda, then shifted in her seat. "What about your promise to let me handle my affairs without your interference?"

"I promised no such thing. It's a promise I wouldn't be able to keep as far as your welfare is concerned," he returned. "Now, stop this nonsense and tell me what happened," he barked, an open palm crashing down on the table, causing the three Masons to jump.

"I really don't want to talk about it in front of the kids," she said, looking at him from the corner of her eyes.

"A knowledgeable child is a wise child."

She stared contemplatively at him for several seconds, mulling over the significance of his words. She drew a deep breath before complying with the initial request. "I got a phone call."

"I figured as much. What did they say?"

"It was regarding the twins this time."

"What about us?" Stephen asked alertly, looking back and forth between Patrice and Lawrence. "Lawrence?" he added. He then looked across the table at Stephenie, wearing the expression of a brave soldier who knows the end is near.

Lawrence reached out and took Patrice's hand in his before speaking. "Your mother has been getting threats to bomb the concert if she doesn't cancel," he said in a tone that attempted to soften the blow of the message. "Those phone calls you thought were wrong numbers and pranks, weren't."

"But why? I don't understand!" cried Stephenie.

"Neither do we, sweetheart."

Patrice's mouth went dry. Just thinking of the message tore at her insides. "I'm sorry. I'm so sorry," she apologized to the twins, regret lining her every word.

"Aw, come on, Mom, you can't blame yourself for something like this," said Stephen.

"I tried not to involve you guys in this," Patrice continued as if she didn't hear Stephen, thinking if only she'd listened to Lawrence this wouldn't be happening.

"What did they say?" asked Lawrence as he stood and pulled her up and into the circle of his arms.

Patrice buried her head against his chest, finding comfort in the familiar feel of his strength and hugged him tightly around the waist. She was almost more afraid to tell him than she was of the implied threat to the twins' safety.

"Come on, tell me," he coaxed, stroking her back gently.

"They asked me if the twins were anti-apartheid supporters," she said in a teary-eyed voice, looking up in his face.

The room grew quiet.

Patrice saw Lawrence's eyes darken murderously, and his nostrils flared with the wrath building inside him. His muscles tensed in her embrace, and she tightened her arms around him, preventing him from moving away.

The twins made their way around the table, their faces ashy with the fear that burned in their eyes. With his hand outstretched, Lawrence drew them into the circle of his and Patrice's protective arms.

"I don't want you guys to worry," he said placing a tight clamp over his anger. "I'm going to take care of it, OK?"

❧ ❧ ❧ ❧

Meandering down the stairs, it dawned on Patrice she hadn't been in the house alone for quite some time. Though she now had the peace and quiet she used to long for, she found it wasn't the ideality she'd imagined it would be. When she reached the middle of the foyer, she wondered what to do with herself. ∗

The twins were gone. Kit and Martin had picked them up an hour ago for a hiking trip in Great Basin National Park somewhere near Las Vegas. Lawrence disappeared while she was in the shower, saying only that he'd be back shortly.

She started in the direction of the kitchen, then changed her mind, going instead to her bedroom. Once there, she turned on the stereo to a high volume, needing the noise to fill the uncomfortable silence. She sauntered aimlessly about the room, stopping in front of the shelf where her latest possession, a sturdy, black lion, stood out from the fragile glass figurines.

She picked up the burnished object and fingered the intricate detailing along its sleek body. The glabrous surface of the miniature king of the jungle was cool against her skin.

Her musings were interrupted by the telephone ringing, she jumped and fumbled with her lion, almost dropping it. After carefully returning the lion to his spot next to the crystalline bull, she strolled unhurriedly to lower the volume of the music. She harbored hope that the caller would grow impatient and hang up.

The streamlined instrument rang several more times before she picked up, "Hello," she answered with irritation in her voice.

"I thought age would have mellowed you out, but I see you're as uptight as ever," the caller delivered smoothly as though he'd rehearsed the line.

The bass pitch, the words uttered in a slow, seductive and measured rate were all vaguely familiar. She knew that voice, but couldn't put a name to the speaker. "Who is this?"

"Aw, I'm disappointed. I know it's been a long time, but I didn't think you'd forget."

No, Patrice hadn't forgotten after all, as shocked recognition raced through her. "Don? Don, is it really you?" With a tight grip on the phone, she dropped onto the side of the bed, her mouth open.

"Yeah, it's me, Patti girl. Every girl's dream and her lover's nightmare—the heart-breaker, the baby-maker, the Don Juan of day and nighttime, and in-between time—willing, ready and able to make you all mine. The . . ."

"All right," she said tiredly, putting an end to the radio rap he used to use when opening his show. She ran her fingers through her hair. Questions, a million of them, were crowding her brain. "How did you get this number?"

"I still have a few friends left in this town, even though you tried to turn everybody against me."

"Oh, cut the crap," she said sharply—thinking some things never change. "What do you want?"

"You haven't talked to me in almost fourteen years and all you can say is 'what do you want?'" When her only reply was a bored sigh, he said, "I'm hurt. I'm really hurt, Patti. I was hoping you'd invite me over so we could talk," he coached, "catch up on each other's life."

She held the phone away from her ear to stare at the instrument, disbelief contorting her features before replying. "That's not possible, Donald. Besides, we don't have anything to talk about. And I want you to lose my number."

"Don't hang up on me, Patti."

That soft tone with its menacing threat cut away the years of separation, transporting her back to the time when succumbing was the easiest, and by far, the safest thing to do.

"Look, Don," she started in a rationalizing tone before her mind balked, rejecting obedience to the fear that that voice evoked. "I don't have time to talk to you, I'm busy."

"Feeling brave now," he laughed tauntingly. "Your boyfriend must be there. But that's all right, Patti, I'll forgive you this indiscretion. When can we get together?"

"We can't, Don."

"I really need to see you, baby." His use of the endearing term made her cringe. "I want to see my kids. Can I at least visit my kids?"

Springing up from the bed, she replied, "At no time. Not now, not ever!"

"I figured the bitterness would have been gone by now and we could at least be friends," he said. "I would like for us to be friends, Patti."

"I'm sorry, Don," she spoke quietly, in control, and without apology, "but it's a little late, and friendship is out of the question. Good-bye." She set the receiver in its cradle.

No sooner had she turned to leave the room than the phone rang once more. She debated whether to answer, sure it was Donald calling back. *I am going to have to find a way of getting rid of him before he really becomes a nuisance,* she thought, while picking up on the fourth ring.

"Don," she said with exasperation, then fell silent.

Patrice's body began to tremble, talons of fear tore at her insides, ripping her apart as she listened to the messenger.

"You really out to give apartheid a try, Ms. Mason. You're denying Stevie and Stephie a wonderful growing experience."

Denial was wretched from her as she cried out, "No! No!" clutching the receiver to her bosom as she slumped to the floor.

"South Africa has some beautiful parks. Rather than hiking, you think they might enjoy a safari?"

Then the prankster laughed. It was a loud, wild laugh that lingered in Patrice's head even after she hung up the phone.

≥⪢ ≥⪢ ≥⪢ ≥⪢

Lawrence paced, never more than two or three feet from the phone in

Patrice's kitchen. He was crazy with worry, and stopped inconstantly to touch the back of the apparatus as though the power to make it ring was at his command. He had already removed his sweater because his activity made him hot; and even now, the white undershirt he wore was beginning to cling to his skin.

He looked at his watch. It was after eleven. The last time he saw Patrice was around three, roughly eight hours ago. He had gotten back around five-thirty, expecting her to be here. When she hadn't returned by six, and the twins phoned from Las Vegas to let her know they'd arrived safely, he alerted Ross that she was missing.

"What do you mean, missing?" Ross had asked.

"I mean she's not here and hasn't been since I got back right after leaving you!" he barked impatiently.

"Maybe she went shopping. What's three hours to a woman in a store?"

"Patrice is not like that. Plus, she never would have missed the twins' call," he said with gut-wrenching conviction.

"Speaking of calls," said Ross cautiously, "did you get around to what we discussed?"

"Yes, and you were right," he replied. The dime-size bugging device he had found in the phone in her bathroom was wrapped in a plastic bag in his coat pocket. "I'll get it to you as soon as I can. I don't know why I didn't think to check it out a long time ago."

"Maybe you're too close?" suggested Ross sagaciously in a soft, rhetorical tone.

"Yeah," breathed Lawrence. "But I don't think she went shopping. And I don't want to leave in case she calls."

"OK, how do you want to handle this?"

"You've got an army of informants out there, find her," he said with quiet desperation in his voice.

Charles and J.T. had been called, as had the radio station. No one had seen her. Lawrence didn't know who else to call. So many different scenarios about her whereabouts had been painted in his mind he didn't know what to think anymore. All he could do was wait and hope she was safe.

The phone rang, jarring Lawrence from his turbulent musings. He snatched the phone off the hook, "Hello." He sagged tiredly against the wall, "Oh, hi, Roger," disappointment in his voice. "No, she's not here at the moment. Yes, I'll tell her you called." He replaced the phone, dropped in a chair at the table, and propped his head in his hands.

"Patrice, where are you?" he whispered harshly, not with anger, but with frustration at his powerlessness.

He sprang from the chair and began to saunter about the room, his hands in his pockets. All this waiting and not knowing was eating away at him. Just as he began to entertain thoughts of going out to search for her himself, he heard the front door open and sprinted from the kitchen.

ॐ ॐ ॐ ॐ

"Where have you been?" Lawrence asked, crushing Patrice to him. He pulled back to examine her with hands that trembled and shook as they touched her face.

She mistook the glaze in his eyes, and asked anxiously, "Lawrence, what's the matter? Is it the twins? Are they all right? Have they called?"

"The twins are fine," he replied quickly to allay her fear. "It's you I've been worried about. Where have you been?" Giving her no time to answer, he pulled her to him urgently, his head descending to capture her lips in a painstakingly gentle kiss. "If you scare me like that again, I'll throttle you," he promised in an affected voice.

"I'm sorry," she said, smiling tenderly into his face. Now that she had the opportunity, she read the look in his eyes for what it really was. "I didn't mean to upset you. I should have called. I guess I wasn't thinking. Forgive me?"

"You're safe, that's all that matters," he said, drawing an exhausted breath. "I think I need a drink. How 'bout you?"

"Yes," she sighed in a whispery voice. "Just let me hang my jacket up and I'll join you in the living room."

He nodded agreeably, and stole a quick kiss from her lips. He watched her go down the hall to her room as though afraid to let her out of his sight before heading to get a much needed drink.

When Patrice joined him, he was sitting on the couch, drink in hand. She picked up the brandy filled glass from the table and took a small swallow, then set the drink down.

"Want to tell me about it?"

She smiled wanly, remembering there was a time when he would have insisted strenuously and not asked quite so politely. But the smile fell, replaced by a thoughtful expression. She folded her hands in front of her, wondering where to begin, how to make him understand her decision.

"You know," she started hesitantly, "I've never been politically active. I mean, pass voting and making a few contributions, politics of any sort was far removed from my life. At least, that's what I thought." She fell silent and dropped to her knees next to him. "I didn't see any connection between running a radio station and the politics of the world. But, this apartheid thing, I don't know."

She picked a piece of lint on the leg of his pants before staring him directly in the eyes. "When I began to understand what it meant, that people were killing and being killed for something more precious than equal or civil rights, I felt I had to do something. I didn't know what specifically, but I have access to a powerful medium, and the authority to use it the best way I can."

Patrice hoped she was making herself clear. His face was so damnably aloof, she didn't know if he was purposely being that way as not to influence her, or whether he understood what she was trying to say.

She lightly pounded his thigh, then pushed herself up.

"Apartheid is wrong in so many ways I can hardly count them. But I can feel the injustice as though I'm there in the middle of that violent hatred." She stopped to take a sip from her drink. "To answer your very first question of where I've been. . . ." She took another sip of the brown liquid. "When I left, I didn't know where I was going. I had to get away from the phone, the instrument of my despair." With a bitter smile, "My personal apartheid, if you will."

"You got another call."

She briefly closed her eyes and shook her head. "Yes. Suggesting my children would somehow benefit under apartheid rule," she said with a hollow laugh. "I sped out of here like I was being chased by a demon. I guess I was in a way. I drove around for hours, trying to convince myself that my children were safe. There was a lot of you in my rationale," she said softly, smiling at him.

"But fear—god, that's an ugly word!—won out, so I went to the station and wrote this eloquent announcement about why we had to cancel the concert. Of course, there was no mention of the threats," she added matter-of-factly, but her eyes glazed with unshed tears. Lawrence took the drink from her hand and gently pulled her next to him.

"I tore it up." There was pride in her voice. "Don't you see, I couldn't do it. It would be like living under apartheid rule. Having someone telling me how to live my life. Before long, he'd be calling to give more orders, making more demands. I'd be a hostage to him and my fear, and so would my children, and so would you. I can't live like that, Lawrence. No one, nowhere on this earth should have to live like that!"

Though he hadn't said anything, nor showed any emotion, his mind was absorbing what she said and relating it to an experience close to him. There were a lot of mistakes made in Vietnam, a lot of waste of human life and property. And he didn't understand a lot of it, primarily because he didn't want to remember his part. But the bottom line was the same. He'd fought for a people he didn't know, just so they could have an opportunity at free choice. *How could I call myself a freedom loving man and not do the same for the woman I love?* he thought, squeezing her to him.

"I know, baby. And I won't let that happen," he pledged, brushing his lips across her forehead.

"Do you think I did the right thing?"

"As long as you believe it's right, that's all that matters to me. "I'll back you up regardless."

"Thank you," she murmured against his chest, wrapping her arms around his waist. "I'm so tired," she yawned.

"Come on," he said rising, "let me put you to bed," and scooped her up in his arms.

CHAPTER ❧ FOURTEEN

Never have I had so little and felt so good, thought Patrice. It was as though a rainbow were planted in her heart and now beamed its colorful rays throughout her body.

She was sitting behind her desk at the station, twisting a pencil between white teeth and daydreaming—sweet remembrances of the weekend burning in her mind. The joy she felt spilled out in laughter. Lawrence Woodson had ruined her for life. She had told him as much when he brought her breakfast in bed yesterday morning.

"I could get use to this."

"Then maybe you should come to the table," he had teased, giving her a purely masculine grin. She tried telling herself if wouldn't always be that way, but she couldn't and wouldn't believe her own warning, not for a moment.

The bell on her private phone rang and assuming it was the man now occupying her thoughts, an uninhibited smile came to her face, and she picked up, saying, "Hi," in a lazy, seductive voice.

"Must have been expecting somebody else to call," the caller complained. "I know that sweet sexy voice ain't for me."

Patrice bolted to attention, "Don, what do you want?" she asked, her voice now hard and cold.

"I was hoping you were in a better mood today, since you were so busy

Saturday and didn't have time to talk to me. Now that you've had a chance to get used to me being back in your life, I figured you'd give me a few of your precious moments during business hours."

"Nothing's changed, Don. You're completely out of my life, and I'm still busy."

"Then I'll just get right down to business."

"Oh?" Though her tone was casual Patrice was suffering a paroxysm of apprehension.

"Yeah. You see, I've been invited in on a big deal that could make me a very rich man. But, well you know how it is. Or, at least, you should, you didn't always used to be a big shot general manager," bitterness had crept in his voice. "Anyway, I'm a little short on the up front dough. And I know you wouldn't want to deny me the opportunity to enjoy financial independence like yourself."

She should have guessed immediately that he wanted something, and silently cursed herself for believing even momentarily that it was anything other than money prompting his call.

"No way," she retorted.

"Here's the deal I'm prepared to offer," he continued as though she hadn't spoken. "You loan me fifty g's, and I won't take you to court for joint custody of my two darling children. They're kind of tall for their age, aren't they? What are they, thirteen, fourteen, now?"

Patrice was speechless, and when her voice returned, the outrage she felt caused her words to trip over each other unintelligibly. "I...You... How dare...I...." In response to his callous snickering, she screamed, "You sick animal! No judge in his right mind would allow you within one foot of the children you deserted long before they were born!"

"A judge might not," he snarled, "but I'm right across the street from this very expensive and very private school where you send them. It must cost you a pretty penny, Patti."

Sheer black fright squeezed her chest, wringing the blood from her face. Feeling as though she were going to be sick from the bitter taste in her mouth, Patrice clamped her hand over her mouth.

"Don't worry, Patti," he cajoled. "I'm not gonna touch your precious children. Unless," he paused significantly, "you don't get me the bread by Friday."

She jumped up from her seat and began pacing around the desk, rubbing her forehead with an agitated hand. The deadline flashed across her eyes in bold letters and the days of the week sped through her brain in fast-forward motion.

"Where do you expect me to get that kind of money from?" Her attempt at a placid composure failed, her cracked voice echoing in her ear.

"You still chummy with 'Red' aren't you? I hear she's a big time vice-president at a bank in town."

"No. I won't do it," she replied hotly without thinking.

"Then, my dar-ling," he crooned, "you get it by any means necessary. Or, I'll take those kids faster than you can say ra-di-o," he warned. "That's fifty thousand by this Friday."

Believing he was about to hang up, she asked, "How will I reach you?" in desperation.

"You won't. I'll contact you. And Patti, now that I think about it, make that a gift, not a loan."

He hung up on Patrice, leaving her clenching the phone. The disconnected tone grated in her ear moments before reaching her consciousness, and she silently replaced the receiver.

Patrice's body began to shake uncontrollably, and she hugged herself tightly. "Do something! Do something!" her brain commanded, badgering the stupefied inertia into relinquishing its hold over her.

With clumsy fingers, she punched out a number on the phone, deciding the first course of action. In her impatience for someone to answer the ringing line, she nervously rapped the top of her desk with a pencil. *Finally!* she said to herself before speaking, "Mr. Carrington, please. Then let me speak to his assistant, Mrs. Hamilton. Yes, I'll hold."

Just as she was replacing the receiver, Ellen Conway walked in carrying a handful of letters. "I need your signature on these so I can get them out in the noon mail," she said, placing the papers on the desk.

"Marie," said Patrice, rubbing the back of her neck and shoulders as she looked around the room. She corrected herself, remembering Ellen was filling in for a sick Marie. "Ellen, I'm sorry," she apologized, "they'll have to wait." She picked up her briefcase from the side of the couch, explaining, "Something urgent has come up and I have to leave. Where did I put my purse?" she asked in agitation, scanning the room.

"Right here," said Ellen, looking at Patrice curiously as she pulled open a drawer on the desk, then held up the leather handbag. "Marie told me this is where you usually keep it. And I'm to remind you not to forget the cancellation announcement. Marie said you'd know what I was talking about."

Patrice looked at Ellen with a blank expression, then snapped her fingers, remembering she hadn't notified the staff of her latest decision. "No, I'm supposed to go over that in the staff meeting, but that will have to be cancelled, too," she replied, scampering across the room to get her overcoat. "Everything is on hold," she added while sliding her coat on.

"Now, you know you have a banquet for the hair-care people tonight. Is that off, too?" asked Ellen, taking notes.

Patrice wished Marie were here, then she wouldn't have to deal with these little tedious decisions. She'd just have to trust Ellen.

"Just handle it, Ellen, OK?" said Patrice. "I'm gone and won't be back today." With her hand on the doorknob, added, "I'll call tomorrow and update you."

🐚 🐚 🐚 🐚

"My money is on this one," said Lawrence, passing the photo across his desk to Ross.

"Aww, come on, Lawrence. There's been nothing unusual going on here," he added, shaking the photo before turning it face down on the desk. "I think you're grasping at straws."

"Call it intuition. Have you had time to check for fingerprints?"

"Give me a break, you just got it to me last night."

"I'm sorry," Lawrence said, "I know I'm pushing," he started, then fell silent. He got up from the chair and began strolling around the room, a pensive expression on his face. "Something is gonna break real soon." He turned to face Ross. "I can feel it, R.J., I can feel it."

Though Ross didn't always agree with Lawrence, he'd come to trust his instincts. "I'll get a man on Patrice and one on the twins before the morning's out."

"Good."

"I've already put a tap on her phone at the station."

Lawrence whistled. "Boy, is she gonna love that."

"She won't know unless you get a guilty conscience," Ross tossed at him with a significant lifting of his brow.

Lawrence chuckled. "No man, not this time," he said, smiling in memory of what had occurred in this very room. It hadn't been funny at the time, but the ending made every bit of the hell he'd gone through worth it.

The sound of a beeper went off and Ross pulled a small, gray gadget from his inside coat pocket.

"It's my man monitoring her calls," said Ross standing to lean across the desk to reach the phone. Before picking up the receiver, the phone rang. He answered, "Hello. Who's calling? Just a minute." Holding the receiver out to Lawrence, "It's Dr. Black's secretary."

Lawrence looked at his watch. "Tell her I'm on my way."

Ross relayed the message, then cleared the line before dialing.

"We have a meeting with the regent's chairman," Lawrence said to Ross, straightening his tie. "Let me know what's going on. If it's urgent, have my secretary come and get me."

Ross nodded as Lawrence walked out.

?& ?& ?& ?&

Patrice bounced up from the couch to resume the pacing she'd started ever since she walked in the house from picking up the twins. The rote speech the cops had delivered still rang in her head.

"Since no crime has been committed, Mrs. Mason, there's very little we can do. It's your word against his. If he has any traffic violations, then maybe we could pick him up and ask him a few questions, but it wouldn't be official. It's like I said before, no crime has been committed. Our hands are tied. I'm sorry."

"Damn you, Donald!"

She fell to the couch and wrapped her arms around her legs, burying her face against her thighs.

"Why didn't you tell me your ex-husband called you?"

Patrice shuddered at the ruthless emotion in his voice, cold and exact, before looking up. Lawrence was standing in the doorway like a post, arms hanging rigid, waiting. Raw hurt glittered in his eyes.

She opened her mouth to explain, but the feeble excuse on her lips wouldn't come. A new anguish seared her heart as she realized there was no reason good enough to salve the wound. Her lids slipped down her over eyes, stinging with new tears and she shook her head from side-to-side.

"Where are the twins?" He asked tiredly while tossing his coat over the back of the couch.

"In their rooms. I sent them upstairs," she replied, too ashamed to face him. She felt the couch sag when he sat down, not near her, but on the opposite end. And then she did look up and followed the direction of his gaze. He was staring up at the picture over the fireplace, his hands loosely clasped between his legs. She reached her hand out to him.

"Lawrence?" He stiffened, and she pulled her hand back.

The silence between them stretched, the air thickening with unspoken pain and despair. Torment was eating at her from the inside, having her lover near, yet so far away.

"How did you find out?" she asked in a small voice.

"That's not important," he replied. "What's important is what do you plan to do about it?"

"I don't know," she shrugged. "What do you think I should do?" she asked, anxious to break down the wall he'd erected, one brick at a time if need be. He tilted his head to stare—his eyes were icy and distant. "Please don't look at me like that," she cried, sliding across the seat to wrap her arms around his shoulders, which tensed in her embrace. "No, don't," she begged, squeezing him tightly. "Please."

"Do you still love him?"

She looked at him incredulously through her tears. "Are you serious?" she asked, scooting away from him. "Is that what you believe? After what's happened between us, how could you even think that?"

"You tell me what I'm supposed to think," he said with jealousy and hurt. He sprang from the couch. "The woman I love gets a threatening call from her ex-husband, but she keeps quiet like she's trying to protect him. I have to find out from some stranger monitoring her phone that her ex called more than once!" he stated. "Tell me Patrice, what am I supposed to believe?"

"You bugged my phone at the office?"

"Yes, I did," he replied loudly. "And, I'm having the same done to these phones!" he said in a tone daring her to disagree.

"Are you two having an argument?" asked Stephenie in a casual tone from the doorway. Stephen was at her side.

"I thought I told you to go up to your room," said Patrice.

"Your mother and I are having a disagreement," replied Lawrence.

"Since you're just having a disagreement and not an argument, can we go and get something to eat?" suggested Stephen. And sliding his hand under his sweater to rub his stomach, added, "I'm starved. When we get back, Stephenie and I will go back upstairs and let you finish your disagreement in peace. We promise, don't we Stephenie?"

≈ ≈ ≈ ≈

"Come eat something, baby," called Lawrence, strolling into the living room. He wore an apron over a light blue shirt with the sleeves rolled up to his elbows.

"I'm not hungry," Patrice said, kicking her boots out the way. She crossed her legs at the knee and folded her arms across her middle in disgust, then stuck her thumb nail in her mouth.

"I know," he said, sitting next to her and folding her in his arms, "but you need to come sit down with the twins." He kissed her cheek lightly, his warm breath fanning the side of her face. "They're trying real hard to be brave for you, but they're as nervous as kittens."

"Yes, I know," she sighed tiredly. "They've been my one shining moment of success. Everything I've worked for means nothing without them. And I'm the one who has put them in danger. . . ." she stopped, unable to continue.

"That's not true and you know it. They know everything you've done was done for them. And they're proud of you. Stephenie was praising your name when we went out, like she was trying to sell me a product. Mark my words, when you get your own station, you won't have to look further than the front door for a manager."

"She told you my secret ambition?" Patrice asked, amazement in her voice.

"No, your son did that," he corrected gladly.

A proud smile curved her mouth and contentment warmed her as she snuggled her head against his chest.

"You've done a good job, Ms. Mason," he said in a tone filled with awe and respect.

She swallowed the lump that formed in her throat. "Oh, Lawrence, if anything happened to my babies..." she started in a voice that came from far away.

What she'd felt over the thought of being forced to cancel the concerts did not come close to comparing with what she was feeling for Donald. The hate she harbored towards him was absolute, and untainted by remorse. It was a tiresome, frightening feeling, but unequaled when stacked against the menace he posed to his own children.

Patrice pushed herself upright, her hands balled into hard fists. "I could kill him with my bare hands. To think that he could even utter the threat to take my children!"

"Hush now," Lawrence cut her off, not liking the irrational sound in her voice anymore than he did her declaration. Even though he understood the venomous hostility circling her thoughts, he knew that people who reacted emotionally often made costly mistakes. He took her hands and gently pried open her fingers. "Nothing is going to happen," he vowed. *When or if it gets to that point, I'll just have to be standing by. And heaven help the poor bastard then.*

She stared into his eyes, and a sense of strength overwhelmed her. "I love you," she whispered, her palms flat against the wall of his chest.

"In spite of my overbearing, overprotective and jealous nature?"

"Because of them," she affirmed. Her face became radiant, a smile emerged, and it was filled with life and with love.

In one forward motion, Patrice was crushed against Lawrence, and his mouth fastened on hers for a kiss that sponsored shivers of delight.

"Come on." There was a faint tremor in his voice as he turned her about face. "Before I embarrass both of us." He marched her to the dining room, where the twins were whispering to each other across the table.

"Mom, are you OK?" The question was from Stephen, who stood while Lawrence seated her at one end of the table.

"Nope. I'm better than OK," she replied with a giddy sense of pleasure, her happiness pouring in laughter.

"Dig in," encouraged Lawrence, sitting at the other end. "It's not as good as your Mom's, but it's filling," he said, lightening the mood.

Patrice filled her plate, while her twins watched, uncertain at first, before following her example. Cartons of Chinese dishes of rice, vegetables, chicken and shrimp were passed noisily around the table.

Together, Patrice and Lawrence generated a family atmosphere throughout dinner, and the twins bounced back with their usual witty bantering. She knew had it not been for his presence, she wouldn't have been able to pull it off.

Though dinner had been a wonderfully relaxed affair, reality was never far away. Lawrence wondered how much longer he could sit quietly on the side-line, while his woman wrestled with possibly the biggest decision she's ever had to make as a parent. As she gazed into the toasty fire with her arms wrapped around her huddled form, she seemed totally lost.

The sound of the doorbell startled Patrice from her reverie. Undaunted by Patrice's curious glance in his direction, Lawrence went to the door and returned with Ross Kinney.

"Good evening, Ms. Mason," he said, flashing a boyish grin.

"Mr. Kinney," she greeted with a nod.

"Have a seat, Ross. Can I get you something?"

"Not now, thanks," replied Ross, dropping into the couch nearest him. "First, I want to fix up your phones," he said, digging into his satchel.

"Do we have to do that, Lawrence?"

Ross said, "Look, that can wait. I'm sure you're anxious to hear what I've found out. . . Maybe a cup of tea isn't a bad idea. Please, Patrice."

When Patrice left the room, the men sat. Ross pulled a notebook from his satchel, murmuring, "I'll leave the stuff in the trunk of your car, and you can put it in when it's convenient."

"Thanks, R.J."

"Anything for a friend. And a fee, of course," he chuckled. "Now..." he said, opening the notebook.

"Let's wait until Patrice gets back," said Lawrence.

"You sound like a man who's known hot water," teased Ross.

"Bathed in it as recently as a couple of hours ago, as a matter of fact," Lawrence returned.

"It happens to the best of us. Does she have any friends?"

Moments later, Ross was holding his cup of tea while explaining to Patrice and Lawrence, "I was able to trace the origination of that computer threat."

"How?" Patrice wanted to know. "The power went out in the whole building. The police said you trace a computer call the same way you do a phone call. You have to the keep the caller on the line for three minutes."

Ross took a sip of the hot, minty liquid before answering. "I got lucky. This is good," he said slightly lifting the cup. "What brand is this?"

"I'll buy you a case," said Lawrence, impatient to hear the latest developments. Since Don had come on the scene, he'd begun to revise his earlier suspicion that somebody at the station was involved, namely Marie.

"Part of your suspicion was right," Ross directed at Lawrence, then to Patrice, "A radio station employee is involved, but not at KHVY."

Though relieved none of her employees were involved, Patrice still found it hard to believe that one of her competitors would help her ex-husband.

"KFFY AM," supplied Ross, singing the station's call letters rhythmically.

"That's absurd!" exclaimed Patrice, springing from her seat. "That was the first station I worked for," she said excitedly, marching to stand near the fireplace. "I know Arnold Maxey very well. He'd never do a thing like this."

Raising a hand in mock surrender, Ross stated, "I'm not saying he did it or authorized it. But somebody who works at that station with access to the computer did."

"How? Why?" she asked.

"The how is simple," replied Ross with a self-satisfied grin on his face. "Whoever had access got a little too cocky. And, as most overly conceited people do"—he smiled knowingly—"they had to leave some sign that they're more clever than anybody else." He shook his head before continuing. "A whole game was designed. And very creatively, I might add. They covered their game using the billing codes the station has for its clients."

"Not that many people in the station would have that kind of access," Patrice pointed out quietly, knowing how guarded that information was kept. "Wait a minute," she added, snapping her finger, "Client billing codes? But wait a minute—KHVY is not a client of KFFY."

"That's what threw me off," said Ross, scooting to the edge of his seat. "Until," he added, "I figured that the billing codes assigned Heavy and the concert halls that received the same message you did, all had the same billing entry dates. But," he accented, "they didn't have instructions assigned to the real clients."

"So, now what do I do? Call Arnold up and ask him if he knows someone at his station has been sending bomb threats on his computer?" asked Patrice sarcastically. She dropped to the couch in disgust and crossed her arms.

"Not yet," replied Ross. "I have an idea who the culprit might be," he said and cast a sly wink in Lawrence's direction, "but not a motive."

Lawrence thought to speak up, but decided against it. Instead he pulled Patrice into his embrace and kissed her lightly on the forehead.

Ross continued, seemingly disinterested in the affectionate display he'd seen from the man, who as recently as two months ago he would have bet a grand would never let a woman get under his skin. He wondered what powers Patrice Mason had.

"A young college student . . ." started Ross.

"Who drives a red sports car," interrupted Lawrence.

"Name's Tracey Tarrant," he said, looking at Patrice for recognition. At her non-acknowledgement, he said, "Don't worry. I have a couple of leads I haven't tracked down yet. Do you know a man calling himself Jay Roberts?"

"Not off hand," replied Patrice. "What does he do?"

"Do?" said Lawrence snidely, unable to keep the disdain from his voice.

"He told your secretary . . ., " started Ross.

"My secretary?" asked Patrice, cutting a side-long glance of anger at Lawrence.

"Uh, well, like I was saying," continued Ross. "He told Marie he was a car salesman. And as far as we can tell, she doesn't know he sells shoes.

"In the store right across the street from the station," Lawrence supplied.

"But, they have an interesting, shall I say, relationship," finished Ross.

"Mr. Kinney, certainly Lawrence has told you of my disdain for the snooping into my employees' personal lives. As long as it doesn't concern the station, they can do whatever they please as far as I'm concerned."

"Come on, honey. R.J.'s only doing his job. If he didn't, he'd have me to deal with."

"Something tells me I might stand a better chance with you, Larry."

"I'm sorry, Mr. Kinney."

"Ross, or R.J., please. I keep looking over my shoulder, waiting for my Dad to step out from some corner or something."

"Excuse me." Everyone turned to see Stephen, standing in the doorway. "Mr. Woodson, telephone."

Lawrence excused himself and left the room.

"It's not that I'm ungrateful, Ross. I guess I'm feeling overwhelmed. Lawrence seems to have called in a platoon of people and I . . . " she fell silent, embarrassed by her outburst.

"He doesn't want to take any chance on anything happening to you or your children," said Ross quietly, weighing her with a critical squint. "I'm sorry, I was out of line."

"No, you weren't," sighed Patrice. "I'm the one who should be ashamed," she whispered in a contrite voice. "Can I get you more tea?"

ва ва ва ва

Martin and Kit arrived unexpectedly, bumping into Ross on his way out. The couple had been on their way to an evening of elegant dining when they detoured at Kit's insistence. She had phoned earlier and learned of Don's extortion from her god-children.

Kit and Patrice were sitting in the dimly lit sun porch off the back of the den, looking across the way at the men battling the twins in a game of Pictionary. Every now and then, Patrice observed Kit's eyes seek out Martin.

Kit's enthrallment with Martin was understandable, she thought, seeing him as she imagined Kit did. He was devilishly handsome in the French cut, pearl gray suit, his firm mouth curled as if always on the edge of laughter. The fact that he'd lasted as long as he had spoke volumes, for Kit was as bad as she'd been when it came to men—they were both very picky women.

A swath of wavy hair fell to Martin's forehead, and when he pushed it from his face, his compelling blue eyes sought out Kit, as if assuring himself that she was near.

While Patrice was delighted for Kit, her mind kept straying to the fifty thousand dollars she had to come up with by Friday. Deep consternation shadowed her face as she drummed restless fingers on the glass table.

"Will you stop that?" said Kit, reaching out to clamp Patrice's hand to the table.

Patrice wiggled her hand free, then dropped them to her lap. Barely two seconds passed before she began the rapping again.

"Talk to me," urged Kit. "What's going on in that brain of yours?" When Patrice didn't respond promptly, Kit whispered harshly, her teeth gritted, "Patrice!"

"I've got to come up with that money, Kit, and I don't know where I'm going to get it from," she murmured, then stuck an index finger in her mouth.

"Certainly you're not serious! You can't be!"

Four heads turned in their direction, and both women fell silent.

"Yes, I am," Patrice whispered firmly.

Kit slapped her hand against her forehead in exasperation as Patrice jumped up. Receiving curious glances from the game players, Patrice hurriedly passed them and went straight to the hall closet. She pulled down a leather bound book labeled "Family Business" from the top shelf and marched off to her room. After getting a pencil from the night table, she crawled to the middle of the bed and opened the book.

"What are you doing now?" asked Kit, startling Patrice with an abrupt entrance. Kit glanced over Patrice's shoulder, and a knowing look came over her face. She dropped on the side of the bed and crossed her legs at the knee, a satin shoe peeking from under the long, shimmering turquoise gown.

"I'm not going to let you mortgage this house, or sell your stocks, or any damn thing else to get money to give Don," she said in a belligerent tone.

Patrice returned Kit's stubborn gaze, and lost the staring contest. She threw the pencil on the opened book and pressed a hand to her head, grappling with the best way to make Kit understand why she had to do any and everything in her power to protect the twins.

"We're talking about my children's safety," she said simply. "I won't rest one minute worrying whether or not Don will make good on his promise."

"And what's to stop him from coming back in two weeks, holding their safety over your head for another fifty thousand? Or even more?" Kit argued logically.

Patrice sighed deeply, then pressed her lips together and stared up at the ceiling. She was totally vulnerable—Don had her between the proverbial rock and hard place. She had asked herself 'what if' a million times.

"I'll just have to take him at his word," Patrice said finally, voicing the only hopeful answer she could muster.

"Fat chance!" retorted Kit, raising fine, arched eyebrows as she sprang to her feet. She stared at her friend with the most incredulous look Patrice had seen. "I don't believe you," said Kit, shaking her balled fists. "When has that creep's word ever been truthful?"

Silence filled the room as Patrice recognized the undeniable fact Kit pointed out. They both knew Don was the biggest liar in the world. If the truth would serve him better, he'd lie anyway. Yet, the risk to her children robbed her of reason.

Her dark worried gaze followed Kit's agitated prance about the room. "Kit," she pleaded, "you of all people must understand how I feel."

With her hands clasped together below her chin, Kit replied in an emphatic voice, "I do. I really do," she added, returning to sit on the edge of the bed. "I look at them now sometimes and I'm amazed that they're the same two people we used to cuddle like baby dolls." Her voice took on a wispy quality as she relived both the wonders and the horrors of experiencing those growing years. "I remember relieving you when they were going through colic, teething, potty training, swimming lessons, piano lessons, not to mention the arguments you and I had, and still have about their clothes. Yeah, I understand. They're my kids, too, you know."

"Then you have to agree that I have to do anything in my power to get Don out of our lives, no matter the cost."

"Good grief, Patrice, it's not about money!" said Kit. "We wouldn't even have to leave the house to come up with fifty thousand. I'm against us giving in to Don's extortion! Let the police handle it," she pleaded.

"They can't handle anything unless there's something to handle!" replied Patrice angrily, rolling off the bed. "I'm sorry, Ms. Mason, but our hands are tied," she mimicked in a mocking tone. "The police have demonstrated time and time again that they are not the people I want to entrust my children's lives with," she added, pacing around the room, her arms crossed. "I just can't take that chance. I'm going to give him the money," she said conclusively, at which Kit uttered an explitive. "But, he'll have to meet me at my lawyer's office and sign a statement that he'll stay out of our lives."

"Of all the stupid . . . dumb . . . asinine . . . Oooo, forget it!" rambled Kit excitedly. She threw up her hands before stomping from the room, slamming the door behind her.

Patrice sighed and slumped to the floor, her back leaning against the bed. A tentative knock at the door interrupted her turbulent thoughts, and she dragged herself to her feet. "Come in."

The twins lumbered into the room. The stern pout on Stephen's mouth and the sad glaze in Stephenie's eyes convinced her she was making the right decision.

"Did you guys win?" she asked, forcing a gaiety she was far from feeling.

"Dad wouldn't really steal us would he?" her daughter asked bluntly.

"I don't want you to worry about it. It's not going to happen."

Though her reply was courageous, she prayed silently. Patrice shoved the notebook to one corner of the bed, making room for the twins to join her. Seated between them, she draped her arms across their shoulders.

"You two little crumb-snatchers mean more to me than anything in the world. I hope you know that. In any case," she added seconds later, "I'm going to make sure your father never bothers us again."

"Aunt Kit said you're going to pay him off," Stephen said in sullen belligerence.

"Yes. I'm going to make him sign a statement in front of a lawyer."

"But what if he doesn't sign?" the twins asked as one.

Patrice licked her lips nervously before replying, "He will."

The twins fell quiet, basking in the security of their mother's arms. However, both quietly wondered what it would be like if she were wrong and their father kidnapped them.

"Mom," Stephenie started, "did you love him?"

The shock of the question held Patrice temporarily immobile. *How can—should I answer that? she wondered.*

"I believed I did at the time," she said in a shallow, choking voice. In the another region of the house, Patrice heard the rumble of masculine laughter coming from the family room. Lawrence's voice was easily distinguishable; its full, hearty baritone color was recorded in her brain. A secretive smile softened her face, and a light shone in the honey gaze, "I realize now I was infatuated with a pretty face and a smooth talker."

"Because of Lawrence?" suggested Stephen rhetorically.

Patrice chuckled, "Yes, because of Lawrence," with a broad grin.

"How did you meet, uh, tck," her son stammered when hard pressed to utter the paternal title given biological fathers.

She laughed, ruffling his hair. "You can call him Don."

"He hasn't been a father, and I don't think he deserves the title," Stephen justified gruffly.

"All right, all right, calm down," she said indulgently.

"What was he like?"

Should I tell them the truth? That their father was a cruel, petty man who was so sure the world evolved around him. And that he always had to be in the spotlight and didn't care who he hurt to get there.

"I heard about him before Arnie hired him," she said in a trance-like tone, remembering the big build-up the station had created around the great, 'Don Juan' coming to KFFY. "Then when I saw him in Arnie's office, I thought he was the most beautiful man I'd ever laid eyes on. He always wore black silk, except during winter when he'd exchanged silk for leather. Always black, and the shirt was always opened to expose his chest, and his pants fit like gloves."

"Sounds like a sissy to me," Stephen commented.

"Back then, we called it sexy," she said in a teasing tone, then fell solemn. Her heart fluttered mildly as feelings of guilt surfaced.

"I know we've never talked about it, your father I mean. Have you missed not having a father?"

"Aww, Mom," cried Stephenie boringly.

"No, I want to know the truth," she said seriously.

"We certainly didn't miss the bas... I mean, Don," retorted Stephen, springing to stand by the window.

"I never thought to tell you about him. It was a topic I didn't want to remember. Maybe I was wrong about that."

"No, you weren't, Mom," said Stephenie. "Stephen and I hardly ever thought about it. With so many of our friends whose parents are divorced, it really wasn't a big deal. Except maybe a few times at programs and stuff," she shrugged, "we sort of wished our Dad could see us."

"Are we like him?" asked her son, shoving his hands in the back pockets.

She wondered if her son needed assurance that he hadn't inherited undesirable traits. She knew then that neither of her children was prepared to learn what she discovered about Don soon after marrying him.

She hadn't been treated like his lover; slave was a more apt description. If she didn't drop everything to see to his needs, he would behave like a petulant child and hurl degrading names at her—and this was when he was in a good mood.

"No, you're nothing like him," she replied.

"How long did you stay married?"

They had gotten married in May; she was pregnant with the twins in July; Don left that October to accept a position in Chicago. Six months after the twins were born, divorce papers were delivered in the mail. It was too callous a story to recant.

"A little over a year." Legally, it was the truth.

Stephenie rubbed her tear stained eyes, while Stephen stared sternly at the ceiling.

"Oh baby, I know it's painful," she said consolingly, smothering Stephenie in her warm embrace. "But it's all right."

"We made out better without him," Stephen proclaimed.

"I second that," echoed Lawrence, coming into the room.

He seemed pensive, not disturbed or angry as he took in the picture of his three Masons. Pain favored the expressions of the twins, while contrition singed the edges of Patrice's eyes. They were his now, and any zealot posing a risk to their world was asking for a fight. Donald Hollingsworth would soon learn Lawrence Woodson did not possess a forgiving, benevolent nature when his family was disrupted.

"I've made a decision," he announced stoically to Patrice, "And I don't want any arguments from you."

Her breath trembled in her chest, and she nodded her head in compliance, saying softly, "All right, Lawrence."

"I'm going to give you the money to pay off that sniveling creep," he said, his tone void of emotion. "If," he added conditionally, "and only if, he signs a statement that he will never, ever," he stressed emphatically, his finger knifing the air, "try to contact you or the twins."

Learning her head back, she eyed her lover suspiciously and swallowed hard.

"Are you joking?" she asked, studying his face.

"No, I'm not," he replied seriously. He sat beside her and smoothed her hair with his hand. His tender gaze spread like wings to cover Stephen and Stephenie.

"I love you," he declared with intense pleasure. "All three of you. More than I'll ever be able to explain. I want you happy. And if you're sure this is what you want to do," he said directly at Patrice, "I'll go along with it."

She knew what it cost him to come to that decision. It wasn't the money; Kit had been right on that count, but giving in to Don was against Lawrence's nature.

Patrice reached out and drew him into the circle of her embrace and loved him with her eyes. Her lips found their way instinctively to his and kissed him intimately, uninhibited by the witnesses looking on.

They pulled apart fractionally to stare tenderly into each other's eyes before warm smiles turned into the laughter of giddy teenagers. The twins soon joined and converged on Lawrence clumsily with hugs and kisses. All four rolled off the bed and onto the floor, smothering each other with love.

That's the way Kit found them when she pulled Martin into the room.

Experiencing a mild attack of jealousy at being left out, she asked, "Can I join, too?"

Patrice looked at her best friend and extended a hand, "If you don't, I'll really be mad at you." The women embraced before they were pulled into the tussle on the floor.

Martin leaned against the frame of the door, his blue eyes wistfully watching the lively family portrait.

CHAPTER ❧ FIFTEEN

Something is being overlooked, Patrice thought, *but for the life of me, I can't fathom what it could be. Maybe I could think if I didn't have so many people following me,* she speculated, while pulling into the parking garage at her office. However, throughout the day, there was comfort and security in knowing that she was being watched.

Lawrence and the twins showed up at the station that afternoon. They had an early dinner before Lawrence had to leave for a business meeting at his Houston office. It was late when she heard from him again. He called her around midnight, and not from his office, but from the hospital. J.T. had gone into labor; his godchild was about to be born. Lawrence didn't know how much longer he'd be at the hospital or if he would come to the house afterwards. Just as Patrice prepared to settle down for a restless night, he appeared.

The light peeking from the bathroom cast a silhouette of the couple lying in bed, bathing them in a yellow haze. Patrice's head was resting on the taut smoothness of his sun-kissed chocolatey chest, his heart singing in her ears.

"Mr. Woodson, you wouldn't be so dangerous if you'd sit down," he said, repeating the scolding tone of the nurse he'd nearly knocked over.

"If that's how you're going to act when we have a baby, I may change my mind," teased Patrice.

"No way, lady." He bent his head to kiss her cheek. "I plan to be right there in the room with you, making sure the doctor doesn't foul up." A wistful sigh passed his lips. "Otherwise, I would go crazy," he chuckled. "A boy is next."

"What?"

"I have two girls and one boy. It's time for another boy." J.T. had given him a goddaughter, and counting Stephenie, he had two girls.

"Sweetheart, it doesn't work like that," she replied.

"Trust me."

"I never would have pegged you for a big family man," she said with a chuckle.

"At least a basketball team."

Shifting her body to slip on top of his, she gazed thoughtfully into his eyes. His look, even in the semi-dark, was so galvanizing that it sent a tremor through her. He heard her sharp intake of breath before she whispered, "What are you going to do with all these children, Mr. Woodson?"

"Lots of things," he replied, toying with the long strands of hair falling around her face in a dark cloud. "Everything. I'll even show them how to ledger their personal accounts," he added with amusement.

She kissed one of the flattened nubs on his chest while sliding her arms around the firm waist. "I'm sure you'll be great at it," she murmured against the warm flesh.

"Yes," he said with a sudden energy that surprised her, as he reversed their positions. "And I can hardly wait to start. As soon as we finish this mess with Don, I . . . ."

"Why did you have to mention his name? I was having such a great time forgetting he existed."

"And I want you to keep on forgetting him," he mandated softly, with a hand under her chin.

The silence between them stretched with sweet sexual tension before she broke the quiet, thinking she could never say it enough, and would never tire of repeating the words. "I love you."

He kissed her first with his eyes, twin beacons leading her to love with their halolike glow. His mouth swooped down to capture hers in a kiss that fanned the heat that had been smoldering just beneath the surface. She heard the faint sound of ripping fabric, then felt cool air touch her skin briefly before his warm flesh pressed her to the bed. They made love until their weary bodies could take no more. Patrice's last thought before succumbing to the numbed sleep of a satisfied love was, *Yes, it gets better and better every time.*

ðà ðà ðà ðà

Lawrence was awakened from an erotic dream in the middle of the night by an intimate weight that settled on him. The pressure felt so right, so natural that his usually quick reflexes relaxed with the pleasant sensations possessing him. Slowly, his eyes opened and locked onto Patrice, who looked very much like all she wanted to do was to enjoy him as greedily as possible.

She flashed a knowing smile. " I didn't think you'd mind," she whispered, an amatory brightness in her eyes. Her fingertips, with their butterfly touch, were moving with slow inevitability across his extensive chest, rustling the field of tiny hairs.

"I thought it was too good to be a dream," he replied, his voice raspy with sleep and anticipation. He felt himself sinking deeper into the bed under her tingling caresses. Her thighs were velvet entrapments at his sides and he laid still, letting her have her way with him.

Something had caused Patrice to spring up suddenly from a sound sleep. It wasn't an uneasy feeling, the perception of an intrusive noise, or anything that she could put her hands on. She had clicked on the night light near her side of the bed, and then turned to wake him. But decided not to—at least not right away.

Settling comfortably on her hunches, she had found herself studying his full, dark-skinned face. The corners of his mouth curved upwards, a slight smile fixed there. As instinctively as she guessed the nature of his pleasant sleep, a hand went to her stomach. The feeling that had propelled her to awaken had begun to unravel, forming a clear picture.

A basketball team. A quiet joy bubbled within her. She imagined her stomach full and bulging with child. Lawrence's child. She had no doubts he would be a wonderful father. He deserved fatherhood more than any man she knew, or was ever likely to meet.

Even in sleep there was a vibrancy about him that excited her—the way he breathed, the facial hairs stirring ever so slightly, the rhythmic rise and fall of his chest. He smelled of fulfillment, she thought, and felt a warm blush spread through her as she remembered the passion shared between them not so long ago.

Yes, she had noticed these things before. This observation only confirmed what she had already come to accept as fact—she would never tire of being with this man. Her dream lover was a lover's dream come true.

Embers of want and need had fired her daring, severing ties with demure propriety. Patrice had felt free in her wantonness, and her senses demanded that she touch him: she began by stroking his soft hair. She followed the long line of brows down to the prominent line of his jaw, and before she realized it, she had mounted him. It was at this moment that Lawrence had opened his eyes.

"Like what you see?" Lawrence inquired on a breathy moan, eyes at half-mast.

"I love it," her sassy tongue replied, hips gyrating over him in slow-motion. Her efforts were rewarded when all the air expelled from his lungs in one wild gasp. Stretching her softness over him, Patrice sought his mouth, which parted in anticipation of a kiss. She played with his lips: tongue tracing the firm outline between mustache and beard, lips pulling his between her teeth to suckle gently.

Lawrence tried to speak between her teasing tongue—to say what, he didn't know—but his vocal chords stalled, and his stomach twisted with the hard knot of need. His manhood swelled to life. She was forcing him to communicate his desire for her in a purely carnal fashion.

Passivity was never in his nature, so he drew Patrice against his entire length, and his hands began to make heated paths up and down her back.

She gloried in the mold they made, enraptured by the feel of his arms around her, his mouth wandering up the tingling cord of her neck. His chest hairs were stimuli to her already sensitive flesh. With her hands gripping his shoulders, Patrice began to sway her hips over his in seductive rotation. She felt his body shiver beneath hers, and soon sampled the pleasures of his lips.

Touching her with wild, hungry caresses, his mouth massaged hers with provocative insistence. He rolled them over, reversing positions. Patrice savored the thundering of his heart against her breasts, and delighted in the fierce heat of his hardness against her.

When he explored her mouth, she tasted him with a new hunger, and felt bereaved when he left her mouth to drop kisses over her skin. His mouth closed softly over the burning sweetness of a hardened nipple, and Patrice felt her body and willpower slip away as naturally as the breath she expired in a tremulous sigh.

Before, she had found him more than adept in bed; now, she felt much more so. The slightest touch from his tender hands effected a barrage of sensations in her, and time and time again, she cried out, praising his name.

Driven beyond anything she had ever experienced, Patrice reclaimed her former position, to become the master of the bodies love-dancing in the dim light.

She found a stubby nipple among a patch of hair and lavished it with her tongue. Tending the taut skin stretched over his chest, she dug titillating fingers into the flesh between the outline of his ribs. Loving hands were soon joined by tender lips, her tongue making a velvet path down the center of him.

Lawrence squirmed under the onslaught of the sensations Patrice evoked in him and from him as she moved down his feverish body. He explored the soft lines of her shoulders, her back, with hands frantic to close around her. But when her mouth closed around his tumid desire, those same hands that had sought to hold her tightened into fists that alternately beat and clutched at the bed.

No woman had ever been allowed to touch him in such a manner. In the back of his mind, he had believed he hadn't missed anything. Now, he became a willing participant in the pleasure of her intimate exploration. *Patrice*, his mind called in delight. Only this amazingly loving woman possessed the power to create this enigmatic blend of pain-pleasure, weakness-strength without threat to his masculinity. He trusted her and knew that for whatever she drew from him, she would also give back. He was humble as he was proud. And aroused beyond belief.

"Please...Please...Please."

Lawrence didn't recognize the cries that poured from his mouth as his own; Patrice was deaf to his pleas, attuned only to satisfying the man who had become more important than life to her.

"Patrice," he grunted, his body learning sensations he had no idea were possible. Lawrence pulled her head back up to him, to plant greedy, desperate kisses about her face before his tongue darted between the opening between her lips. He lost himself in the kiss as surely as his fierce tongue explored the inner recesses of her mouth. Patrice gave herself freely to the passion of the kiss, and helped Lawrence position her legs to bend at the sides of his waist. He then slid a hand between their perspiring bodies—the separation barely discernible—to tantalize the silky hairs at the meeting place of her thighs; an unerring finger delved into the warm, welcoming wetness awaiting him.

"Lawrence." This cry was different—half plea and half a demand for conquest.

"Now, Patrice, now," he commanded on a torn breath. He kissed her gentle, hard; and with her guiding, possessed her in one thrust. It, too, was gentle, hard.

A veil of poignant passion swirled around them, shrouding the bed. Only two people and one goal existed in the world Lawrence and Patrice created. It was a place of color, where tender emotions and the forever-kind of warm sensations enjoyed a loving environment. The room was silent, save for the sounds of the man and woman earnest in their search for fulfillment.

Lust and love became fast, lasting friends. And with each deepening thrust came unspoken signals of a sealed love.

ૐ ૐ ૐ ૐ

While Patrice dressed the next morning, she saw the cashier's check for fifty thousand dollars on her dresser. She smiled, bittersweet, ever mindful of all that the money symbolized—the end of one painful chapter in her life, and the prologue to a new.

When Lawrence had made the offer, she was so caught up in what he was really offering that she hadn't stopped to think about it. Now, a sense of foreboding enveloped her: I don't relish having to tell him I can't accept the money.

Don is my problem, and I don't want the overlap from an old life polluting the new. And to use Lawrence's money to that end, she believed, would be tantamount to having a permanent reminder of the past. Patrice folded the check in half and placed it in her drawer among her lingerie. *I'll return it,* she thought, *after I've loved him into submission.*

When Patrice arrived at the station, she made arrangements with the bank to get the money that afternoon. Next, she contacted her attorney, who advised her against submitting to Don's extortion and warned that even a signed statement would be broken by someone of Don's twisted personality. She persisted, and he relented, grumbling about clients who paid for advice and then disregarded it.

❧ ❧ ❧ ❧

The Friday of reckoning arrived and Patrice couldn't wait for it to be over. Unfortunately, the day had hardly begun. While sitting behind her desk she was unable to concentrate on any of her reading; her eyes kept straying to the telephone, willing it to ring.

She sighed wearily and rubbed the ache between her shoulders. She hadn't gotten any rest last night, and neither had her family. She'd run them ragged with her morbid excitability, partly due to guilt for the secret she kept from Lawrence.

He had been almost as nervous as she, though he hid it well from the twins. But she knew, and it really showed this morning when she refused his offer to accompany her to work. She had dressed in a hurry—hoping to avoid just such a confrontation. He was prodigiously beautiful, blocking her bedroom door, his well-muscled shoulders bulging from a white undershirt.

"Why are you being so stubborn?" he bellowed, his eyes imperious flashes of frustration.

"I'm not being stubborn," she replied calmly, sliding a slender foot into a black high heel shoe, "you're being irrational." She stepped into the other shoe. "It doesn't make sense for you to sit around my office waiting," she added, standing in front of her dresser to apply make-up.

"But it makes sense for me to sit around my office all day, wondering what's happening twenty miles away and knowing I can't do anything if this doesn't go the way you planned?!"

"Nothing's going to happen," she replied in an even tone, "except when Don calls, I'll have him meet me at my attorney's office and he'll sign the statement." She applied lipstick, "I'll give him the money," and smacked her lips together, "and that will be the end of it."

"I don't like it," Lawrence grumbled.

"Lawrence," she turned to face him, pleading, "you promised."

He shook his head violently as his finger wagged in her direction, he said firmly, "This is the last time, Patrice."

"The last time for what, baby?" she asked innocently.

"The last time I let you have your way." She smiled sweetly. "I mean it," he affirmed, folding his arms commandingly across the firm chest.

Patrice didn't realize the laughter she heard was her own as she remembered the stern countenance Lawrence had tried to maintain. But his eyes, twinkling with affection had given him away.

Patrice closed her eyes momentarily and was instantly assailed by a spasm of panic. *But there is still Don to contend with, and he poisons practically everything he touches,* she worried.

Patrice stretched her arms over her head, then slowly pivoted, looking over the contents of her office as though seeing everything for the first time. The status she had once associated with this room was no longer here, for the enticing mystique of power was gone. She had Lawrence to thank for that. He'd taught her by example there were other important things in life—even more important than having a successful career. Climbing to the top in radio was all she'd known and worked toward for so long. This readjustment in priority would take a little getting used to, even though it had already found her receptive.

Struck by a sudden impulse to get out of the office, she headed to the production room where she knew she'd find Roger. When she got to the room where the station's commercials were cut, a red light flashed over the door, signaling that a taping was in session. She peeped through the small window carved near the top of the thick, sound-proof door and saw Roger sitting behind the massive electronics board. He looked up and saw her. The red light dulled, and she went into the room.

"What brings you to this side of the track?"

"Just taking a break from the paper work. Don't let me keep you from yours though."

"I was just trying out some of the sound effects on this board. Want to hear some?" he asked enthusiastically.

"Not really."

"Have you and lover-boy had an argument already?" he ventured.

"No, nosy," she replied chuckling. "Not that it's any of your business."

A light on one of the control board's panels lit up, and Roger picked up the phone behind him. "Production, Roger here," he said. "Yeah, she's here. OK, I'll tell her." He held the receiver to Patrice, "Line four's for you."

The announcement set off an alarm bell in her head. "I'll take it in my office," she said, rushing hastily from the room. She stumbled as she raced through the maze of hallways to her office, her anxiety increasing with each step.

When she got to her office, she slammed the door shut, then leaned against it, taking several deep, tranquil breaths. Looking more in control than she felt, she walked over to her desk and picked up the phone.

"Hello," she said in her professional tone.

"Has he called yet?"

She was relieved it was Lawrence. He tied her up with lengthy questions about her day before ringing off with a promise to call back later.

She moved aimlessly about the office, unable to concentrate on anything, as she fantasized about all the wonderful and exciting things she and Lawrence would do when this was over. A few of her ideas included the twins. *And, after a while, a baby,* she thought with gladness bubbling inside her.

Before she knew it, it was five o'clock and time for the regularly held evening meeting with the sales staff. They were in high spirits because of the new business accounts they were accumulating, and itched to party. The sales staff invited her to join them at a new club, but she feigned a heavy workload and asked for a rain check. She was finally able to immerse herself in some of the paperwork, which helped to take her mind off pending confrontation.

Just as she was about to write on her notepad, the buzzer on her phone went off, a short, harsh sound. The pen she held was suspended in mid-air, and her flesh shuddered with an ominous chill. She stared blankly across the room at her phone, floundering in an agonizing maelstrom of indecision. She bit down on her lip until it throbbed, and chastised herself for forgetting that this was not an ordinary day.

Her glazed eyes flew to the hands on her watch. It was after six! The buzzer went off again, this time longer and more raucous than before.

Scampering across the room she picked up the receiver. "Hello," she said breathlessly, clutching the handle between her hands.

"I'm down in the lobby. Clear it with security so I can come up."

"I thought you were going to call today!" she said accusingly at him.

"It is today, sweetheart. Now get them to let me up."

The next voice she heard was that of Mr. Simpson, the night security guard who was stationed at the main desk. Not knowing what else to do, she instructed him to let Don come up to the station.

When she hung up, her mind warned, "This is not the way it was supposed to happen," replaying the business-like scenario she'd envisioned. She eased down into her chair, coaxing herself not to panic, trying to think of a plan before he arrived.

Only she and Ken, the six-to-ten announcer were still in the station, but he was locked up in the control room. Impulsively, she called him on the hot line.

She drew a blank; she forgot the number and cursed. She slid a panel out from her drawer where every extension in the station was listed, then punched the seven digits to the control room's blue phone.

The line rang over twenty times before Ken answered. "Ken, call security downstairs and have them send up a guard. Don't mention I told you to call," she stressed. "I don't want anybody to know I called down. You got that?" At his, "Yes, ma'am" reply, she replaced the phone.

Her heart thumped uncomfortably, and her palms were beginning to perspire. She leaned her head against the back of the chair and closed her eyes in an effort to compose herself. She could not and would not allow Don to know just how frightened she really felt. The only thing left to do was pray that Don wouldn't become unreasonable and that everything would turn out fine. The buzzer rang on her phone again, this time alerting her that Don was at the station's door. She pressed a button on the side of the phone and sat back to wait.

Even though Patrice had left her office door opened so as not to be startled by his entrance, nothing could have prepared her for the sight of Don. There was little of the handsome and stylishly dressed man she had married years ago. This Donald Hollingsworth looked unkempt, and the white suit he wore was baggy on the thin frame. A slicked-back wig alerted her that his appearance was phony; he was dressed like a seedy character in a stage play. His eyes remained unchanged throughout the years—no amount of make-up could conceal their true character. What she once thought were bedroom eyes, no longer beamed a seductive light, but were drawn into nearly closed slits, exuding a quality she was hard pressed to define.

"Hey, babe," he said as he strutted into the room and slowly scrutinized everything in sight.

Patrice got up from her chair and stepped from behind the desk as he approached.

He first inspected the certificates and plaques on the wall before turning his attention to the picture of the twins on her desk. He looked at her, his head cocked at an angle, scanning her face and figure intently. She thought she recognized a wistfulness lurking in the round, black eyes, but it was quickly replaced with a malevolent smirk.

Donald walked around her desk, his finger tracing a line around its edges. His face rearranged itself into a secretive smile, an odd combination of evil insolence and pleasure. He passed by her, sauntering to the bookshelf where he fingered the books housed there.

She couldn't read him, and that disturbed her more than any physical threat. What has caused Don to become this shell of a man with the soulless eyes?

He pulled the KHVY Arbitron book from the shelf and flipped through the pages like a card dealer shuffling a deck of cards. Deliberately, he let it fall to the floor. When it landed, the loud thump caused Patrice to flinch.

He chuckled, then sat on the side of her desk, inches from where she stood, and stared at her with disdain. It was then that she recognized jealousy and hatred flaring out of his eyes. She also realized his forboding disposition was no act, and experienced a growing uneasiness under the hostility radiating from him.

"You got it all, didn't you babe?" he said bitterly. "A high powered radio gig that pays a lot of bread. Just what you always wanted. Forgive me if I don't offer my congratulations."

"You had the same chance I had," she retorted calmly, faking false bravery.

"And you took it away," he said in a soft voice, looking at her from the corner of his eyes. "Over twenty years in the business gone after you'd been on the job for only six, lousy months."

"What are you talking about, Don?"

He pushed himself up, and Patrice quickly stepped back, fearing an attack. He laughed and walked away.

"I know you got one here somewhere, where is it?" he asked, looking through the books on the case.

"What are you looking for?"

"The policy book. The one with the rigid rules that cost me my job." He began tossing books on the floor. "The one you wrote and that everybody accepted as though it were a doggone bible. I made KTOP the number one station in the market, and all I got to show for it is a damn policy book, and you don't even have it on your own shelf! Ain't that a blip?"

He cast a sidelong glance at her, and seeing her nonplused expression, said, "You didn't even know, did you?"

"Know what? What are you rambling about?"

"I'm D. J. Holly, baby," he said, expanding his arms wide. "I know you heard of D. J. Holly, the number one jock in all of Atlanta."

The name didn't register to Patrice, and it showed on her face which added fuel to his anger.

"You know, you're a cold bitch," he said nastily. "I bet if I were a woman, I could have been president of the company by now. But not you. You ain't go never get no higher than what you are now," he taunted, then laughed as if a funny thought occurred to him. "If you were good on your back, maybe you could make it. But we both know, honey," he said conspiratorially, "that you are stiff."

Patrice regarded him cooly, her head held proudly, refusing to allow his venomous remarks to find their target.

"What's the matter, babe? My jokes ain't funny enough for you now? You used to think so. In fact, everything I did used to be fine with you," he said, reaching out to pinch her cheek. She deflected his hand by raising an arm protectively—her insides cringing at his touch.

Undaunted by her rejection, he continued, "You don't want to remember that you looooved"—he made the word sound like an abomination—me, do you? Yeah, you did. Until you became a goodie. Wanting to stay at home. Hah! And babies. . .I hooked up with you for a laugh—you looked at me like I was God in the flesh. But after a bit, nothing I did was ever good enough for you, was it? You were climbing that ladder—weren't you college girl? But you still let me under your dress," he sang, then erupted in a fit of laughter.

The sound seemed forced and unnatural to Patrice, and fear spread its cold fingers up her spine. *Where is that security guard? Ken hasn't made the call.*

Suddenly, Don fell quiet, and his eyes narrowed and hardened. "You always had to prove you were better, brighter, a real high achiever. There you were, your belly growing big with my kids." he said mockingly.

"Don, you need help," she said before she could stop herself.

But he didn't hear her for he was lost in memories. "Oh, that's right. Everything you have should have come to me," he said, slamming a fist down on her desk—knocking over the photo of the twins.

In an instinctive move, she righted the frame, daring to steal a glimpse at the smiling faces in the photograph. Don never commented on how beautiful his children are, she thought.

"The car, the nice house, the fancy job—it should all be mine. Mine! And what do I have?" he continued, "What? Nothing!"

"You left, Don. Not me. You left. Remember?"

"You damn right I split. I saw what was happening. And it's still happening. Every time I turn around, I hear or read something about the energetic woman on the rise in radio. I couldn't go nowhere without hearing something about you," he spat. "How stupid I was, feeling sorry for this poor, lonely, college student. Then you turned right around and stabbed me in the back."

"That's not true," she defended hotly, then cursed her wayward tongue. Sparring with him was the last thing she needed. She knew, by his distorted irrational drifts into the past, that fueling the discussion was an unwise lead.

"But that's all right now, because you're going to pay for the way you've destroyed my life, my career. You're going to pay through the nose," he snarled. "Where's my dough?"

She felt the nauseating sinking of dread. "Uh, you were supposed to call," she hedged, backing from him into the corner of her desk.

"Where's my damn money?" he shouted impatiently edging towards her.

"It's at my attorney's office," she replied, unable to control the waver in her voice.

"What?" he said with disbelief, backing from her fractionally, his hands looped inside the pockets of his coat. "I told you to have the money when I called. Don't hand me this crock about an attorney!"

"I was prepared to give it to you," she said, licking dry lips nervously, "providing you signed a statement swearing not to ever approach me or the children again."

"Providing? Swearing?" he murmured to himself, before turning his rage on her. "You dumb, stupid bitch! If you know what's good for you, you'll get my money here, right now."

She shuddered. All she could think was that everybody else had been right and she, wrong—dead wrong and foolish to believe Don would sign anything. And if he had, the chances of his return were certain, for his fixation on her was too strong for him to abandon the past and start afresh.

"Didn't you hear me?" he asked in a dangerously quiet tone, jolting her from her silent reverie. "I said get my money over here."

If I give in this time, he'll come back—again and again. The twins will never be safe, nor will I ever be free of him. He could decide to kidnap them anyway. Don doesn't just want money, he really wants me to suffer, to beat me down to nothing.

*Patri*ce screamed when suddenly Don slapped her viciously across the face with the back of his hand. Stumbling, she fell against the desk, a trickle of blood dripping from the side of her mouth.

"Don't screw with me, Miss Anti-apartheid," he said between clinched teeth.

"So—it was you!" she said accusingly. "It was you who sent those threats."

"What bomb threats? I don't know nothing 'bout no threats," he denied, suddenly on the defensive.

"Then why did you call me Miss Anti-apartheid?"

"Haven't you listened to your own station? You do remember that KHVY is sponsoring an anti-apartheid concert and festival?" She stared suspiciously at him with a critical squint, looking for any signs that he was lying. "That's rich," he laughed bitterly. "That's really rich. What the hell do I care for some protest concert? Them folks in South Africa can do any damn thing they please, as far as I'm concerned. It ain't got nothing to do with me."

"If not you, then who sent those threats?"

"You're stalling," he snapped, grabbing the collar of her blouse. He snatched her to him, his vile breath heating her face as he ordered, "Call that attorney and tell him to get his butt over here right now with my dough. Or I'll beat the living daylights out of you."

Fear, ugly in its vividness glittered in her dark eyes. She kept them glued to his face, while trying to convince shaky legs to function. She raised her hands to protect her face from the next blow when she heard a loud crash and watched as Don's body was hurled against the wall like a rag doll.

"Lawrence," she cried in a suffocated whisper.

Lawrence pulled Don up from the floor by the collar and began plummeting his face and body with long, aching blows. "I'll kill you, you little..."

Don's attempts to ward off the punishing blows were ineffective. He could hardly stand, except for the painful help he received from Lawrence's vicious grip around his neck. Blood was gushing from his nose and mouth as he begged and pleaded, "Come on, man. Please man."

Patrice cried out for Lawrence to stop, but there was no indication that he'd heard. "Lawrence, you're going to kill him," she screamed, tears gathering and trickling down her face. "Stop—Stop it! Oh, please baby, stop before you kill him. He's not worth it." She ran to grab his arm, trying to prevent another brutal fist from plunging into Don's already battered body.

Her pleas must have gotten through to him, for he let Don fall to the floor in a heap, coughing and sputtering on his own blood. Lawrence stood over Don; his legs straddling the pitiful specimen. His breathing was labored; his fists clinching and unclinching at his sides. There was a barbaric gleam in his eyes—his attack would have continued until he had severely maimed, if not killed, the man on the floor.

"If you so much as think of Patrice or the twins again, I'll finish what I started. There'll be no place you can go. There'll be nothing, or no one to stop me from ending your miserable existence."

Lawrence looked over at Patrice and saw the blood on her mouth. Releasing a loud, guttural howl, his hands closed into marble fists and naked animosity blazed in his eyes. Patrice dared to grab one fist as he lunged for Don, crying softly, "No more, please. For me—no more."

He stared at her as though anesthetized for a brief second, then unspoken pain and remorse appeared on his face. Crushing her to him, Lawrence whispered soothingly, "Baby, I'm sorry. So sorry," as he gently rocked her from side-to-side. He pulled away slightly to look down at her, concern and regret alive in his gaze. He lightly touched the bruise on her face before gathering her back in his arms. "Damn," he cursed harshly.

"Shhh," she soothed, basking in the protective arms cradling her, "I'm fine. Everything's all right. It's over."

"Ms. Mason! Ms. Mason!"

Her name was called frantically, before Simpson and Daniels came barreling into the room, guns drawn.

"He's all yours," Lawrence said to Daniels, leading Patrice from the room.

CHAPTER ✦ SIXTEEN

*I*t was cold and black outside, but warm and cozy inside the Lincoln as the big car moved smoothly through the downtown streets with its sparse traffic.

Patrice was quiet and contemplative as they made the short drive to the police station. Second guessing her actions and thoughts leading up to the confrontation with Donald crowded her brain. Though the threat of danger had been removed, she wasn't basking in relief.

The only thing she knew for certain was the love she had for the big bear of a man at her side. She smiled with the keen sense of pleasure she felt from that certainty, for nothing else mattered. She'd seen a vulnerable side of him that both frightened and pleased her, but tonight he'd shown her that there were no limits to his love.

"Honey, I wish you'd let me take you home and put you to bed," said Lawrence. "You don't have to do this tonight."

"And I'd like nothing better than to go home and be pampered all night long. But I wouldn't be able to forget, knowing it would be there for me tomorrow."

"I just hate to see you have to go through this tonight when there's no rush."

"I'll be all right. I have you by my side." Her lips found the side of his mouth for a tender kiss, then she lay her head on his shoulder.

"What are you thinking about?"

"Something Don said," she answered after a while. Feeling him stiffen, she brought his hand to caress the side of her face and smiled into his palm before placing a kiss there. "He denied having anything to do with sending the bomb threats."

Patrice couldn't see his face frown.

They fell silent for the remainder of the ride. When they arrived, Lawrence tried again to dissuade her from going in, but she refused with a stubborn shake of her head and got out of the car without waiting for assistance.

Resigned, he placed protective arms around her shoulders and steered her inside the building and through several narrow, poorly lit corridors. They weaved past uniform officers escorting handcuffed prisoners and other police personnel going about their duties.

Taking one cold hand in his, Lawrence ushered her pass the set of swinging, double doors, marked "Criminal Investigations Division>

Officer Daniels spotted them from where he stood at a door near the end of the hallway. "Mr. Woodson, Ms. Mason, down this way," he said, motioning with his hand.

Before reaching the room that Daniels had retreated into, Patrice came to an abrupt stop, a curious expression on her face. Lawrence also stilled and peered down at her. Before he could open his mouth to speak, dawning came over his features, for he too heard the familiar voice Patrice recognized coming from a partially opened door.

"Please, I'm tired. I already told you I don't know anything," cried a young woman in a tearful voice.

"You delivered those threats! You helped plan the whole charade! What did he promise you, eternal love?" demanded a male interrogator harshly.

"No, you've got to believe me," the woman exclaimed chokingly.

"Admit it. Make it easy on yourself. He's going to be charged with a felony, and you, with aiding and abetting a felon. Is that what you want?"

"Why do you want to protect that animal?" That, from a female interrogator. "Because you love him? Well, he loves you, too. That's why your face looks like it does, all swollen and bruised. And guess what, he has another woman. Another gullible, young," she stressed, "woman— girl really, nineteen years old."

"Admit it," shouted the male interrogator.

Just then a police woman escorted a woman, no more than twenty years of age down the hall and through the swinging doors. Patrice recognized the young female without knowing her. The hopeless, swollen eyes, red from crying, the dejected slump of her shoulders, even the way she allowed herself to be led, told the story of misplaced love.

From the room a woman's voice screamed, "I didn't do anything wrong. Maybe I shouldn't have told him where she lived. . . but I didn't know. . . ." Then the door was kicked shut before Patrice could hear more of the damning confession. But she'd heard enough, and though she didn't want to believe it, there was no denying the evidence: *It was Marie.*

Lawrence held her firmly by the shoulders, staring at her with concern.

"Lawrence." His name fell like a desperate plea from her lips as she fought to maintain control over fragile emotions. She fell against him, wrapping her arms tightly round his waist, and closed her eyes.

"I'm sorry," he whispered while rocking her gently in his embrace. "I'd give anything in the world for it to be different."

She slowly opened her eyes to see Ross Kinney come into the hall from a room not far from where she and Lawrence stood. She stared at Lawrence, then followed his line of vision to Ross, who was approaching them. Regret was written on both men's faces.

"I didn't know how to tell you," was all Lawrence said, his tone sorrowful. He turned to Ross and shook his outstretched hand. "Thanks a lot, man."

"Don't mention it," Ross said to Lawrence, staring with sympathy at Patrice. "Have you told her yet?"

"That young woman," she said, pointing towards the steel doors, "was Tracey, wasn't it? And here," she pointed to the closed door where the familiar voice had been heard, "that was Marie's voice I heard." Her matter-of-fact tone belied the anger, betrayal and pity she was feeling. "He used both of them. He lied to them just as he lied to me."

Lawrence merely shook his head. He saw the bitter tears before they began to fall from her eyes and crushed her to him, muffling the anguished cry as she sobbed pitifully into his coat.

"Do me a favor and tell Daniels I'll call him tomorrow," Lawrence said to Ross. "I'm taking Patrice home."

"No!" she protested, wiping her eyes with the back of her hands.

"Yes."

Neither his tone nor expression allowed room for argument. She acquiesced and let him guide them, retracing their earlier path to exit the police station.

꒳ ꒳ ꒳ ꒳

Snatches from the past several eventful hours scrolled rapidly through Patrice's mind. Much of what she remembered from the time she left the office until she stepped inside the front door of her home was now one giant blur. She was sitting in bed, propped up by a stack of pillows behind her back, dabbing a cold towel against a bruised lip. The swelling had gone down since leaving the police station, and only a slight tear at the corner of her mouth remained. She considered herself mighty fortunate that this was the only physical scar of her ordeal.

She set the towel on the night table next to the bed and folded her robed arms across her chest. The house was quiet; even the sounds of Lawrence's showering had ceased. She stared at the bathroom door, wondering what was keeping him and hugged her knees.

She didn't want to be alone with her thoughts. Not yet, anyway.

Lawrence had filled her in on the details leading up to his arrival at the office on their way home. Donald J. Hollingsworth, known as Jay Roberts to Marie, and J. Don Holly to Tracey, had been under Lawrence's watchful eyes since this morning.

Lawrence, believing he was following Jay, was led to Tracey's apartment. It was there that Lawrence met Ross. When Lawrence overhead Tracey refer to Jay as J. Don, he elected to keep tabs on the man with the two names, while Ross followed Tracey to class.

Ross confronted the college student and tricked her into confessing about the bomb threats she helped J. Don send. Intimidated by the threat of jail, Tracey spilled the whole story, implicating Donald, whom she hadn't heard from until this week. She didn't know about the extortion; she only knew that he had called to say they were about to come into some big money.

Marie hadn't been so fortunate. All she'd gotten for her part, small though it was, were false promises. Patrice understood, if not condoned Marie's actions. Marie had allowed herself to be manipulated for one of the oldest reasons in the world for which women made fools of themselves— love.

Patrice shook her head sympathetically, for she too had fallen for the exterior trappings, love-blinded to the contents inside. She knew the difference now.

We could have lost everything tonight, she reflected, shuddering as horrible, vivid visions of Lawrence killing Don flashed in her head. She hoped to never see that crazed, out-of-control look in his eyes again.

Am I capable of murdering a person? she wondered. The image of Lawrence and her children in danger solidified in her mind, and the answer found voice in a resounding, "Yes."

"Yes, what?" asked Lawrence, who appeared at the bathroom door, a large towel tucked around a trim waist as he briskly rubbed his head with another.

She whistled admiringly of his long, hairy legs and replied, "I was just thinking out loud," an amusing grin brightening her expression. If she lived to be a hundred years old, she'd always enjoy looking at him, regardless of his state of dress or undress.

"Must be some heavy thinking," he said, sitting on the side of the bed, looping the towel around his shoulders. "How's that lip?" he asked, touching her mouth with caring fingers.

"It's fine," she replied, taking his hand in hers and holding it under her chin. "I was thinking about the incident with Don."

Several beats passed before he said anything. Finally, "And?" He didn't try to mask the intensity of his irritation at the mere mention of Don's name.

A kind and understanding smile turned up the corners of her mouth as she gazed mellifluously at him. She caressed his face with loving strokes before wiping the frown from his forehead with gentle fingers.

"You know, I behaved pretty irrational about the whole thing," she said at last, dropping her hand. Her smile cracked and humility shone in her eyes. She let out a long audible breath before continuing, "I used to think I was indestructible, not physically, but where it really counted, up here," she said, tapping the side of her head with her finger. "I was wrong. Nearly dead wrong," she murmured solemnly. "Practically everything I did was wrong."

"Hindsight is great," he said with quiet emphasis.

"You think I'm being hard on myself, don't you?" Her tone was edged by a lack of self-compassion as she eyed him thoughtfully.

"Yes, I do," he replied in a warm voice that began to thaw her austerity. "You reacted like a lioness protecting her cubs. You can't fault yourself for that. It comes with the territory."

"What territory?"

"Of caring and wanting to protect those you love. When you open yourself to others like that, there are inherent risks involved," he said with the wisdom of one who knows. "That's one of the things about you that attracted me. You weren't afraid to take risks."

"If only I hadn't made so many mistakes along the way."

"And you'll make more." He reached out and touched her hand. "We don't always make the right choice or know where our decisions might lead us. But that doesn't mean we should stop striving to do, to be the best we possibly can."

Silence lingered in the room. Lawrence watched as the battle she fought with her emotions played across the light tan features. He wished she didn't have to go through this punishing retrospection, but recognized the act as part of the normal healing process following the trauma.

"How have I lived so long without you?" she asked staring at him with a sweet musing look.

"I'm not sure," he replied flippantly, holding her chin to kiss her gently on the mouth. Then his tone changed, matching the serious expression on his face. "You've done a damn good job and I won't let you underrate your accomplishments because of a bizarre situation."

"Thank you. I needed that," she said, the beginning of a real smile spreading across her face, as she basked in his approval. "I need you, too. You've been wonderful through this entire nightmare."

"And now you don't need me anymore?" He feigned hurt.

She grabbed the ends of the towel around his neck to pull his face closer. "I'll always need you. Forever."

A thunderbolt of love struck his heart, then burst, spreading its loving light throughout his body. His hands locked around her spine, pressing her to him as he captured her mouth in a kiss that made her heart pound with a pulsing rhythm. When he released her, the very air around them seemed electrified.

"Speaking of always and forever," he said, kissing her tenderly with his eyes, "we have some unfinished business."

"Hm?" she uttered absently, her eyes fastened on his mouth. She had an aching need for another kiss.

He got up and went to her dresser, then returned with a piece of balled tissue paper. He opened it, revealing the folded check.

Patrice's hand flew to her mouth. "I was going to tell you about that."

He raised his brow suspiciously. "Please, let's not argue tonight. I'm just not up to it."

"That's not really what I wanted to talk about," he said, a mysterious light in his eyes. He held up his hand; her engagement ring was on the tip of one pinky. "There's a little matter about a date. You do recall agreeing to marry me, as in love, honor, cherish and obey?"

"Oh, no, mister!" she exclaimed with laughter in her voice, sliding the ring onto her finger. "Those vows will definitely be rewritten."

"Don't change the subject."

A sweet gasp escaped her throat when his warm hand stole inside the robe to caress bare skin. "When?" he asked against her mouth, his probing hand sending currents of desire through her. She moaned into his mouth when his tongue teased pass her lips, and his palm grazed a sensitive nipple, sending a shock wave through her entire body. "When?" he demanded urgently, beginning to feel the flush of sexual desire he was promoting.

"When what?" she teased breathlessly, her hands engrossed in exploring the contours of his muscular chest. She heard the sharp intake of air he sucked in and sighed with the heady sensation of her power.

"When are you going to marry me?" he said, pushing the robe from her shoulders. Gently, he eased her down onto the bed, his seductive gaze sliding downward from her eyes to the tan creaminess of her neck and breasts.

"After the concert at Banneker University," she said while planting delicate kisses on his heaving chest.

"Before," he murmured raggedly, placing a tantalizing kiss in the hollow of her neck.

Patrice moaned softly as he centered himself over her and wrapped willing arms around his neck; her body pulsating with need. He raised up on his hands on both sides of her head and began showering her body with kisses before his tongue teased one nipple to attention.

Her breathing was reduced to gasping pants and sighs as he slowly slid down her body and back up again. "Be-fore," he coaxed, teasing her ear with his whispering hot breath.

"Yes," she cried, pulling his head to hers to reclaim his mouth in a hungering kiss.

Patrice wanted to tell him she'd marry him any day, any time, any place he named. In fact, there were lots of things she wanted to tell him. But everything could wait until later. After all, they had all the lovely tomorrows.

《◈ 《◈ 《◈ 《◈

They reached for each other several times during the night before grand promises and plans gave way to sweet dreams as they fell asleep in each other's arms.

An annoying sound penetrated Patrice's sleep, and she stirred. Lawrence heard it too, and sat up, trying to isolate the intrusive noise. Both simultaneously realized that the door bell was ringing.

"The twins!" they said as one. Instantly alert, both jumped out of bed and began scrambling around the room, looking for something to put on.

"Coming!" called Patrice, hurrying to the front door, tying her robe in place. Lawrence was on her heels. She pulled the door open, and the twins rushed into her arms, spouting greetings and questions.

A clean shaven, crisp looking Martin, pushed a sleepy, complaining Kit into the house. "It's too early to be up," grumbled Kit, dropping onto the first couch she reached.

"Yes, we know, sweetheart," cooed Martin, sitting next to Kit and folding her in his arms. "We tried to give you a little more time," he whispered secretly to Lawrence, "I had them ring the bell, but as you can see. . ." he shrugged, pointing to the twins pulling Patrice down on the sofa between them.

"Don't worry about it, Martin," replied Lawrence, covering a yawn behind his hand. "Anybody for coffee?"

Kit raised her head half-heartedly, a "please" expression on her face, while Patrice looked at him hopefully. He left the room, rubbing the sleep from his eyes.

"Tell us what happened first," bubbled Stephenie. "And don't leave anything out."

"Not now, please," begged Patrice. Yawning, "I haven't had a shower yet."

"I can't believe you guys were still in bed. It's almost eight o'clock. What have you been doing?" fired Stephen.

"Is it that early?" whined Kit, curling her legs on the couch.

"I'm afraid we have a night owl who can't get up in the morning," Martin said before kissing Kit tenderly on the forehead. "Poor baby."

"Why don't you two run and help Lawrence?" Patrice suggested to the twins.

They looked at her significantly before agreeing, "All right," reluctance tainting their voices.

Kit lifted her head to examine Patrice closely after the twins had left. "You look none the worse for wear."

"I'm surprised you opened your eyes wide enough to notice," retorted Patrice, resting her head against the back of the couch.

"There's very little that escapes my notice, even if I am half dead. Like that tiny scratch on your mouth. I pray it's from passion and nothing else."

Patrice ignored Kit's observation, replying cryptically, "Likewise," eyeing Kit and Martin. Two red stains suddenly appeared on Kit's cheeks, and she teased, "Why Katherine Margaret, I can't remember ever seeing you blush before."

"You're hiding something," Kit accused, reading Patrice's mind.

"You keep your mouth shut," Patrice threatened.

Martins' eyes had been darting back and forth between the women, trying to follow the mysterious conversation. Eventually, he succumbed to the thought that it was probably best that he not understand.

"Lawrence gave us a partial report last night," he said, adding tentatively, "but I'm afraid he didn't mention anything about a ring," nodding in the direction of Patrice's hand.

"I didn't even notice it!" wailed Kit, suddenly wide awake. "Does this mean the case is finally closed?"

"Yes. Don was arrested, as were his accomplices."

Kit didn't miss the bittersweet expression that briefly shadowed Patrice's visage. "Lunch, tomorrow," she declared as the time for a more intimate discussion.

"Is there a chance of him posting bail?" posed Martin.

"Officer Daniels promised to let us know if he does, but I don't think he can come up with the money."

"But what if he does get out?" Stephenie was heard asking as she, Stephen and Lawrence returned with a full coffee tray.

"You don't have to ever worry about him again," replied Lawrence, setting the tray on the coffee table.

The twins accepted his firm contention as the final word on the matter and began helping him serve coffee.

A comfortable silence fell over the room. Stephen, however, had a curious gleam in his eyes, looking back and forth between his mom and Lawrence. Stephenie noted his strange scrutiny and knew something was going on. She tapped her foot imperceptibly to get his attention and tilted her brow, looking at him inquiringly. He scowled and moved away from her, undaunted by her attempt to discourage him from doing what he felt he had to do.

"Lawrence, " he queried in a man-to-man demeanor and tone, "I don't want to give you the impression that we're ungrateful or anything like that . . . ."

Stephenie tackled him and covered his mouth with her hand. "Pay him no attention, Lawrence. He's always tacky before he gets breakfast."

Stephen wrenched her hand away and glowered. "Will you stay out of this? I was talking to Lawrence."

Martin hid his amusement in his cup, while Kit covered her face, feeling embarrassed for Patrice.

"Not like this, you klutz!" said Stephenie.

"We've got a right to know," replied Stephen hotly, his elbows reared back in defense of his position.

"What is it you've got a right to know, son?" asked Lawrence, setting his cup on the saucer.

Stephen gulped for Lawrence's calm tone caught him unexpectedly. "I was just wondering what your intentions are regarding our mother," he said respectfully.

Stephenie groaned, rolled into a ball, and covered her face. Martin could no longer contain his laughter, and Kit belted him in the middle, then looked sympathetically at Patrice.

"Does this answer your question?" Patrice asked her son, holding out her ringed hand.

Stephen buried his face in his hands; Stephenie shrieked and grabbed her mother's hand to get a closer look at the dazzling stones.

"It's gorgeous! Look, Stephen! Isn't it beautiful?" she exclaimed.

Patrice took a sip of her coffee before turning to Lawrence. "Do you think you can instill some tact in this kid," nodding in her son's direction, "or is it too late?"

"Oh, I don't know," replied Lawrence, picking up his cup and resting back against the couch. "I kind of like his style," he added, taking a sip of coffee. "There are no crossed signals, so you always know where you stand."

❧ ❧ ❧ ❧

🐦 🐦 🐦 🐦

Dear Reader:

We hope that you have enjoyed *Love Signals* by Margie Walker, just as much as we have enjoyed working with her on this book for you.

We are very proud of this series featuring black women in love. As the months go on, and as we expand and enlarge the dimensions of this fresh approach to romantic fiction, we hope that you will not only greet **Romance In Black** with welcoming hearts, but it is also our hope that MARRON PUBLISHERS will be included in and warmed by this embrace.

For the convenience of our readers, subscriptions are available for those who wish to receive both **Romance In Black** releases quarterly. A discount of up to 25% is offered to those who decide to participate in our special "family" service. This service also entitles you to a free three- or six-month subscription to **Dark Secrets,** our new bimonthly newsletter showcasing contemporary short stories and poetry.

Should you decided to write Margie Walker, or wish to receive further information on any of MARRON PUBLISHERS' publications, please contact: MARRON PUBLISHERS, P.O. Box 756, Yonkers, NY 10703. Or call 1-800-766-0499 for fast subscription service.

Marquita Guerra
Marquita Guerra
Publisher

Sharon A. Ortiz
Sharon A. Ortiz
Publisher

P.S. New writers—sharpen your pencils! Guidelines for the **Romance in Black** series are available at your request.

🐦 🐦 🐦 🐦

ROMANCE IN BLACK

Love Signals by Margie Walker

Patrice Mason, the general manager of a Houston radio station, and Lawrence Woodson, Vice President of Banneker University, clash over an anti-apartheid concert sponsored by KHVY Radio. As bomb threats and pranks jeopardize the project, Patrice wonders if Lawrence is yet another distortion in her world, or is the attraction a viable love signal.

Island Magic by Loraine Barnett

Follow Rhonda Baptiste and Alan Hussein, assistant editor and managing editor of *West Indian World* magazine, from their exciting meeting on a subway platform to the development of their mutual respect and love. The action surrounding these two lovers is played out in New York and Barbados.

Posters of RIB covers are available for purchase. For details, contact: MARRON PUBLISHERS, P.O. Box 756, Yonkers, NY 10703.

- - - - - - - - - - ✂ - - - - - - - - - - -

- - - - - - - - - - ✂ - - - - - - - - - - -

DARK
S E C R E T S

Let MARRON PUBLISHERS stimulate your visual and literary senses. Subscribe to this refreshing bimonthly newsletter designed to appease your craving for a finely crafted short story or an inspiring poem. Explore the vast dimensions of love, the intricacies of family relationships, or the complexities of the human and ethnic experience.

You'll not only enjoy the works of our upcoming writers, but share the visions of many talented artists as you view **Dark Secret's** original illustrations and photography. And for you aspiring writers, MARRON's bulletins featuring resource organizations, seminars, lectures, and workshops will keep you informed, updated, and motivated.

Share in America's growing awareness of its vast cultural diversity—join our family of readers!

Oh, and remember: **Dark Secrets** is free to **Romance In Black** subscribers!

---✂---

DARK
S E C R E T S

☐ **YES**   ☐ One Issue $3   ☐ One year $15   ☐ Two years $29
                                          (6 Issues)   **(12 Issues)**

☐ Maybe. Please place me on mailing list;
  or mail a free copy to :

☐ Payment Enclosed   ☐ Bill me

NAME ————————————————————————

ADDRESS ——————————————————————

CITY ———————————— STATE ———————— ZIP ———————

PLEASE ALLOW TWO TO FOUR WEEKS FOR DELIVERY

Call 1-800-766-0499 to claim your free T-shirt or leather bookmark when you refer a friend.

---✂---